The Wrong Kind of Falling

Books by Whitney Amazeen

<u>Carefree</u>

One Carefree Day

One Day Too Late

Something Bright and Burning

<u>Meadow Hills</u>

A Summer of Dandelions

The Wrong Kind of Falling

<u>Little Birdie</u>

Stages

A MEADOW HILLS NOVEL

The Wrong Kind of Falling

WHITNEY AMAZEEN

For my bestie, Cait.
The kind of friend everyone else wishes they had.

Playlist

1. *Tuesday* — NEIL FRANCES
2. *parking lot* — Allie Paige
3. *Hello My Old Heart* — The Oh Hellos
4. *Harvest Moon* — Poolside
5. *Charmed* — Σtella, Redinho
6. *Woodland* — The Paper Kites
7. *The Kite* — Luisa Marion, Noah Floersch
8. *If I'm Honest* — Trousdale
9. *Take It or Leave It* — Great Good Fine Ok
10. *Would That I* — Hozier
11. *What If I Love You* — Gatlin
12. *Kiss Me* — Sixpence None The Richer
13. *2000 Miles* — Gatlin
14. *When U Saw Love (ft. Babygirl)* — ELIO, Babygirl
15. *Bloom - Bonus Track* — The Paper Kites
16. *YLIOF* — Laity
17. *Hey Girl* — Stephen Sanchez
18. *Iris* — The Goo Goo Dolls
19. *I Won't Last A Day Without You* — Carpenters
20. *Kiss of Life* — Sade

"And now these three remain: faith, hope and love. But the greatest of these is love."

1 Corinthians 13:13

The Wrong Kind of Falling

September

Chapter One

BASH

I, Sebastian Black, have a grand total of two things on my mind most of the time. Number one is mixed martial arts. It's non-negotiably what I think of most, more than anything else in the world. Most people would probably assume my obsession with fighting stems from anger issues, but on the contrary, it's something that calms me. Among the many other benefits of my favorite sport, knowing I can protect the people I care about in a confrontation makes me *anything* but angry.

The second thing that's always on my mind is food. As someone who works out and trains frequently, I eat more than the average man. And I admit, eating high-quality foods and protein can get expensive, but it's always been made possible by my massive bank account.

Correction, Bash. It used to be made possible.

I can't deny my gratitude for all the perks being wealthy used to offer me in life. This doesn't, however, change the matter of my stomach, which is tragically empty at the moment.

A feeling I'm experiencing more and more lately.

I watch my younger sister, Ingrid, sling her bag over her shoulder as I shuffle to the kitchen. "Are you off to work?" I ask and then wince. It's a stupid question. Of course she's off to work. She's wearing her all-black waitress attire and her daily scowl.

Ingrid shoves a pen into her twisted-up red hair, leaning against the doorframe. "Unfortunately." She opens the door, promptly stalking outside without a single word of farewell.

I'm used to this sort of behavior from my dear sister, but I walk her out, anyway. I shuffle outside behind her, the crisp autumn air biting cold against my exposed face and arms. Suppressing a shiver, I reach into my pocket for my lighter and regrettable pack of cigarettes. Ingrid turns on her heel when she hears the flame from my lighter spark, but I make no pause. "You should smile more, Innie." I inhale a puff of my fiery crutch to keep warm. "You'd probably come home with better tips." I know smoking like this is the worst possible habit for someone whose entire future depends on lung capacity and stamina, but I'm living off canned soup and desperation for now. My bar for pre-fight fuel these days is low.

And unfortunately, my current predicament has left me more on edge than when I was doing well with quitting.

In one swift movement, Ingrid captures the pack from my fingers, her eyes sharp as daggers as she glares at me. "And is it too much to ask for you to quit smoking? It's expensive. Get a job."

"Ingrid." I take it back from her, prying it from her fingers, one at a time. A good-humored smirk graces my lips, knowing Ingrid is all bark and no bite. "I pawned my beloved Rolex, remember? My money bought this, not yours. Besides, this is my last pack, and I won't buy another. I promise to keep my hands busy with distractions after this, as usual." I tuck it back into the pocket of my green, flannel pajama bottoms for safekeeping. "Besides, I'm not nearly as hirable as you. Not unless you've found help-wanted listings in this little town asking for someone to throw a deadly punch."

She practically bares her teeth. "Awfully convenient that there are no MMA gyms or local fight clubs around here. Especially since you're the one who got us into this mess. Yet here I am, forced to work."

"You can always go back to Mummy and Daddy if you have a problem with it. I didn't ask you to stay with me, did I?"

"No. But here I am."

I glance at the time on my phone. "And *I'm* headed to church in a few."

"Your favorite place. Perfect. Go stuff your pockets." Her hard exterior melts into amusement as she opens the car door. She tosses her bag in. I swear I hear a chuckle escape her lips.

Laugh all you want, Ingrid. With all the free food I've been bringing back, I know better than to let my personal opinions get in my way, no matter how challenging.

For someone who loves God but feels uncomfortable at church, I tend to avoid it as much as I do decaf coffee and serious relationships, so this has just been another hurdle to add to my ever-growing list. And as someone who's never struggled to buy anything until now, it was too hard to admit my current circumstances to Harvest Valley

Church—a place full of people who are surely as judgmental as they come.

Besides, the last thing I want to do is seem like a charity case to anyone, especially since this is my own doing, but there's only so much hunger a person can take before desperation kicks in.

As pathetic as it is, neither my sister nor I have ever made a true meal in all our lives. After our parents cut us off two months ago, we've been living off canned food and cheap bread because Ingrid's paycheck doesn't cover enough for us to eat till we're satisfied. The girl never smiles, so she rarely gets tipped. I'm pretty sure her resting face is a deep-set frown, despite her only being nineteen. Still, I'm thankful it's enough to cover the essentials—limited food, toiletries, and the hefty utility bills that have been arriving by mail, thanks to Mum and Dad. They've given up going paperless just to torture us.

I need to keep building muscle mass to stay in my weight division, and I'm used to eating much more in order to do so. But these past two months, my stomach has been pretty vocal that it's not satisfied.

I inhale the scent of crisp Maine air as I touch Ingrid's arm. She freezes, waiting but not turning to face me. I squint at the grassy hills towering over us through the brightness of the morning sun, trying to find a way to finally convince my sister to let me suffer alone. "You really can go back. I won't be angry, you know."

Ingrid is silent. When I'm being genuine with her like this, I know she can't tease me for returning from church each week with pockets full of buffet food instead of just asking someone for help.

"Oh, stop." Ingrid rolls her eyes. "And thank Logan for the both of us, will you?"

If it weren't for Logan, we'd probably starve, I think, remembering my unease when our neighbor invited me to a men's weekly breakfast at his church here in Meadow Hills. I chose to overlook the church part in favor of the breakfast and have yet to regret it. I always bring some back for Ingrid, and as a thanks, she keeps her antagonistic comments coming my way.

Ingrid avoids my gaze as she gets in her red convertible. Despite my guilt, I bite back a smile. Why our parents let us keep the cars, I have no idea. Maybe it was a slight moment of guilt for leaving us completely penniless, but I'm not going to complain.

I drag my socks on the cobblestone drive as I go back inside, take a hot shower before I dress, and get in my own beautiful, black and white '73 Camaro. When I'm driving it, I can almost pretend I'm not poor for the moment. Just for a bit, I'm back in Woollahra, the suburb of Sydney where the air smells like eucalyptus and generational wealth, and no one's ever had to pawn their Rolex. Though I wouldn't go back even if I could, this beauty is a bright spot in my otherwise dismal situation.

A light flashes on the dashboard as the car roars to life. *Check engine.*

I frown. "Check engine? For what? Bedbugs?" Learning the inner workings of automobiles isn't something I've made a habit of engaging in. Not when I've always paid for the best in the business. *But now,* I realize, *might be the time to start.* Dad's not here to give me grief over wanting to get my hands dirty for once, and a mechanic is out of the question. Neither Ingrid or I can afford one now. Not in our current predicament.

As I navigate the clean, well-manicured streets on the way to Logan's church, I can't help but admire my parents' taste in "investments." My mother grew up here in Meadow Hills, and after inheriting her parents' old lake house, she and my father renovated it within an inch of its life and rebranded it as one of their "seasonal residences." It doubles as their East Coast base, a short drive from their auction house in Portland—where they spend every June and July selling overpriced estate collections, antique furniture no one actually wants to sit on, and paintings that all look the same to me but apparently go for seven figures.

They're big on prestige, my parents. Big on appearances. Which is probably why they've spent the past decade globe-trotting from Woollahra to Maine, chasing the summer like it's a tax write-off. I'll give them this, though—trading Sydney's winter drizzle for lakeside afternoons and seasonal farmers' markets? Not their worst decision.

However, this is my first autumn here. I've never stuck around past July, and I'm usually only here on occasional business with my parents. So I've had no idea what to expect. But now that I'm here for my first September, and for once, free to explore and let my surroundings sink in, I finally see it all.

The towering maple trees at every turn are unreal and serene, and for this early in the season, there's an offensively substantial amount of yellow-orange leaves and cold weather to accompany the sunshine. The way they flutter down in slow motion, gathering in crunchy, satisfying piles along the sidewalks, feels like something out of a postcard.

Porch steps are stacked with pumpkins and baskets of mums. Every gust of wind carries the scent of pine needles and woodsmoke, and the air is just crisp enough to sting my nostrils in the most pleasant way.

Despite my initial reluctance to fall for the town I've been "stranded" in, I can't deny its appeal.

It's so—I wrinkle my nose—*lovely.*

I park at Harvest Valley Church and breathe out a deep sigh. My thoughts ring with alarm in my head: I made it in one piece, and now I've got to go inside if I want a hot meal.

You can do this, Bash. You did it last week, and the past few weeks before that. This time will be no different.

This isn't the first church I've stepped foot inside. In fact, the one my family attends in Australia is the only place I felt more judged than I did at home. It was a constant hub of rude comments and passive-aggressive implications endlessly hurled my way. It started when I began smoking cigarettes at eighteen and only became worse when I got my first tattoo shortly after. Any friends I had were no longer allowed to speak to me, so I learned how to be content without them.

But still. It feels as if I've never been allowed to be myself without apology. So, after wrestling with my decision, a lot of praying, and hoping God wouldn't be disappointed in me, I decided not to step foot in a place like that again.

I get out of the car and roll the sleeves of my designer button-up. I glance at the bare spot on my wrist where my Rolex used to live before I pawned it a few weeks after Mum and Dad decided I needed a lesson in obedience. Checking the invisible time is just muscle memory now.

Did I get anywhere near what it was worth? Of course not. But it's been enough to help keep bread and peanut butter in the pantry, along with a sad ration of gas here and there. Plus, the phone bill I can't afford to lose, and cigarettes—my most loyal, toxic companion. They're currently burning through my remaining funds faster than I can.

I drag a hand through my professionally-cut blond hair, which has grown just shaggy enough to look like that 90's curtain hair men used to have. It's been two months since I was exiled to small-town Maine, and I'm finally starting to look like someone who belongs here—lived-in, broke, and unbothered.

"Bash, my man!"

I turn my gaze toward Logan, the saving grace himself. He's already propped against his truck like he's in a car commercial—tall, effortlessly cool, and somehow making a hoodie and joggers look like designer couture. Not only does the guy have smooth dark skin that looks moisturized by divine intervention, but also a face so absurdly symmetrical it offends me on a spiritual level.

If I didn't like him so much, I'd start a petition to have him removed from public spaces for the safety of everyone's self-esteem.

It's become a routine of ours to meet in the parking lot before breakfast. I arrive, sulk about my life, and try not to overthink everything. Logan interrupts my sulking.

"I'm starving," I tell him by way of greeting.

He chuckles, shoving his fists into the pockets of his joggers. "Chill, my dude. There will be plenty to eat." Logan flashes a smile that reveals his nice teeth, made whiter by the contrast of his dark skin.

The two of us walk into the building together. My

stomach growls louder with each step I take, and when the scent of sausage and crispy bacon hits the air, I nearly collapse. *See, Bash? It's not completely hopeless. God will provide for you if you keep having faith. Don't give up just yet.*

The familiar sea of faces smiles at us. People I'm still struggling to remember nod at me, and I return the gesture.

Logan and I get in line. As usual, the back of the room is cramped with tables and chairs. A long, buffet style table holding all the food is perched near the large window at the entrance. When it's our turn, I take a plate with shaky hands, willing my knees not to buckle.

"So, what's new with you?" Logan asks, spooning some blueberries onto his plate.

"Besides the obvious?" I laugh without humor. "My car wants me to check the engine. No idea why yet."

Logan shrugs one shoulder. "I can take a look at it if you want."

My spine straightens. "Really? You'd do that?"

"Sure, no problem. I can help you Sunday morning after church, if you come."

I nod. "Thanks, mate."

As I add potatoes to my plate of waffles, I realize what I just agreed to. Even though I have nothing but gratitude toward Logan, I know it's only a matter of time before he and the rest of the members of Harvest Valley show their true colors. The moment they get to know me and see my flaws, they're going to shun me like my last church did.

Coming to Tuesday brunch for the food was a stretch to begin with. But now Sundays too? I'm not prepared. Besides, Sunday morning is a time I typically spend training—Rocky style, since I can no longer afford a gym membership or the fuel to get to the nearest one out of town.

I try not to mope.

I'm going to have to come, for the good of my vehicle.

I follow Logan to a table and proceed to eat in silence, partly because I'm ravenous, and also because I'm still trying to work out my new training schedule for the week. Logan inhales his food, and when his stomach appears to be nice and full, he pats it like a well-behaved pet.

Someone approaches the table, and I recognize him from all the previous meals I've attended. "Hey, Steve," I say.

"Hi, Bash." Steve reaches out to shake my hand. I can't help but notice the way it slightly shakes, and how Steve swallows hard, like he's afraid of me or something. Unfortunately, this is something I've gotten used to since I started training seriously. Logan is one of the few friends I've made who doesn't seem at all intimidated by me, and it's part of the reason I like him so much.

Logan nods at Steve. "Bash will be joining us in his first ever church service this Sunday."

Steve looks so excited, it makes my stomach sink. "Awesome," he says. "I'll see you there."

He walks away, leaving me to contemplate how I ended up here.

"This is great, man." Logan rubs his hands together like he's about to dig in for supper, though he just stuffed his face full of French toast and eggs. "I knew you'd join me eventually."

"Don't get too used to it." Staring off at the table of men next to us, I watch Jason clap Bob on the shoulder, all smiles to be here. "This is a one-time thing. And besides," I add with a grin, "you know I'm only here for the food."

Logan laughs. "Well, there won't be much more than donuts and coffee on Sunday. Sorry to disappoint you."

"It's fine, mate."

He relaxes in his chair. We're the only two seated at this particular table, which is probably for the best. The last thing I want to do is get *involved* here. Network. Make friends. By some unspoken rule, Logan and I always sit apart from everyone else, but that hasn't stopped them from occasionally coming to me. Introducing themselves. Getting to know me, or trying, at least. It's to be expected after all. This men's breakfast group meets every Tuesday. Things are bound to get more personal eventually.

I just need to get out before that happens.

"You know," says Logan, "I think your parents cutting you off was God's way of leading you here."

"Well, if there's one thing I'm grateful for, it's that He got me away from my parents," I mutter.

His brows narrow as he meets my gaze. "You've never told me why they cut you off, you know."

I smirk at the table. I don't like people rummaging around in my personal business, so normally I'd tell him to mind his own, but Logan means well. "In July, I debuted with my fight promotion, Munera, against the very explicit wishes of my parents. Then I told them I was done working for them. Doesn't get much worse than that to members of high society."

I try not to get angry as I think back to the last night I worked an auction with them in Portland, the same night my fight showed on TV. I remember my parents, in a rage I've never known they were capable of. Them draining all my accounts and leaving me to rot in our Meadow Hills lake house. "When you ignore our rules, you don't get to spend our money, Sebastian," my mother spat. "You're twenty-five years old. You'll just have to make do with your fight money now, since this new whim is so important to you."

"Fight money?" I laughed. "What fight money? I don't have any sponsors yet. This was my first professional match and my next one is four months away. I'll maybe get two grand. Calm down, Mother."

Calm down was probably the worst thing I could have said to her.

The rest seemed to happen so fast—Ingrid, refusing to go back home with our parents. Them promising she wouldn't get any more money from them if she stayed with me. I must have done something right as her big brother, because when she had to choose between money and me, she picked me. And two months later, she's still here.

And if their dozens of phone calls lately are any indicator, my parents definitely expected us to both come crawling back by now. But the thing is...I don't care about their money. I've always wanted to be free and on my own. I just wish things hadn't played out the way they did.

"I'm sorry that happened," Logan says, breaking me out of my trance.

I shrug. "It's nothing more than a manipulation tactic. They want me to come back home, so they're punishing me by cutting off my access to money. They think I'll come running back to them any day now."

"That's messed up." Logan rubs the back of his neck and frowns. "Will you, though? Go running back to them?"

"No. They'll only let me come home if I give up

fighting because they want to keep training me to take over the family business. And there's no way I'm doing that. Besides, I don't want to go back."

"Have you heard from your parents since all this happened?" Logan asks.

"Oh, yeah." I lean back in my chair. "Mum calls about once a week to remind me I've made a terrible mistake and to convince me I should come home. She mentions how badly I need her and Dad's money every time."

He nods, frowning like he's processing my words. And I admit it's a lot to process for me, too. I still can't decide if my parents are against me fighting because they think I'd be better off running their business someday, or if they simply have no faith in my fighting abilities.

No faith in me.

To them, I'm nothing but an embarrassment.

"Logan! Bash!" The youth pastor approaches us, sauntering over from across the breakfast hall. He has long, dark hair in dreadlocks and a wide smile I can't seem to hate, much as I try. "Glad to see you here."

"What's good, Hayden?" Logan grins at him. "Guess who will be back here Sunday morning, bright and early?" He elbows my side. I want to kick him.

Hayden's eyes widen. His grin transforms into a laugh. "No way! Bash, that's awesome. I'll save you a seat next to me."

"No," I cut in. "No, really, you don't have to do that." This is exactly what I've been trying to avoid. I refuse to start getting finagled into this lot's inner circle. To become part of this small town's community without my permission. But as much as I'd like to get out of coming back on

Sunday, I can't help but feel obligated to attend in exchange for Logan taking a look at my car.

"Nonsense." Hayden slips his hands into the pockets of his baggy cargo pants. "See you Sunday!"

"Yeah." I nod, hoping he'll mistake my grimace for a smile. "Yeah, I guess you will."

I mingle for a bit longer before telling Logan, "It's time for me to go, mate."

He nods, pulling me into a one-armed hug. "Thanks for coming, man."

I don't linger another moment. I make for the exit, practically sprinting in the car park for my Camaro.

And barrel headfirst into someone carrying a cooking pot.

Before I can process what's happened, the contents of the pot splash over her shirt and face, soaking her.

I swear loudly. "I'm sorry. So sorry."

The woman blinks in surprise several times and sets the pot on the ground. She stares down at her ruined white T-shirt for a moment before glancing up at me.

My breath catches in my throat as I take in her face, deep bronze and heart-shaped, framed by her hair, which looks like a jet-black curtain of ink spilling around her. Her eyes are a vivid green that do funny things to my body. A few noodles from the—soup, is it?—stick to one side of her hair, yet she still might very well be the most beautiful woman I've ever seen.

"It's no problem," she says.

No problem? She can't mean that. I don't answer immediately, still struck by her excruciating attractiveness. I clear my throat. "I find that hard to believe. Look what I've done to you." I pluck the noodle off the end of her hair and show it to her.

She giggles. "I'll be fine."

"I've wasted your dinner."

"It's not mine." She bites her lip, making blood rush through my body. "It was for the soup kitchen."

I frown. "Oh." *Nice. You really are a winner, Bash.*

But she offers me a lopsided grin. "Thankfully, they've already eaten. These were just the leftovers."

"Still," I say. Her gaze locks onto mine, drawing me in, so I take a step closer. "At least let me take you out to make it up to you." My own words give me pause. *What am I thinking?* I don't do relationships, and I don't have much right now, but I'd gladly spend what little cash I have left from my watch on her.

"No, don't worry about it." She shakes her head, but that smile still lights up her face. It's the kind of smile that makes me feel happy just from looking at it. Infectious.

She picks up the pot and regards me once more, tilting her head sideways and squinting through thick lashes. "Bye."

I reach out a hand toward her involuntarily. "I—"

But she's already gone, halfway across the car park toward a white sedan. And I'm left staring after her, wondering who on earth she is, and why I suddenly feel the need to find out.

Chapter Two

ROMILLY

IN THE QUIET hours before the sun rises, I can never resist a good bath.

And as much as I love my sister, privacy isn't always easy to come by around her. Thankfully, our impromptu sleepovers at my place are never more than weekly, but I sometimes wonder what Zara's reaction would be if she tiptoed to the bathroom at four in the morning and found me in the tub, under my blanket of bubbles and hot water injected with essential oils. Candles are currently lit around the rim of the tub, and my favorite paperback of secret, romantic poetry is in my free hand.

Zara would probably do a cartwheel if she saw me right now. She'd overreact and take this as the evidence she's been wanting that I'm not as resistant to relationships as I put on.

I scan the page in front of me as the water laps over my chest and stomach. The flickering, scented flames thicken the air around me, and I try to push away the longing thoughts that enter my mind as I read.

Beneath the quiet moon, your touch ignites me,
A fire in my veins that burns and lights me.

And then *his* face flashes behind my eyes. That tall stranger from church with the tattoos, the Australian accent, the blond hair and blue eyes. And that voice.

His intense stare as he held up that noodle. *Look what I've done to you.*

My thoughts dance around at a dizzying speed from the memory.

No.

I'm usually so good at keeping men out of my thoughts, and it's not often I find a man attractive enough to make me reconsider why I avoid thinking about them in the first place. While this guy was probably the finest man I've ever seen, there was also something more than attraction between us. I know I couldn't have imagined that unspoken chemistry we had because it was so strong, it practically strangled me with its presence.

Even though I was covered in soup, I wanted to keep standing there, keep talking to him, keep staring at that grin of his—half charm, half trouble—as well as those blue eyes carrying mischief the way a cloud carries a storm.

And being as lonely as I am, sitting in a bathtub reading love poetry definitely isn't helping.

Heart pounding, I force myself to try to think of something else. Just because I'm finally living on my own again doesn't mean I have an excuse to start daydreaming. I'm independent, like I've always wanted to be, and I've been so good lately. My thoughts have finally been in check. And then *he* had to go and ruin it by asking me out, because now here I am imagining what would have happened if I said yes.

Besides, I tell myself, *just imagine what future Romilly would think if she knew you were entertaining such things. She'd be disappointed. You're living your dream as a dog groomer and shop owner. You don't need anything else to manage, and the last thing you want is to get hurt again.*

After soaking for another thirty minutes, I pull the plug in the tub and let the water drain, then grab my folded towel from the wooden stool perched beside me. I dry off and, with a sigh, hide the book in my toiletry bag.

When I'm dressed in a pair of baggy jeans, a cream knit sweater, and leather jacket, I complete my weekly silk press on my naturally curly hair and apply a light layer of makeup. I'm singing during worship at church today, so I might as well get ready now.

I make my way down the creaky hall, careful not to wake my sister. If my brother, Aiden, were here, he'd probably sleep just fine, but Zara will pop out of bed like a toaster pastry at the sound of rain falling. I plan to let her sleep in since it's practically her love language, and since she has a key, she has no problem letting herself out.

It's going to be so strange when she goes off to college next year. Unlike most of our friends, my sister and I decided to start a dog grooming business instead of going to college, but once it failed after a few years, and we were both forced to move back home, she decided college was the path for her after all. Since I couldn't stop grooming if I tried, I was desperate to make my new, solo shop work out. And it did. The moment I started making enough to be out of my parents' house and back on my own, I found this place. And though this tiny, historical cottage isn't perfect, it's charming and it's mine. Now that I'm twenty-seven, it seems appropriate for me to finally *stay* on my own.

I start up the stove and make my favorite breakfast, oatmeal topped with cinnamon, sliced apples, and bananas. I take it to the table and settle in, careful not to step on the flicking tail of my sleeping cat, Jasper, who is in a cozy, curled-up ball beside the chair I settle into. He's wearing a green knit sweater I bought him from my favorite boutique, and like always, seeing him in it makes me smile.

Crossing my legs, I dip my spoon into the bowl of oatmeal. It will be time to head to practice before the service soon, but while I eat, I always try to read at least one verse. And today's doesn't at all seem like a coincidence.

"So I say, walk by the Spirit, and you will not gratify the desires of the flesh."
–Galatians 5:16

I wince. *Okay, God. I hear you loud and clear. No more fantasizing about the hot newcomer.*

"You smell nice."

I start in my chair when I realize Zara is standing right next to me. She folds her arms across her pink satin pajama top. A few strands of her hair escape her matching pink bonnet. "Stop doing that."

Her eyes round in fake innocence. "Stop doing what?"

"You know what." I fix her with a glare. "Stop appearing out of nowhere and trying to scare me every time you're here."

"No idea what you're talking about, to be honest." She sniffs the air. "Why do you smell so nice?"

I blush, thoughts of my hopelessly romantic lavender-oil bath rushing back to me. "I don't smell nice."

"Yes, you do. You should smell like sweat and morning breath, but you smell like a candle shop instead, and it's weird."

"I took a shower, Zara."

"I take showers, and we use the same stuff. Why don't I smell like you?"

I back away from her approaching nostrils. "Okay, enough!" I stand from my seat. "I have to go to practice now. See you in a few hours."

She arches an eyebrow at me but lets me walk away from her. "I will find this secret perfume of yours and make it my own."

"Whatever."

"You can't stop me," she promises.

But I cut off her voice as I close the front door. Shaking my head, I bite back my smile. Of course she notices how I smell the one time I take a bath while she's here. Still, I'm really going to miss her. Meadow Hills is a small town. Without her in it after she leaves for college in Portland, it's bound to feel vast and empty.

I hug my coat against my body as I walk to my car. Late-September in Maine is comfortably cold, and the abundance of red and yellow trees surrounding the town can't be beat. As I drive along the narrow stretch of road, I can't help but admire the sleepy hush all around at this hour. The railings of the gazebo at the town center are covered with numerous cats. A fluffy white one is perched at the base, and it yawns just as I peek out the window.

Not to mention, the lights are just turning on at Old Joe's diner, and I spot Joe himself through the white marker illustrations on his windows of the maple lavender latte he serves every autumn. He's unstacking chairs from atop his wooden tables as he readies his restaurant for the day. Seeing him awake at this early hour always makes me feel less alone, somehow.

The only church in town is only a couple miles down the road. As the familiar building approaches from the other side of the windshield, warmth enters me. It feels like another home.

I park and get out of the car. My old boots clop against the sidewalk as I near Harvest Valley Church. I open my purse and approach the back entrance to find my key, fishing around inside until the cool metal meets my fingertips.

"Can you spare some change?"

My gaze jumps to the old man sitting on the parking curb a few feet away. He's not holding a cardboard sign, but his clothes are worn and tattered, his eyes crazed with a literal hunger that makes my heart feel like it's clenched in a fist. Though I've seen him around town lately, this is the first time he's ever interacted with me.

"Of course." I find my wallet in my still-open bag and fish out my last ten dollars, a tip from a dog grooming job I did last week. "Here." I hand the money to the man, and he takes it.

"Thank you." He stands and stretches his shoulders. "Thank you so much. This will buy me breakfast."

A gust of cold wind makes me shiver. "If you come back on Tuesday, I'll serve you a nice, hot breakfast myself."

His answering smile lights my insides. "I'll hold you to that." He stretches out his hand for me to shake. "The name's Herman."

"Romilly." I shake his hand.

"See you Tuesday." He nods at me and makes for the crosswalk.

I turn back to the rear entrance of the church and unlock the door. I flip on all the lights as I enter, ignoring the small twinge in my stomach. I'm the first one here again. I shouldn't be surprised though, because I don't know anyone else as crazy as me, willing to wake up at four in the morning to get here at five-thirty.

Still, the emptiness is all too familiar.

I flip on the lights to the backstage room. The only thing that stirs in the room is dust, but the rest of the music team will be here soon.

I get a cup of water from the dispenser in the corner, clap all the erasers resting on the whiteboard together to dust them, and review the list on this week's worship songs, even though I have the order memorized.

Anything to fill the empty time.

Harnessing the power of distractions is all too familiar to me these days, and I'm starting to get creative.

I clear my throat and start my vocal warm-ups. I have to admit, singing into such prominent silence is always jarring at first, but after a few scales and arpeggios, my ears adjust to the sound.

"I'll never get over your voice. It's so unfair."

I jump at the sound of Hadley's compliment, placing a hand to my chest. "You scared me."

"Sorry." She chuckles and sets down her guitar case, pulling out her pearl white Strat. "I was going to say something as soon as I got here, but *girl,* you had me entranced. You're like a freaking siren or something."

I blush. "Thanks."

A hum of voices sounds from the hall and the rest of the worship team fills the room. Jake with his travel keyboard, Eddie with his drumsticks, and Martin with his bass.

"Good morning everyone," I say.

"Morning, Rom." Eddie taps his drumsticks together with a silly grin on his mouth. "First one here again?"

I shrug. "I had nothing else going on."

"Why don't we do something about that?" Jake winks at me. "Just say the word when you're ready for me to hook you up with my cousin. Allen, remember?"

"I will." But the thing is, I won't. I pick up my water cup from the low table next to me and take another sip. Shift my feet on the carpeted floor. Avert my gaze from Jake's.

"He's a real catch," he promises.

"I'm sure he is."

Hadley squints at Jake. "Leave her alone. She's over dating. Let her be the strong, independent woman she's trying to be."

"Fine. Just trying to help." He purses his lips and then adds, "But you don't have to spend all your time alone or volunteering at shelters to be independent, you know. You can have a man, too. You're allowed to do something for yourself."

"I know. Thanks, Jake." I try not to get irritated with him, because I know he's just trying to be nice. But what he doesn't understand is that I'd rather be alone, no matter how unnerving or depressing my loneliness feels.

It's bad enough knowing how untrustworthy men are, even the ones who seem promising. I wish I could find a way to make myself not care about romance, love, or relationships after what my ex, Cole, put me through.

But it's hard.

I *do* care.

With a sigh, I point to the song list on the wall behind Jake. "Shouldn't we practice?"

He tries to hide his scowl. "Fine."

After three rounds of our worship set, it's safe to say we're all warmed up. There's still time to kill before the first service begins, so we all take a rest, seated on the foldout chairs in our small, well-lit space.

"Sorry for nagging you, Rom," Jake says. "I just—"

Hadley huffs out a sigh. "What is with you, Jake? Just let it go." Her polite smile is starting to wear thin, and not just because she and Jake used to date, but also on my account. I feel a wash of gratitude for her.

"Fine, yes. Sorry." He holds up his hands. "I'm all done." He gets up and stalks to the bathroom without another word.

I nudge Hadley with my shoulder once Jake is out of ear shot. "You doing okay?"

"Fine." She shrugs. "It feels like we've been broken up for years instead of months, the way we've been fighting like an old divorced couple."

I touch her shoulder. "But it hasn't been years. So if you need to talk, I'm here."

She nods. "I know. Thank you." She's silent for a long moment and then with a sniff, says, "He was never really a good fit for me anyway."

"Yeah, you're probably right." It's partly a lie. I thought

for sure they were going to get married, but I have a feeling it's what she needs to hear, especially after she dumped him for smothering her. Sometimes I think she regrets it, but who am I to judge? I don't want to be in a relationship, either. Because I hate the part that comes *after* believing I've finally found my person. The part where "my person" shows his true colors, after the damage has been done and I've already become emotionally invested. The part where he lets me down.

Everyone lets down the person they love eventually.

Hadley interrupts my thoughts with a hug, then stands. "All right. Let's get ready. We're on that stage in less than an hour."

I clear my throat. "I was just thinking the same thing."

Chapter Three

BASH

MY MOTHER really has the worst timing. In the entrance of Harvest Valley Church, just as I'm about to lift a crispy, glazed donut to my lips, she calls. And I'm ravenous. But she's still my mother, so I answer.

"Yes, mum?"

"Sweetheart, please just come home and drop this nonsense."

My stomach tightens the same way it always does when she voices her disapproval of the things I love. Of the things that make me... *me*. "I'm sorry you think my dream is nonsense, mother."

A sigh. "And I'm sorry you think choosing violence is a worthy career."

I try to control the heat boiling in my veins. *Deep breath, Bash.* But I just can't let it go. I refuse to let her continue to belittle anything I care about that she doesn't approve of. "The problem for you is that it's what I want, isn't it? It's that you didn't choose it."

"Don't be ridiculous. Come home. I'll make ribs. Your favorite."

I grip the phone so tight, my knuckles are probably white. "See, that's the part I don't think you understand. I'd rather be on my own and hungry than back with you and Dad, being controlled. I am never going to want to run the auction houses, okay? I can't stand to be in them. I never have." What I don't admit is that part of me does feel a little abandoned that my parents were so willing to toss me to the curb for choosing my own path for once. But still, the other part of me—the bigger part—finally feels free.

She's silent. I imagine her cheeks turning pink, the way they only do when she's enraged. "That's how you see it, is it?" Her voice slightly quivers. "And I suppose you think you're on your own right now, do you? Don't forget, you're still living in *our* lake house. Even though it might not feel like it, your father and I are still supporting you. You have no idea what it's like to be on your own for real, Sebastian."

My pride flares. The frustration I've been suppressing each time she calls finally breaks free, and there's nothing I can do to keep it from affecting my tone. "Give me two more months and I will. My next fight will pay enough to get me out on my own."

A light laugh sounds from the phone. "Fine, then. I want you out of that house in two months whether you win or not. If you do win, you'll finally see how hard it is to be on your own, in the real world without our help. But if you lose, I really hope you'll give this up once and for all, and *just come home*."

"Give me until November. I'll be gone, win or lose."

And then I hang up. I try not to dwell on the heavy dread settling in my stomach. Because without any sponsors, winning the fight isn't going to pay much at all, and if I lose...I'll have nowhere left to go but home. Unless I get a job. One that will keep me from having to go back to my parents, where life feels more suffocating than comforting.

But you're not going to lose. You're going to find at least one sponsor and win and finally prove to them this is more than just a phase or a whim. This is your passion. And it's a real career. One to be proud of.

I tuck my phone away and finally take a bite of the donut I'm still holding. It's not half bad, so I add three of them to my stack. They're free, after all, and I'm hungry. I fold them into my napkin and balance them in one hand with my cup of free coffee, so I can be welcomed as a newcomer with my other hand. This town is so small, I can't imagine there are many new members, so it's bound to happen. Even though I'm not a new member, and don't plan on becoming one.

"You alright, man?" Logan elbows me, nearly making me spill my refreshments.

"I'm fine." The words are easy. Practiced. As much as I hated being forced to schmooze my parents' clients, doing so is the only job I've ever known besides fighting, and...I'm good at being charming. I know how to wear a pleasant face to hide what I'm really thinking. So when I let the effortless grin fall in place, Logan drops it.

We make our way across a large, grassy courtyard with outdoor seating and string lights hung between surrounding poles. There's an abundance of pumpkins scattered around, along with a heavy maple scent in the air from the coffee station. I almost don't want to go inside. Actually, scratch that. I *definitely* don't.

Logan and I walk through the entryway to a small

auditorium with rows of cinema-style seating. The lady standing at the door hands us each a pamphlet as we enter.

Please, God. Don't let this be a bad experience like my last church.

Soft background music fills the air while everyone finds a seat. I watch as people hug, exchange warm smiles, and engage in quiet conversations before lowering themselves into chairs. Logan grins and gestures to the row of empty seats nearest to us. I take the one on the end, and Logan squeezes between my knees and the backs of the chairs in front of us to sit next to me. At least Hayden, the youth pastor, is nowhere to be seen with his promise of saving me a seat next to him.

Logan whispers, "Thanks again for coming."

My jaw tightens in response. The lights dim, and a collective hush falls across the room. As if on cue, everyone stands up and music plays from all around. Logan rises with me and claps along with the music. A drummer and several other musicians are onstage, playing live. Pretty well, too. I know some of the words to this song but not all of them, and apparently neither do some of the others here, because the lyrics to the songs are displayed on tiny screens mounted on each end of the room.

As unwelcome as I've felt at church in the past, I can't deny how much I've missed this part. The singing. And hearing the voices of those around me singing in unison to the same God we all love makes the back of my throat burn with emotion. I try to swallow it down.

After the third song ends, everyone sits. A slower melody begins playing, and a young woman walks onto the stage and takes the microphone. She lifts it to her full lips and when she sings, her voice comes out soft, feather-light, angelic.

And I'm left staring, transfixed, but not just because of her voice. Because of her *face.* I would recognize it anywhere. It's her. The one from the parking lot. The soup girl. "Who is she?" I whisper. *Oh, great . . . did I ask that question out loud?*

Logan leans in to respond in a hushed tone. "That's Romilly Westfall."

"She has a beautiful voice."

As if she can hear me, Romilly turns her gaze onto me while she sings. Something in my chest does a little dance.

"She does," says Logan. I turn to look at him, and he's staring at her too.

When Romilly's song ends, applause rings around me like an alarm—*wake up, you idiot!* I shake off the stupor I've somehow managed to fall into. Romilly may be beautiful and have a voice like I've never heard before, but the last thing I need right now is to let a woman distract me. This is my chance to show everyone I can make something of myself as a fighter, and that it's not just a foolish whim on my part, or a rebellious streak.

Besides, this is the first time I've ever been free. Do I really want to start something that might tie me back down?

The reminder hits me like a brick wall.

It's what I repeat to myself when she disappears backstage, replaced by the pastor, a fifty-something man. It's what I try to remember as my thoughts drift to her over and over throughout the service. It's what I cling to while scribbling on my pamphlet, drawing little animals and even writing my phone number down like a presumptuous fool.

The service finally ends, and when Logan and I stand to leave, Romilly Westfall herself begins to make her way over to us.

My thoughts scramble as she approaches, each step closer making me feel more like a madman than before. *She's easily the most beautiful woman I've ever seen.*

"Hey, Romilly," Logan greets her.

"Hey, friend," she says. She hugs him, squeezing her eyes shut. I give her face another once-over now that I'm certain she won't notice. She has prominent cheekbones and a cute, round nose with a straight bridge. Her top lip is somehow just as full as her bottom lip, and—I can't help but notice—she has an elegant, long body slightly hidden under her modest but trendy clothing. She's even more beautiful than I remembered. Too beautiful.

When Logan releases her from the hug, she opens her eyes and looks right at me. I expect her to mention the soup incident, but instead, she says, "I'm Romilly. What's your name?"

Something about her tone is confident, but soft—a pairing I can't help but admire. But knowing she might not recognize me from our soup-spill encounter in the car park knocks me into silence and I fail to remember how to speak.

Logan clears his throat and says, "This is Sebastian Black. It's his first Sunday here."

"Bash," I choke out, finding my voice again. "Everyone calls me Bash."

"Oh, nice." She beams. "You should come to men's breakfast on Tuesday, too."

Instead of stating that I've already been attending the dreaded event more often than I'd like, I ask, "Will you be there?" The implication is unashamedly present in my tone.

She arches a brow. Regards me like she's worried for my competence. "No," she says carefully. "It's for men."

Ah. She has a point. And now I feel like a complete and utter fool. Where my typical charm has run off to, I have no clue. I turn to Logan for help, but he's wandered off to talk to someone else across the room. I could strangle him right now.

"It's a really cool event, though," Romilly continues, unaware she's wasting her breath. "There's delicious food, and lots of great people, and the message is always so—"

"I've been to the men's breakfast," I finally tell her. "I go every week. It's *this* I don't do very often. Sundays. Not really my thing anymore."

"Oh." For some reason, I want to kick myself as the glowing smile on her lips dims. "I understand." She pauses and takes a step forward. "And here I was, hoping to see you around here next Sunday."

I note the way her lips remain parted, those lips so plump and pink and irresistible. I want to bite the bottom one. I don't know how to answer her, because after the way I've been treated in the past, I'd rather eat cheese off a dirty shoe than start coming back to church. But the way she's studying me is fogging up my brain. Making me reconsider. A strand of shorter hair on her forehead threatens to fall into her eyes, which now that we're standing closer than before, I can see with certainty are bright green with brown flecks throughout. "I'll come back on Sunday if you let me take you out for coffee." The words escape before I can think things through.

She blinks in surprise. "Oh. Sure." A small smile

appears. "We can go to Logan's house. He makes the best coffee."

"Actually, that would defeat the point. I say coffee, but what I really mean is a date."

She purses her lips, her eyebrows drawn together in worry. "Then I'm very sorry."

Did...did she just politely turn me down? At first I can't be sure, because I've never actually been turned down before. Though I've never dated too seriously, I've *dated*—of course I have. And it's never been challenging for me to secure a date with a beautiful, single woman before.

Maybe she isn't single. My gaze darts to her left hand. I expect to see a wedding ring resting on her finger, but there's nothing other than a simple gold band on her thumb. How odd. It's almost as if she's not interested.

I know the best thing to do would be to forget about her and quit while I'm ahead. I came to the service today, fulfilling my end of the bargain. Logan is going to take a look at my car in a moment. I shouldn't be spending my dwindling cash on overpriced coffee, anyway. But if I wanted to, there are plenty of other beautiful women in the world. If I really wanted to, I could pursue someone who's actually interested in me.

But that's the thing.

I don't want a relationship right now.

I need to focus on my career, and as a member of this church, Romilly is probably just as judgy as the rest of them. She'll want even less to do with me once she learns more about me.

Yet, her hooded eyes and the way she keeps leaning toward me say different. And there's something clearly magnetic between us, something strong enough to make me think she might just be playing hard-to-get, so I might have to ignore my better judgement here.

I lower my voice a notch, letting the charisma I was raised with seep into my tone. "If you let me take you on one date, not only will I attend church next Sunday, but I'll *continue* attending the men's breakfast. And I'll also let you answer all my aching questions as a newcomer to your church." *No need to let her know you'll be out of here as soon as you win your fight.*

She stares at me, pondering, and at first I think she's going to tell me to get lost, but then I see it. The barest hint of a smile. The slightest twitching of her mouth. "Fine. One cup of coffee," she says, and then winces, closing her eyes and shaking her head a little. "I mean...I would love to have coffee with you, Bash." Her voice is saccharine, almost too sweet, and it wraps around my name in a way that makes my body feel warm and light.

"Great." I flash a grin, ever the smooth gentleman. "Then here's my number." I hand her the pamphlet I received at the beginning of service, scribbled on with doodles.

She frowns at it. "Is that...a zebra?" She rotates the paper to gauge the drawing from a new angle.

"It is." I point to myself. "Penned by yours truly."

She laughs, the sound unmistakably instinctual. And then she clamps her mouth shut like she's worried she's offended me. But her lips remain upturned. "It's very good."

"And right there is my phone number." I reach over and point to the top corner of the page. My face is closer to hers with me leaning over the paper like this, and I can smell the lavender and honey perfume of her hair. Of her skin. It must be her body wash.

"Wow, you sure had that ready to go, didn't you?" A funny expression crosses her face. "Do you...write your phone number on the program every time you come to church?"

My face heats with embarrassment, but I try to hide it. "Of course not."

She narrows her eyes, but her lips form a thin smile. "I'll see you tomorrow afternoon. For coffee."

"Where should I pick you up?"

"I'll text you the place to meet me. Now that I have your phone number." She waves the paper in the air like a tiny flag. "Bring your Bible," she adds before walking away.

"I don't have a Bible." At least, not here in Meadow Hills. It's still back in Australia. But she's already gone, off to greet someone else, and I'm left staring after her, once again.

Chapter Four

ROMILLY

BEFORE I LEAVE CHURCH, I find my family to hug them goodbye.

"You sang so beautifully, honey," my mom says, smoothing my hair back. "But you look exhausted. Are you getting enough sleep?"

"Of course. I'm fine." I smile at her and my dad, who wraps his arm around her waist.

Aiden gives me a fist bump instead of a hug, probably because of the game he's streaming on his phone in his other hand. One he can't take his eyes off. I remember how annoyed our parents were when he first took up the gaming hobby, but when checks started coming in the mail, they couldn't deny how impressed they were at what he was making for a high schooler.

Last, I give Zara a tight squeeze. "I'll see you soon. Let's have another sleepover."

She nods. "We gotta get them in while we can."

"Stop reminding me you're leaving for college. It's not like you're going tomorrow. We have a *year*."

She laughs.

I head to my car and get in. I'm about to put it in reverse when Logan Henry knocks on the passenger window.

Smiling, I roll it down and wave at him. As angry as the majority of men make me, I can't help but feel a soft spot toward Logan. Maybe it's because he's like a brother to me, but I feel like if there were such a thing as a trustworthy man, it would have to be him.

Bash on the other hand? Everything about him so far screams "do not trust me."

"I'm glad you got to meet Sebastian," he says, reading my mind. "I actually just finished looking at his car. The dude has a blown head gasket. Expensive to fix, but at least his car will still run for a while. He's a real nice guy."

"I'm sure he is." My smile feels forced. If only Logan knew just how much Bash has been on my mind since I first bumped into him. And I didn't even know his name then. It irritates me that I now have another detail about him to try to block out of my silly fantasies.

Logan sighs. "He's going through kind of a tough time. I'm wondering if there's any work we can find for him here."

"W-work?" I struggle to remain composed. "You want to give him a job?"

"He really needs it."

Thoughts swarm in my head of my conversation with Bash just before I got in the car. I agreed to a date with him. *A date.* Something I'd never in a million years normally do. But the way he made flutters course from my hairline to my toes with that charming, dangerous twinkle in his eye and that easy grin clearly affected my ability to think straight. *If you think it's bad now, just imagine what it will be like if he works here with you.* "How badly?"

Logan blinks in surprise, unable to hold back an uneasy chuckle. I'm not sure I've ever questioned helping someone in need before, and he's definitely taken aback. "I'm thinking pretty bad, based on some private things he's told me."

Private things? Curiosity pricks me, but I ignore it. If Logan doesn't feel right about spilling Bash's secrets to me, I'm not going to push him. And this is about more than just me. It wouldn't be right to turn away someone who needs help because I can't get a hold on myself. My shoulders sag. "I guess we could use an extra leader for autumn camp. But wait...is he even a Christian?"

"Bash? Oh, yeah. He's just a little rough around the edges. And you're right." Logan claps once and points at me. "He would be perfect."

"You think so?" I scrunch my nose. Bash has a lot of things written all over him, but "church camp leader" definitely isn't one of them. And he already said so himself. *It's this I don't do very often. Sundays. Not really my thing anymore.*

But Logan nods. "Absolutely."

"I'm meeting him for coffee tomorrow, so I'll offer the job to him then."

When he lets that sink in, his answering smile is blinding. "Oh, are you? Interesting. *Very* interesting. I really think this is all part of the Lord's plan, you know?"

My cheeks catch fire. "He has questions about Harvest Valley, that's all. I agreed to answer them."

Logan's eyebrow doesn't move from its elevated position.

"Anyway, I have to get to work. I'll see you Tuesday." Before he can respond, I back out of my parking spot and drive away.

My thoughts are in a fluster as I drive to my cottage. I'm not sure what Logan finds so interesting about me having coffee with Bash, but I'm not sure I like it.

Shaking the irritation away, I park in my cracked driveway. I almost forgot the reason Zara spent the night, but when I step inside and see the freshly painted interior we worked on yesterday, my spirits lift. My kitchen walls are now sage green, complementing the natural honey oak cabinets and white countertops. I smile as I check out the living room next, now a calming sand tone instead of the aggravating red it was when I first moved in.

It looks beautiful.

I can't help but feel a strong sense of pride when I realize how much all my hard work has paid off since last year. Sure, I'm working myself to the bone to be able to afford renting on my own, but it's worth it. Not having to rely on anyone else for anything is worth it.

Speaking of work, I need to get going, I realize, glancing at the time on my phone. Even though it's Sunday, I've scheduled myself a full evening to make up for my morning off the clock. Thankfully, my grooming salon is only a short drive from here.

Before I go, I find my cat, Jasper, curled up inside my old Miss Meadow pageant crown atop my dresser. This is his favorite place to sleep in my room, and I sometimes wonder if it's his way of reminding me to smile. Though I've aged out of that pageant, winning funds for the homeless was the award I was granted more than once, and that knowledge always makes me happy.

I rub Jasper's fuzzy head with a grin. "I'll see you tonight, buddy."

The Paw Spa often feels like a sanctuary to me. I know most people probably don't feel that way about their place of work, but I can't help the rush of relief I experience every time I enter mine.

I love the sound of the clippers and shears, snipping and buzzing away the thick manes of Doodles and Aussies. The various scents of puppy shampoos and canine colognes. I love the wagging tails of my regular clients after a few long weeks of separation while their fur grows out between cuts. But most of all, I love the distraction work offers me.

Here, there are no lonely thoughts.

And it's a good thing, too, because I spent every last dime of my savings on the buildout for this quaint, private dog grooming salon.

"Hey, Romilly," my bathing assistant says. She has one hand under the belly of a golden retriever who keeps trying to sit on the elevated work table where she has him standing. The tray between our stations carries my expensive, professional dog-grooming clippers.

"Hi, Lana." With a smile, I glance around the salon I worked so hard on, admiring the teal accents on the doors and ceiling. The color very much complements the warm wood paneling. There's a blush pink wall behind the check-in desk and a cozy seating area with coral-pink chairs, giving the space the inviting, boutique feel I envisioned. A wall displays my colorful array of leashes, collars, and pet clothing for sale, adding a touch of whimsy. The faint scent of high-end hair products lingers in the air, along with the pumpkin spice candle glowing on the reception desk. They both do their job to mask any typical kennel smells.

It's just me and Lana here, as usual, and it looks like she's already gotten started with bathing and drying Cindy, my first dog for the day. I feel a wash of gratitude. I couldn't make this work without her. In order to afford the payments on this place and my cottage, I have to groom at least thirty-six dogs a week. And there's no way I could do it alone.

I stop at the front desk and open the schedule on the computer to see how many more dogs I'll be working on today. Three are currently booked, with my first one—a Rottweiler named Betty Lou—arriving in less than an hour. Excitement bubbles in my gut. I haven't seen Betty Lou in over a month. Her pet parent, Paige, is a ballet instructor who I've seen around town but formally met and befriended at last year's Miss Meadow pageant, and seeing her on my schedule always lifts my spirits.

But the feeling only lasts a moment, because I open the mail next. And instead of my usual bills, a notice stares up at me.

With shaky hands, I read it:

Dear Ms. Westfall,

Due to rising property maintenance costs, insurance premiums, and local tax adjustments, this letter will be serving as formal notice of a 25% rent increase in accordance with the terms outlined in your lease agreement, effective on the first of next month.

All other lease terms and conditions will remain unchanged.

Sincerely,

Karen F. Lattimer

Meadow Hills Commercial Properties

I sigh, setting the notice down. This is the last thing I need right now. Though I'm grateful to have Lana as my bather, I've finally managed to get to a place where I feel comfortable operating without my last groomer, Agatha anymore.

It will be fine, Romilly, you'll just take on a few extra dogs every day. It will all work out.

Still, I can't stop myself from sending Agatha a text, because I'm already working so much, and it would be nice not to have to add even more to my plate.

ME

> Hey! Any chance you'd want to come work at The Paw Spa with me?

AGATHA

> I've told you, sweetie. I'm working in Portland, now. But thanks for the offer.

I try to swallow back the burning in my throat.

ME

> To be honest, I could really use the extra hands around here. I just got hit with a rent increase

AGATHA

> Oh, honey. I'm sorry. Unfortunately, after the way things ended last time, I don't really feel comfortable coming back. I've told you that.

ME

> But this building is in much better shape than the last one. I'm not closing down over expensive repairs again. Besides, I'm renting now! If anything happens, it's up to the landlord.

It takes Agatha a while to respond, and I clutch my phone tight as I wait.

AGATHA

> That's good. But have you seen your online rating? Only 3 stars.

ME

> I can get that rating up easily.

AGATHA

> I'll tell you what...if you can get to 4 stars, I'll consider it.

My chest lightens at the sliver of hope. *You hear that, Romilly? All you have to do is get to four stars!* But I have no idea how to do that when I'm not sure why my ratings are so average to begin with. I pull up my business page online and read the reviews. Most of them are merely star ratings with no text, but one catches my eye from an anonymous user.

```
Cute shop, and I love Romilly, but
she really needs to hire another
person. It takes too long to get an
appointment because she's always
booked, and her grooms take forever
to finish. Might get my dog groomed
out of town next time.
```

Throat tightening with emotion again, I close my eyes. *Help me find a way to make this work,* I pray. *Please, God.*

With my mind in a haze, I set up my station, arranging the clippers, shears, and brushes neatly, while making sure everything is within easy reach. Then I fluff the cozy beds in the kennels and adjust the framed portraits of today's canine clients above their designated spots, smiling at the familiar faces. Even though it's an extra task, I switch out the photos daily depending on who's coming in. Each dog has their own little nook separated by teal gates against the long wall, a touch I'm particularly proud of. It's all about making them feel at home.

By the time Paige walks in, I'm practically bouncing on my heels. She must have come straight from work because she's wearing loose sweats over a pink leotard. "Is that my favorite girl?" I say when I see Betty Lou. As I approach them, I notice Paige's mouth set in a slight cringe. And then I mirror her expression when I take in Betty's short, black and brown fur, caked in mud. Her nails are practically curling, they've gotten so long.

Paige laughs uneasily. "She had a little too much fun chasing a stray chicken around this morning. It's been hard to keep her off the sofa while we've waited to come in."

"That's okay," I laugh. "How do you feel about a shave?"

Her dark gaze turns sheepish. "That bad, huh?"

"I'm kidding, Paige."

She visibly relaxes. "Okay good. But I honestly would have gone with it, Rom. You know I trust you. And it doesn't help that I'm chronically gullible."

I laugh and capture the leash as she passes it to me. "I'll take Betty Lou from here. It will be about two hours for her bath, brush, and nail trim. I'll give you a call when she's done."

"Thanks," she says, waving at her dog. "Be good, girl."

I walk Betty Lou through the barn door to the back of the salon where we keep the wash tubs. Lana meets me back there, holding a leash with Koda, a matted, black Goldendoodle on the other end. "Trade ya."

I hand her Betty Lou to wash and take Koda. While we're back there, I shave him down to within an inch of fur. "I'm sorry, boy," I whisper. And I am. I love his curly, black fur. But unfortunately, shaving all the fur off doodles is one of the things I do most at work. It's practically my bread and butter since their fur gets easily matted without daily brushing.

With all his fur gone, Koda is a breeze to wash. I scrub him down with a delicious, toasted almond shampoo, and he sits perfectly under the powerful velocity dryer. When I bring him back out the front of the salon, I notice Lana facing the mirrored wall, dabbing her eyes with a tissue. Betty Lou is tethered by leash to the metal loop in the ground near my grooming table. When Lana sees me, she scurries back to the table and the room grows quiet.

"What is it? What's wrong?"

Lana bites her lip. "Ugh. I was going to try to wait until after today to tell you."

My stomach flips. "Tell me what?"

"I'm leaving Maine at the end of the week. I got into that computer science program in Colorado I was telling you about. It was all so last-minute. Remember I told you they put me on the waitlist? Apparently someone dropped out, so I get to take their spot."

Instead of answering, I secure Koda to the tether at my

station. For a moment, I don't know how to respond, but then Lana adds, "I was hoping today could be my last day of work so I can spend the rest of the week packing. You can find a replacement for me, right? Easily."

I nod my head, mumbling, "Of course, Lana. And congratulations. I'm so happy for you." But inside, it feels like I'm about to crumble. First the rent increase, now this? Am I doomed to have my business fail a second time?

It took me months to find Lana. It's been hopeless trying to secure someone dedicated enough to push through the challenges that come with being a dog bather, especially in a town as small as Meadow Hills. Besides me, there's only one other dog groomer in town. And thanks to my last business failing, Agatha has made it clear she can't trust working with me unless I somehow raise my rating. But now that Lana's leaving, it's probably only going to plummet even further.

With effort, I smile and turn my back to Lana so I can finish the rest of Koda's groom.

We work in silence the rest of the day, but the voice in my head is anything but quiet as it screams at me, *there goes all your hard work, Romilly. You're about to be right back to square one.*

Chapter Five

BASH

I SPEND way too much of Monday morning sitting out back by the lake after getting ready for my coffee date with Romilly. The water shimmers and stretches out like a glittering blanket, rippling under every gentle breath of the wind.

It's inherently peaceful out here, and for that reason, it's my favorite place to read my Bible. Or rather, to read verses on my phone in my Bible app. I've already showered, and the wind blows into my nose the smell of the hair products I save for special occasions, now that I can't afford to buy more once they run out. I even ironed my clothes for the day.

I feel like I'm a teenager again.

What is it about this woman that makes me want to impress her so badly? I have no idea. I don't even know her. But maybe after having coffee with her today, I'll finally be able to move on and think about something else. Like finding sponsors, getting into a gym so I can properly prepare for my next fight, or figuring out how I'm going to fund my ridiculously expensive car repairs. Anything that doesn't involve asking my parents for help.

When I glance back at my phone to continue reading, a verse I've seen many times before stands out at me.

> "He replied, "Because you have so little faith. Truly I tell you, if you have faith as small as a mustard seed, you can say to this mountain, 'Move from here to there,' and it will move. Nothing will be impossible for you."
> –Matthew 17:20

The tension in my body eases as I read it over and over. Though my financial situation has been causing me stress, this was exactly the reminder I needed to have more faith in God's goodness and power.

By the time noon arrives, I look in the mirror and realize I've given every past version of myself a run for his money—my overgrown blond hair is combed and gelled in place, with only a few tendrils escaping at the front. I know for a fact the white button-up and light wash jeans I'm wearing bring out my eyes, and my most pricey, unused cologne clings to my skin in a way I know would drive most women mad.

Even Ingrid notices when I enter the living room. She sniffs the air from her spot on the sofa. "What smells lovely?" she murmurs.

I point to myself. "That would be me."

"Ew." She wrinkles her nose. "Never mind."

"Oh, come on, sis." I plop down on the loveseat adjacent to where she's sitting. The stone fireplace is lit below the TV in front of us, which is currently playing a cooking show. I want to laugh because I doubt Ingrid will find a way to make something edible out of the scarce ingredients we've been buying. "If you think I smell lovely, I can only hope Romilly agrees."

She frowns. "Romilly? What's a Romilly?"

"Romilly is a she, not a what. And I'm meeting her for coffee in less than an hour."

She snorts. "Well if she has any sense, she'll stay away from you." Thankfully, Ingrid isn't referring to the untrue rumors back home about me being a womanizer. She's just giving me a hard time because, well, she's my little sister.

"Let's hope she doesn't have any sense, then. What a disappointment that would be."

"Ah." Ingrid's face brightens. She stands and walks to the kitchen island a few feet away and picks up an envelope. "Speaking of disappointments, look who wrote us." She waves the envelope in the air before handing it to me.

I scan the name in the upper left-hand corner.

Mr. and Mrs. Black.

My gaze darts to Ingrid's face. "Mum and Dad wrote us?"

She shrugs, though I note the tension in her shoulders. "Open it, will you? I've been waiting all morning while you gussied up."

I ignore the jab and tear the envelope open. Inside is a folded note with a check for ten thousand dollars. The note reads:

Ingrid,
Please stop this foolishness and leave Sebastian be. He'll never learn his lesson otherwise.

Come home. And share this with your brother so the two of you don't starve.
    Love,
    Mum and Dad

I resist the urge to tear the check in two, because who am I kidding? Ten thousand is enough for us to comfortably live how we used to for a month or two. And Mum knows it. She's probably counting on this check to remind us what we could have if I withdraw from Munera, come home, and let her take control of our lives again.

I'm about to tell Ingrid what the letter says, but she's already at my shoulder, scanning Mother's words herself and scoffing when she sees the check.

"As if we need that. Get rid of it." She stomps off, making for the stairs.

"Ingrid."

Halfway up, she pauses, turning to me.

"You can go home if you want. I won't hate you for it."

Her icy gaze softens. "I'm not going anywhere. Otherwise I would have, like, as soon as we couldn't afford to buy the nice cheese anymore. And you'd better learn something from that." She gestures to the cooking channel still playing. "Because it's about time you learned how to be good at something other than smashing people's faces in."

I crack a smile. "Love you, too, sis."

She continues upstairs and I glance at my phone. My pulse quickens when I see the text from her:

> Hi Sebastian, this is Romilly. Meet me at Old Joe's on Apple Street?

When I don't respond right away, another message from her comes through:

> Unless you'd rather reschedule because that's totally fine with me

I quickly respond.

ME

> No, that's perfect. I'll be there soon.

I give myself a once-over in the entryway mirror, making sure I still look irresistible. Then I tuck the Bible I snagged from Harvest Valley yesterday under my arm and grip my parents' monetary peace offering in both hands. As tempted as I am to stock up on protein powder, get my car fixed, or start a membership at a gym for training, Ingrid's right. No more. We don't need their money, not a dime.

But that also means no more messing around. No more letting Ingrid carry the weight of our food budget and utilities while I sulk about my situation. It's time for me to contribute.

I'm trusting you, God, I pray. *I'm leaving everything in your hands now.*

And then I tear the check to pieces.

There's no going back now.

On the corner of a quiet brick street, across the gazebo by town hall, Old Joe's Diner comes into view looking like it's been pulled straight out of a postcard. Ivy trails down its striped green and white awning, and a chalkboard sign out front advertises fresh pastries and maple lavender lattes.

I find Romilly already seated among one of the mismatched tables sprinkled throughout the diner when I enter, and momentarily pause when my stomach growls, thanks to the scent of pumpkin spice, freshly-baked goods, and espresso mingling in the air with the clinking of steaming coffee mugs. I can only hope my cologne is effectively drowning out the smell of the cigarette I just smoked, because I'd hate to ruin the mouthwatering aroma drifting around this space.

I take in Romilly before she has a chance to notice me. She's wearing a fitted beige turtle-neck that hugs every curve of her torso. The front pieces of her long, black hair are twisted back and secured behind her head. Her face is tilted down as she reads something, probably the menu.

The worn wooden floors creak beneath as I make my way over to the corner table she's at. When a full three seconds pass without her noticing I've slid into the seat across hers, I frown. *How could someone as beautiful as her be so unaware of her surroundings? It's not safe.*

And then she blinks like she's been abruptly woken up from a long sleep. It's really cute. I try not to smile and fail.

"Sebastian, you're here. Already."

I raise a brow. "Try not to sound so excited."

She laughs. "Sorry. I'm just surprised. I was distracted, reading this." She gestures to a thick, open tome which could only be her Bible.

"Ah, right. Speaking of which..." I plop mine onto the table between us. The thud makes our salt and pepper shakers rattle.

"Is that..." Her eyes scan the text on the front. *Property of Harvest Valley Church.* "Did you steal this from my church?"

I shrug. "You told me to bring a Bible." I slap my hand on the cover. "Bible. Brought by me."

"*Thou shall not steal,* Bash." The words are playful, endearing. I expected her to be angry, but she even giggles.

It makes my teasing grin grow wider. "I didn't steal it. I borrowed it."

"You should have told me you needed one."

"Don't worry, they'll get it back. I promise."

She smiles. "I'm not worried. I'm totally kidding. They'd probably be thrilled you took it, especially since you don't have one."

"Oh, I have one. But it's back in Woolahara where I'm from."

She tilts her head sideways. "Where's that?"

"In Australia, near Sydney." There's a part of me that can't believe we're actually seated together at this tiny café in Meadow Hills. Like before, the pull I feel toward her is impossible to ignore, and the easy conversation flowing between us makes me more comfortable than I've been since my parents left me in Maine. "This place is nice. I've never been here before."

Her eyes get insanely wide. "Old Joe's? You're kidding. How is that possible?"

Her shocked expression makes me chuckle. "I'm typically only in town during summer—well, *your* summer—on business. And my family does most of their dealings in Portland. They don't tend to spend much time at…smaller venues." I clear my throat because the truth is that they'd never come to a tiny little diner like this when they could find something more upscale and notable out of town. And that truth makes me uncomfortable.

Romilly shrugs. "Well, they're missing out. And it's an

honor to be part of the reason you're here for the first time."

Part of the reason? I want to laugh because she's the entire reason. And though I've been trying to appear indifferent since I sat down, I haven't been able to take my eyes off Romilly since I arrived. I stare into her eyes, hoping she'll take notice of my excellent bone structure and let my charms penetrate her disinterest in me.

But she flips open the cover of her Bible instead. She smiles fondly, faintly, at it, like she's never seen one before when she probably reads from it frequently, just like I do.

"So tell me," she says. "How do you know Logan Henry?"

I blink in surprise. "Logan? He lives on the same block as my parents' lake house where I've been staying. I met him while I was on a jog, and he was working on his car. Why?"

"No reason. Just curious." She clears her throat. "He mentioned to me you're possibly in the market for a job?"

It takes me a moment to process her words. "He— what?"

"We're pretty short-staffed for our upcoming autumn homeschool retreat," she continues. "If you're interested, we'd love to have you as a camp counselor." The words come out in a rush, like she's afraid she won't say them if they don't come out fast enough.

"What's an autumn homeschool retreat?" It's all I can manage at the moment.

Her cheeks become an adorable shade of pink. "Sorry, I should have explained. It's..." She drifts off, her expression turning dreamy. I stare at her, transfixed. "Well, it's like a high-energy, week-long *experience* for the homeschooled kids in town. We even get some kids from out of town, too. It will be this October over at Cranberry Pines Campground, right before the snow comes in. We do fun nature activities, have chapel time, and connect with others. It's really fun. The purpose is to give the homeschoolers an avenue to build and deepen long-lasting relationships with each other through the church."

"And you want me to be one of your leaders?" The idea is so comical, I'm almost certain I'm misunderstanding her. Anyone from my church back home would scoff at the idea of me being a camp counselor. All because of the rumors. All because of my appearance. And if I were approached with this job back home, I would rather be a test subject for open heart surgery without anesthesia than spend an entire week stuck in a cabin with any of them. Yet, here this woman is offering me this opportunity while not even knowing me. I can't help but laugh. "Are you sure you want me?"

"Only if you're interested. We'd pay you, of course. You just need to be vetted and go through a background check."

"Romilly. Please don't take offense to what I'm about to say. But I doubt the parents of these high schoolers would ever trust you again if you hired someone like me."

She frowns. "Why? What's wrong with you?"

"Well, there's the fighting, for one. And if that's not enough, there's always the cigarettes, the tattoos, or the—"

"Fighting?" She widens her eyes at me. "What kind of fighting? Like, hurting random people?"

I grin, because she looks so alarmed it's adorable. "I fight professionally for Munera. It's just for sport. But

Logan was right...I do need a job. At least, until my next fight. And that's two months away."

She winces. "And the retreat isn't till next month."

"Yeah, I figured. You can count me in, but I don't know how much help that will be to me at the moment." I keep my voice gentle, because the last thing I want to do is disappoint her when she's being so...kind. Generous. Non-judgy.

Romilly crosses her arms and stares off into the distance like she's trying to think.

Something wet touches my elbow. I glance to the right, where a Labrador retriever stares at me expectantly. It licks my elbow again, and I offer it a gentle pat on the head.

"Sorry about that," the owner, a middle-aged gentleman, says.

"It's no problem, mate. I love dogs."

When he leaves, I turn back to Romilly. She's analyzing me in a strange way that has my eyes narrowing.

"What?" I ask.

"It's nothing."

"Oh, no it's not. Not with you looking at me that way. Tell me."

She blushes. "Um, well...I was just thinking since the church position is so far away, how about a job as my assistant dog bather?"

I clear my throat. "Your what, now?"

"Assistant dog bather. I'm a dog groomer and I desperately—" She breaks off to clear her throat. "I mean, I guess I could use a hand around the shop."

"Dog bather." I'm not sure which idea is worse. Not having any money, or this job.

Grow up, Bash. Stop acting privileged, because you

aren't anymore. And I can't deny that being part of my old-money family without any real responsibilities at twenty-five has unfortunately left me with a very narrow pool of work experience. I dropped out of college. I've never had a common job in my whole life. I've only ever done street fighting before I went professional, which is how I got noticed on social media and scouted by my agent, Max, who got me my Munera contract in the first place. And sporadically assisting with my parents' prestigious auction house also doesn't count as a common job, not by a long shot. But even then, my participation was limited to occasionally attending events, helping with private viewings, or mingling with clients.

I would make a terrible employee.

Romilly pulls her bottom lip between her teeth as she watches me ponder. It makes warmth flood my chest and my brain go foggy.

"I'll do it," I say. "I'll take the job."

"Which one?"

"Both. Even the dog bathing one."

For the first time, her smile slips from her mouth. "Wonderful."

"Does that...upset you?" I search her face. "Because you don't exactly seem thrilled."

She shakes her head. "No. Of course not. I'm just thinking of all the training you'll need."

I try to muster up some false confidence. "I'm sure it's not as hard as it seems, washing a dog or two."

Her mouth twitches. "I'm sure you're right. Can you start Wednesday?"

Training outdoors isn't at all ideal. MMA is a sport only the strongest can endure, and not being able to prepare for my next match properly makes me feel on edge.

I should be in a gym.

I should be sparring right now and maintaining my jujitsu and kickboxing skills. But all I can manage is running and using my body weight or objects around the woods to build muscle. I could ask Logan to spar with me, but he's gearing up for a surfing competition and can't risk possibly getting injured. And thanks to the lack of protein at the house, I've already dropped weight. If I can't maintain my current weight, I might not qualify for my weight class, Middleweight, anymore.

The pressure from my agent should be enough to keep me moving, especially since his last message, which let me know my former opponent got injured in a match, and I'll now be fighting Connor Stronghold—someone slightly more experienced than me and undefeated.

But I can't deny, it feels amazing to get the sweat pumping during my run. Jogging always helps me feel calmer. It's one of my favorite ways to drown everything else out. So I keep doing it. And after spending the rest of the afternoon training, I grab burgers with Logan—his treat, bless him—before I head home.

When I get inside, I set the Bible down on the kitchen island and flip the lights on. The modern, black cabinets come into view, but I almost jump at the sight of Ingrid slumped over in one of the seats, her face pressed against the sparkling, black quartz countertop as she snores.

She's still in her waitress uniform. I can't help but

notice how exhausted she looks, even while asleep. She must be working long, difficult shifts. Something in my stomach tightens. *My poor sister. She's only nineteen and this is her first job.* Hopefully accepting Romilly's offer will help to take some of the pressure off her.

I turn from the kitchen, about to head upstairs, when she opens her eyes. Stretches. "When did you get back?" Her voice is still a sleepy haze.

I grin. "Just now. And guess what, little sis? I got one of those job things, just like you."

I have her full attention now. She sits up straight. Opens her eyes all the way. Frowns. "What on earth are you talking about?"

"I'm officially an employee of The Paw Spa."

A moment of silence ensues, and then she bursts into laughter. She holds her stomach, almost tipping out of her stool.

I frown. "It's really not all that funny."

But she doesn't stop laughing. Not until a full minute passes. Her laughter finally dies down, and she breathes deeply, like she's trying to prevent another bout from starting up. "I'm sorry. It's just that I thought you said you got a job at a *pet salon.*"

"Romilly's pet salon," I growl. "And be grateful. Because now you won't have to work so hard."

"Where did you meet this Romilly gal, again?"

"Logan's church."

She holds up a hand. "Bash, if you really want to spend all your time around a bunch of judgmental jerks, then I'd just move back home with Mum and Dad."

Against my will, my thoughts immediately go to Romilly at the words *judgmental jerks.* To Logan. The two of them simply don't fit the stereotype. But I know she's not wrong about many of the others. "You have nothing to be afraid of, Ingrid. I'm only in this for the money." *And the woman I can't seem to stop thinking about.* "I mean, come on. We need to buy quality food eventually, you know."

She rolls her eyes, folding her arms against her chest. "Speaking of buying things, I got you more goodies." She nods toward the coffee table in the living room, beside the fireplace. From here, I can already see a colorful pile of lollipops and fidget spinners.

"Thanks, Ingrid."

"This time, don't lose the spinners in the woods, and take your time on the lollipops."

"You must really hate the smell of my cigarettes."

She rolls her eyes. "I do. Everyone does. Now, no more excuses about smoking again, you understand?"

I silently mourn the near-empty pack in my pocket. "Cross my heart."

She eyes me with suspicion, so I walk over to the low table and pick up a bright red fidget spinner. I spin it in my hands a few times and pluck a grape lollipop from the table as well, unwrapping it and popping it into my mouth. "You'll be in a smoke-free home again by morning."

Her body visibly relaxes. "I'm going to bed." She stands from her seat and goes upstairs, leaving me alone with my new treats.

When eighteen-year-old Bash took up cigarettes to make his parents angry, he never thought he'd still be struggling with it, at twenty-five. And eighteen-year-old Bash *certainly* never suspected that a childish stack of things like fidget toys and candy could effectively curb the cravings. If

I hadn't lost my last spinner and burned through all the candy before the store had a chance to restock, I doubt I would have been so tempted to turn to this latest pack.

I settle into the leather armchair beside the fireplace. The heat relaxes me as I play with the spinner in my hands. As much as I hate to admit it, I very much enjoy smoking. But if I want to be as healthy as possible for my next fight, it's got to go once and for all. I can't let this vice ruin the one thing that makes me feel unshackled in a world full of structure.

I can only hope the same thing will happen Wednesday morning at my new job—the job that will help me afford to finally get back in the gym.

Chapter Six

ROMILLY

THE SMELL of freshly brewed coffee and warm breakfast fills the cozy, sunlit space of the Harvest Valley soup kitchen. The soft yellow walls make the whole space feel uplifting, along with the warm light fixtures hanging over-head, casting an inviting glow across the room.

"Remember me?" The question carries softly through the quiet hum of conversation and the occasional laughter from our volunteers.

I look up from behind the long serving table, and my face brightens at the sight. It's the homeless man from the other day—the one I gave a few dollars to and promised a hot breakfast if he showed up on Tuesday—which is today.

"Herman! You came!"

He nods, a smile tugging at the corners of his mouth. His worn jacket hangs from his body as he takes in the neat rows of folding tables and chairs, where early guests are already seated. Smacking his lips subconsciously, his eyes flick toward the spread of food. "Sure did. And I'm hungry, too."

"Well, you came to the right place. Would you like a little bit of everything?"

He nods, and I grab the long ladle, dipping it into the pot of steaming, cinnamon-scented oatmeal. I spoon a generous portion into a sturdy, disposable bowl, then add a plate of crispy bacon, fluffy scrambled eggs, and fresh fruit.

Herman takes the plate. "If you don't mind me asking, how can you afford to hand out free food like this? Who's paying for it?"

"The members of our congregation donate so we can do all kinds of things." I smile at him. "Because of them, we're able to help support families in need, reach people in other countries who are living in poverty, and serve breakfast for lovely people like yourself."

His round, fuzzy cheeks grow rosy. "Thank you. Where do I go now?"

I point to the door at my right, on the other side of the counter. "Men's group is right through that door if you'd like to join them. There's plenty of food in there as well. Otherwise, you're welcome to eat in here and go about your day after."

"Men's group?"

"Yeah. I'm happy to walk you over if you'd like."

Herman pauses, his brow furrowed as he thinks it over, then smiles softly. "Okay. Sure, I'd like that."

"Awesome." I untie my apron and set it on the counter beside me. Turning to the group of high schoolers volunteering in the kitchen with me, I give them a quick nod. "I'll be right back."

I meet Herman on the other side of the counter. We walk through the doorway leading to the adjacent room together. As we step inside, we're greeted by a few smiles, along with rows of mismatched but comfortable chairs, and a few round tables scattered throughout the space. Coffee cups, open Bibles, and half-eaten pastries rest on the tables like evidence of a successful morning.

I can't deny that there's a warmth to this room that feels like a gathering at a friend's house rather than a formal meeting. As usual, there are too many familiar faces from Sunday services here for it to feel any other way.

I gesture for Herman to follow me toward a table where Hayden, the youth pastor, is sitting with a small group of men. His expression brightens when he sees us, and he stands, brushing his hands down his plaid shirt and jeans as he grins. "Romilly!"

"Hayden, this is my new friend, Herman." I watch them shake hands and grin. "Do you have a seat for him, by chance?"

"Of course." Hayden gestures to the remaining seat at his table, and the two of them start up a conversation.

I make my way back to the kitchen next door, but stop when I literally *feel* someone's gaze on me. My eyes dart up and land directly on Bash's. He's leaning against a wall off to the side of the room, wearing khaki pants and a white button-up with the sleeves rolled back from his heavily tattooed forearms. The way he's watching me with such intensity makes it hard to look away.

We stare at each other for an embarrassingly long moment. Then he lifts the corner of his mouth and offers me a small wave.

I walk over to him.

As I approach, I take a deep breath. *Why does he have to be so attractive?*

He crosses his arms once I'm standing right in front of him. "Fancy seeing you here."

"Why are you standing all by yourself?"

"Mr. Turner needed a chair more than I did." He nods toward the full table closest to us where old Mr. Turner is eating his breakfast. Guilt slices through me as I notice all the chairs in the room are taken. I make a mental note to bring an extra one in for Bash.

"It's nice to see you again," he says, breaking me away from my thoughts. "But I could have sworn you said men's breakfast was for men." He grins at me. It's the kind of teasing smile that feels like a secret between us, and it makes my heart flutter.

"It is. I'm working in the kitchen today."

He arches an eyebrow. "How many jobs do you have?"

"Too many. Now if you'll excuse me, I should probably get back to this one." *And now would be the moment to walk away. Any minute now. Go, legs, go!*

Bash shoves his hands in his pockets, that huge grin still plastered to his face. "Well, what about after?"

"I'm grooming dogs after."

His smile fades, brows drawing together. "Do you work seven days a week?"

"Six, actually. I always take one day a week off, but I pack the rest of them full. And it's fine. I like working." I shrug like I'm unbothered, but the truth is that I have no choice, especially now that Lana's gone. There's no way I can afford to take any more time off until Agatha, my old groomer, comes back.

"You should take the rest of the day off and hang out with me instead." The low, charming way he says it makes nerves shoot to my toes. His eyes are locked on mine, and it's hard to think straight. I can't imagine what it would be like to do something so careless, but I can't deny the idea excites me.

I shake my head. "Sorry. We can hang out at work tomorrow."

He laughs. "Fine. I know a rejection when I hear one." But he doesn't look at all defeated. If anything, he only looks fascinated. He studies my face with a small smile that makes blood rush to my face.

"I'm...I'm not rejecting you. I'm just busy. Which reminds me—your background check came back great, so you're now not only my employee, but a Harvest Valley Church camp counselor. So, I'll see you tomorrow morning at The Paw Spa. " I don't give him a chance to retort, and as I head back to the kitchen, I replay his words in my head. *You should take the rest of the day off and hang out with me instead.*

Ugh. What is it about him that makes me kinda want to?

The last thing I need is another man tricking me into liking him, or getting me to trust him, only to let me down in the end. Bash may be handsome, but he's exactly the kind of man I need to avoid. He's a professional MMA fighter, and practically textbook for: I'm a bad boy and I will break your heart.

If I could, I'd stay far away from him. But unfortunately, he happens to be my new dog bather, and without him, I might have another failed business on my hands. Since he needs my help too, there's not really anywhere for me to run.

Jasper eyes me curiously when I get home. It's like he knows I brought him a treat, even though I double-bagged the pumpkin loaf I bought from Old Joe's Diner before I stuck it in my purse.

"Hey, buddy." I scratch his head before I even cross the threshold. Jasper paws at my hand and sniffs the autumn air wafting in from the open door. I come in and close it before he can get any ideas about manipulating me into letting him be an outdoor cat. He already gets supervised outings every night, but knowing him, he'll try to push it. He's currently wearing a bright orange sweater from Iris Lily, my favorite boutique in town. Though Jasper has been known to attack random strangers without warning, part of the reason I love this cat so much is he'll let me put him in whatever ridiculous costume I desire, even hats, as long as I pay him treats as compensation.

As I feed him the pumpkin loaf, my best friend, Addison, calls me. I lift the phone to my ear. "Hey, Adds."

She responds with a sigh.

"Uh oh. What's wrong? Is married life giving you trouble?"

"Oh, no. The married part is still amazing. But the stepmom part?" She sighs again with exasperation. "I think I'm failing."

"What are you talking about? Your bonus kids love you." I've never seen four children adore their nanny-turned-stepmom as much as I've seen Perry's children fall head over heels for Addison.

"Today, when I asked Izzy to clean her room, she told me she didn't have to listen to me because I'm not her mom."

"Oh, Addy."

"And then later she apologized and burst into tears, telling me she's just scared I love baby Marina more than her and her siblings because I'm Marina's 'real' mom."

"That's so sad. I hope you reassured her that's not true."

"Of course I did," she says. "But now I'm feeling like maybe she should know more about her biological mother. Like, she should know I'm never going to abandon her like that."

I bite my lip. "As much as I hate to admit it, I'm with Izzy. It's hard to trust people when your situation feels too good to be true."

The line goes silent. "Are you referring to Cole?"

"Hey, you know we don't speak his name. But yes."

"Cole is an idiot. Not all men are like that, Romilly."

I want to laugh and agree with her, to tell her I'm just kidding, that I know Cole was an exception. A bad seed in a barrel of gems. But to say any of that would be a lie, because I don't believe it.

"Um, I'll call you later, okay? Jasper wants his outside time really bad."

Because we're so close, she definitely knows it's an excuse. But like the amazing friend she is, she doesn't call me out on it. "Okay, talk to you soon."

I hang up and glare at Jasper when he meows at me expectantly. "I know, I know. You *do* actually want your outside time."

He cocks his head sideways in response. I'm about to walk him to the backyard, where the fence is high enough for me to intercept any escape ideas he might have, when I notice Zara lounging on the couch in my living room, wearing my purple bathrobe and satin eye-mask. Anyone who's never met her would probably think she's me because of how similar we look.

"What in the world are you doing here?"

"Oh, you know. Just hanging out."

"That's creepy, Zara."

She feigns offense. "You're the one who left your back door unlocked. And you should be thanking me, because I finally decided to return those cute jeans you loaned me, but you weren't here." She studies me, searching my face. "You good?"

"Why wouldn't I be?"

"Anytime you talk to Addison these days, you start moping after. I couldn't help but observe this time was no exception."

"Moping? I'm not moping."

"You're definitely moping." She offers me a pitying smile. "It's okay if you want to be in a relationship, you know. You can admit it."

"That's the last thing I want."

"Really, Romilly." She bites her lip, traces of humor fading. "You've had a weird chip on your shoulder for about a year now. And according to my calculations...that's around the time you and Cole broke up."

"I'd like to not talk about this anymore, Z. Please."

She worries her lip as she studies me, contemplating. And then she nods. "Fine. But I'm here to talk if you need me. I know you have Addison, but I'm here too if you need someone less...happy." She gives me a knowing smile and fluffs her curly hair. "Anyways, your jeans are in your room. I'll get out of your house, now."

"Thanks." I walk her out and give her a hug. "It's still creepy the way you keep appearing out of nowhere."

"I'm nothing if not creepy," she says, a teasing glint in her brown eyes. "And your reactions are always worth it."

I snort, because no one would ever guess how much Zara enjoys getting a rise out of me by her sweet demeanor. I don't even make her take off my bathrobe before she gets in her car because I know she'll be back when I least expect, claiming she's here to return it.

When she's gone, I take Jasper to the backyard. I don't even have to motion him to follow me. He's used to our night routine. When I open the chipped, white single door leading out, he's practically sprinting. I sit on the wooden rocking chair on the porch while Jasper sniffs grass, rolls around, and sharpens his claws on the same post of the wooden fence as usual. The wood is splitting now from all the fun he's had with it.

I take a deep breath, shutting my eyes against the cool wind stinging my face. And I hear Zara's words again.

It's okay if you want to be in a relationship, you know. You can admit it.

Out here, beneath the dark sky speckled with glittering stars, I can be honest with myself for once. I can admit the truth, pathetic as it is.

Zara is right.

I'm lonely, and I hate it.

Despite my efforts to stay busy with work, surround myself with fluffy critters, and volunteer nonstop at church, there's still a void—a longing to share my busy life with someone else.

I can't help but remember the way Cole's soothing presence, his kind voice, and his gentle touch all contributed to me trusting him and believing him when he told me my lack of experience didn't bother him, and neither did my desire to wait until marriage.

And then I remember the night I discovered Cole left Meadow Hills to visit the woman in Bar Harbor he'd been secretly seeing our entire relationship.

Jasper rubs against my leg, purring. I break away from the memory with relief. "Men are scoundrels, aren't they, buddy? You're the only one worth knowing, aren't you?"

He arches his back as an answer. I comb my fingers through his yellow and black fur, letting the texture calm me. Maybe these feelings are resurfacing because of a certain someone I just met who also has a smooth voice, a charming smile, and convincing words.

I may be lonely, but in my opinion, it's better than being naive. And I've simply learned too much to ever trust another man.

Especially one like Sebastian Black.

Chapter Seven

BASH

I'M NOT sure what I expected Romilly's workplace to look like, but it certainly wasn't *this*.

Paw-shaped flagstone leads a pathway through the grass to a small, wood-paneled building nestled between downtown Meadow Hills and a suburban development. It's mostly isolated, save for a horse ranch half a mile down the road and a used car dealership. I open the glass, storefront-style door and step into the entryway. More wood paneling, but this time with teal accents on the doors, ceiling, and curtains. There's an entire wall painted light pink, and a group of coral accent chairs opposite the check-in desk. Behind them is a wall dedicated to displaying a variety of leashes, collars, and...pet clothing for sale.

There are no cages in view. I don't hear the barking and screeching of animals who think they're being tortured. There's a subtle scent of bleach, but it doesn't sting my nose because it's masked by a more intentional, pleasant aroma.

"Good morning, Sebastian."

I smirk when I hear her voice. "Great place you got here," I say, turning to face her. She's wearing normal clothes instead of a uniform: straight leg jeans and a green, bohemian-style top.

Romilly beams. "Thanks. I actually had to move back with my parents to save up enough to afford it. I'm just grateful it all paid off." She opens the picket-fence gate dividing us and motions me to join her on the side of the room.

I follow her to a kennel area against a wall. But it's not just any kennel area. It's a long, horizontal strip with teal gates closing off each section. But the most amusing part of all is the framed portrait of each dog hung above their designated area. She literally has portraits of her canine clients hung on the wall.

I point to the photos. "So, you clearly love animals, but this is a bit excessive, don't you think?"

She laughs. "I just like my dogs to feel welcome. I keep fluffy beds for them here, too. That way they're nice and comfy while they wait for me to work on them."

"I see." *How is it possible that she just got even more adorable?*

"The first thing I'm going to show you is how to prepare the kennels for the day. The photos are kept at the front desk, in the drawer on the right." She points to the line of kennels. "And the pictures aren't just for aesthetics. They're a visual reminder of my schedule for the day, and they get switched out depending on who's coming. So, as you can see, we'll be working on six dogs today, and the order of the photos represents the order in which they'll arrive."

I smirk, examining the dogs. "Dibs on the Chihuahua."

She fights a smile. "You'll take that back, I promise. Besides, you'll be working on all these dogs. Just like I will."

"Wait...what?"

"You'll need to wash, dry, brush, trim the toenails, and brush the teeth of each of them. Those are the duties of my bather."

"Is that all?" She doesn't miss the heavy sarcasm lacing my voice.

"If they need it, you'll also have to express their anal glands."

We stare at each other for a moment as I try to determine whether she's joking. When she doesn't crack a smile or burst into laughter, I contemplate thanking her for the opportunity and continuing back home. Mum and Dad's controlling, oppressive nature doesn't sound half bad in retrospect.

The bell on the front counter echoes through the room. Romilly beams and immediately twists her long, black hair into a bun at the nape of her neck. A little squeal escapes her as she bounces on her feet and gently claps her hands together. "It's Kujo! I can't wait for you to meet him. He's the best. Come on."

"Did you just say *Kujo*?" I blink several times as she heads toward the front desk before processing that this is my life at the moment. *Sebastian Black, working man. And not just any job. She wants you to express anal glands. Why is it again you're so obsessed with her?*

At the front of The Paw Spa is an elderly lady holding a leash attached to a dog larger than she is. His coat is black with a splash of white on the tummy, and his eyes look yellow at first glance. I don't think I've ever seen a more terrifying dog in my life, in fact. His gaze locks onto me immediately, like I'm an intruder in his home. I swear his eyes shine red for the half second he takes me in, and then a loud, booming bark rips through his massive body.

No. No way is she going near that thing. Instinctively, I capture her hand and tug her back before she can approach it, earning a questioning glance from her.

"You can't be serious, Romilly."

Her face clears. "Trust me."

She removes her hand from mine and waves at the lady. "Mrs. Camden, it's a pleasure to see you again!"

"Hello, Romilly." The elderly woman wobbles toward us, extending the leash forward for Romilly to take. "Looks like you have new help around here?"

I resist the intense urge to step in front of Romilly before she can take the leash, in case the dog decides to rip her face off or something. "I'm Bash," I tell Mrs. Camden. "Pleasure to meet you."

"He's The Paw Spa's new bather."

Mrs. Camden looks skeptical as she takes me in. I wonder what she thinks of my crisp button down, my designer jeans and shoes, or my tattoo-covered arms. "What happened to Lana?"

"She's moving," says Romilly. "Packing as we speak."

"First Agatha, now Lana? That's a shame. I really liked her."

Romilly stiffens but pastes a smile on. "Don't worry. Bash here is well-equipped for the job. Or at least, he will be by the time I'm done training him." She pats my shoulder. I'm hyper-aware of the contact, even after she takes her hand away.

"Just so you know, Kujo doesn't like strange men."

Romilly laughs. "No problem. Bash can mostly observe till they get to know each other better."

"All right, then. Well, I'll be going now."

"Bye, Mrs. Camden."

The woman leaves us alone with her...thing. I can't even refer to it as a dog because I've truly never seen anything like it. "What breed is Kujo?" I ask.

"He's a Cane Corso."

Terrifying as he is, I can't help but admire Kujo's strong frame and menacing glare. I even kind of relate to him for a moment because here I am, judging the guy by his looks when the same thing always happens to me. I sigh. "Where do we start?"

She gestures to the dog with her chin. "We check him for any open wounds, matting, or dental problems."

"Alright." But I make no move toward him.

Romilly must sense my hesitation, because she laughs a warm, bubbling sound. "He may look scary, but trust me. Kujo is such a softie." She gracefully kneels to the ground, reaching her hand out to peel back his lips. He wags his tail, letting her examine him, making me feel like a complete pansy.

"Let me try." I model her movements, kneeling down beside her. But when I reach my hand out, the massive canine's lips curl on their own. The skin at the top of his snout bunches together, and a low growl escapes him. I return to a standing position and cross my arms. "Not fair, mate. You haven't even given me a chance to show you I won't hurt you."

Romilly looks amused. "Come on. I'll show you what to do, okay? Then I'll expect you to take over with the other dogs today. But I'll still be able to help you, since this is your first time working with animals."

She leads me and Kujo to the washing area. I swear the dog looks over his shoulder at me a couple times, simply to glare. I try to pay attention as she shows me which shampoo and conditioner Kujo gets every time and directs me on how to wash him by modeling everything for me. She has no issues scrubbing the massive dog down, getting him nice and clean. She even trims his toenails with him right there in the bath, and the dog is perfectly polite, handing her each paw one after the other.

She shows me how to dry him with the velocity dryers attached to the wall, and how to brush his teeth as well.

I can't help but admire her courage, the simplicity with which she performs the task. "What do you need a bather for? You're so good at this."

She blushes. "Thanks. But I need the help because I have to take a minimum of thirty-six dogs a week in order to afford this place and still make a profit. And both washing and grooming them all would take too long by myself. So having a bather on staff allows me to just focus on the grooming part, and it saves me half the time."

"I see. Why don't you hire more groomers as well, so you can make more of a profit and work less?"

"I...um..." She continues in a hushed, embarrassed tone, "The only other groomer in town doesn't want to work with me."

I frown. "Why not?"

"My last business failed, so she doesn't trust me anymore. And I-I totally understand. It is what it is." She stares at her hands as she worries them together, and I'm prevented from answering when another customer enters.

This dog, Janet, is a Yorkie, and much smaller than Kujo. Much more cooperative when I try to pet her, too. Romilly monitors me as I complete all the steps she demonstrated, stepping in occasionally to correct me, and reminding me what to do next.

The more dogs I work on, the more I get the hang of it. It's all new to me, never having owned a pet before. And though I like dogs just fine, it takes me a while to get used to the smell of them when they're wet.

"How am I doing?" I ask her.

She glances over from her grooming table to see my progress with an Australian Shepherd named Rosie. "You're doing fine for now. And don't worry, it won't take long for you to improve. Hands-on jobs like this one make a fast learner out of anyone."

I shake my head. "I'd love to learn how to not make a mess of my clothes. Look at you. No fair." Compared to me, Romilly looks spotless. Her jeans have a few clumps of hair sticking to the bottoms near her ankles, but otherwise, no one would ever guess she's been grooming dogs all day. I, on the other hand, am not only completely soaked, but covered in so much hair, I'm starting to feel itchy.

But I continue. Because I'm determined to do a good job no matter how uncomfortable I am.

When it comes time to bathe the Chihuahua, Romilly hands me a tiny pink muzzle for Angel to wear. "You're going to need this. Trust me."

And she's right. Angel makes sounds I've never heard before as I lower her into the water-filled tub. She snarls, twists every time I touch her. If it weren't for the muzzle, I'd be way too scared to even touch her.

"You're right," I mutter. "I'm eating my words right now."

She giggles. "Told you."

A grown man like me, scared of a dog smaller than my boots.

This is truly a new low for me.

When I walk through the front door, it's six p.m., and Ingrid is putting away leftover spaghetti she must have made while I was gone. I'm exhausted, but I know I don't have a chance of making it past her to escape to my room as soon as I see her face.

Her mouth falls open as she takes in the chunks of fluffy dog hair stuck to my trousers, shirt, and face. The scratch marks on my forearms. The water squishing in my shoes.

"This is too good to be true," she states in an even tone.

"I don't want to hear a word."

"Whoever this Romilly is, I've got to meet her."

I roll my eyes. "Enough, Ingrid."

"I mean it. Look at you, Bash. She got you to *work*. Like, actually lift a finger. I've simply got to meet her. Invite her over for brunch."

"Brunch?" I arch an eyebrow. "You mean you want to serve her food from a can, or what we've been taking from her church?"

"Of course not. We can buy real food, because you have a job now."

I arch a brow. For all the day's moments I spent close to giving up, wondering how on earth I landed myself in this situation, only to push through from sheer determination and stubbornness, I forgot all about the reward portion of my hard work. *The money.*

"I made two hundred dollars today in tips alone, Ingrid."

Her mouth falls open. "How come I never get tips like that?"

"Because you never smile."

She scowls. "Whatever. I'll go to the store in the morning. And I'm working this weekend, but invite her over for brunch next week. I'll cook. When is her next day off?"

"Tuesday," I say, and then realize what she just said. "Wait...*you're* going to cook?"

She sticks her tongue out at me. "I've been learning new recipes. Haven't you seen me watching the cooking channel? I just made spaghetti for the first time."

I scratch my head and then feel a foreign substance beneath my nails. Probably nail grinds or dog dander. My stomach churns. "Fine, then. I'm going to shower."

As I climb the stairs to get to the bathroom, I hear Ingrid whisper to herself, "Simply *got* to meet this woman."

But I hardly register it, because excitement stirs in my stomach.

With this kind of money, I can finally get back into a gym to train.

I turn on the shower. While I'm waiting for the water to heat up, I send a text to my agent, Max.

ME

Any sponsors bite yet?

MAX

Sorry, Bash.

ME

None? Why?

MAX

It's all still the same. You're unproven in your promotion and your flashy debut wasn't enough. Sponsors want consistency. Discipline. Proof you'll stick around and perform.

ME

But I'm an undefeated street fighter.

MAX

Yeah, but they don't have that proof. And that's kind of a running joke in Munera. Every street fighter claims he's undefeated.

ME

But...I went viral online

MAX

You're one of many who have gone viral, and some fizzle out quickly. Sponsors just want to make sure you're legit before they invest. But don't worry. They'll come eventually.

Eventually. But not before my next fight. Which means I won't get the payday I'm hoping for if I win. Not even close.

And that will only keep me right where I am, or worse.

Running back home like my parents want.

Closing my eyes, I pray, *Lord, if this is what you want for me, please help me succeed.*

Chapter Eight

ROMILLY

BASH DOES SURPRISINGLY decent at work the rest of the week. Despite his obvious physical strength, I thought he'd have a much harder time. It does, however, take me a ridiculous amount of restraint to not freak out on Saturday when he gets bit by Shadow, a black Schnauzer.

He's going to quit. He's going to quit just like Lana and Agatha did and leave me to do this all alone.

But holding up his thumb, Bash grins at me. "I'm going to get rabies, aren't I?"

"Why do you look so excited about that idea?"

"Because I'm a man, Romilly. I live for danger. Will I die?"

I shrug one shoulder. "Anything is possible."

"Excellent."

With a laugh, I look for a bandage in my bag, hanging from my station. "All the dogs that come in have to be up to date on their shots, and the system would alert me if they weren't. So, sorry. No rabies today. But here. Let me patch you up, just in case."

He laughs at my concern, pulling his hand away. "No need. I'm fine. I only got nipped."

"Give me your hand, Sebastian." I take it firmly in mine and peel back the wrapping on the bandage.

"I've survived worse wounds than this, believe me."

"I'm sure that's true, but I can't have you bleeding on the dogs, or getting your hand infected."

Once he's all patched up, he inspects his hand, flexing his fingers. His gaze shifts from his hand to my face, making me blush. There's something about his amused, intrigued expression that makes me want to look away. But I hold his stare anyway.

"Did you know you often smell like lavender?"

I blink through the haze of his words. "Lavender?"

"Yes," he says. "It's one of my favorite smells." He turns back to Shadow and unties the dog's tether on the ground loop, then leads him to the washroom in the back. Just like that. As if commenting on the way I smell—which apparently, is his favorite— was no big deal.

Focus, Romilly.

It hits me for the first time how different working with Bash is going to be than working with Lana. My old bather was always so quiet, so professional. But Bash's random compliments and the way he openly checks me out like it's part of the job description isn't something I'm used to.

This isn't going to work unless he and I can coexist professionally. I refuse to mix business with pleasure, especially with the state of my business already so fragile.

Without overthinking it, I beeline to the back room where Bash is elbow deep in the tub, washing a now-muzzled Shadow. I almost laugh at the way he's hunched over like a giant at a miniature sink before I refocus. I place my hands on my hips. "What was that about?"

He looks at me over his shoulder, his brows drawing together. "What was what about?"

"That little comment. About me smelling like lavender."

"You do smell like lavender. Almost every time I see you."

I reach around his massive shoulder and shut off the stream of water. "We need to talk about this."

He frowns like he has no idea what this is about. "Okay. What's wrong?"

My annoyance doubles at his oblivious tone. "I'd like you to know that I take my work environment very seriously. I won't tolerate us intermingling or flirting. Okay?"

At that, he finally turns to face me completely. Shadow glares at him from the tub as he pulls a red lollipop out of his pocket and sucks it into his mouth. The confusion in his eyes has evaporated, and now he just looks like he's trying really hard not to laugh. An annoying half-grin graces his lips. "Okay...but it kinda sounds like you're expecting me to pretend I don't find you attractive. And I'm sorry, but that's not going to happen. We can keep things professional, but I think you're beautiful, and also really distracting."

My brain stops working for a moment. I know I should be glad he just agreed to keep things professional, but there's only one thing I'm focusing on. *He thinks I'm beautiful.* But instead of commenting on it, I blurt, "Where did you get the lollipop?"

"Why?" He smirks and shoves his hands into his pockets. "Do you want one?"

I kinda do, but I shake my head. "No, I do not want one, Sebastian. We're working."

"You can call me Bash, you know. Everyone but my parents does."

I make a mental note that he prefers his nickname, so I don't slip up again. "You're right. I'm sorry, Bash."

He grins. "But Sebastian honestly doesn't sound too bad the way you say it."

I gape at him. "This is exactly what I'm talking about. That was unprofessional."

"You're right."

I expect him to follow his statement with a "sorry" but he doesn't. I sigh.

This is going to be a long two months.

Clearing my throat, I gesture to the dog shivering in the tub behind him. "Shadow is probably getting cold."

Bash takes his time turning back around, letting his gaze linger longer than necessary. When he returns to Shadow, flicking the water switch back on, I take a deep, steadying breath and return to the front of the shop.

Sitting at the reception desk to wait for my next dog is probably the best thing to do, considering how jittery I feel after that interaction with him.

I think you're beautiful, and also really distracting.

I shake my head and send Addison a text.

ME
I think I need to fire my new bather.

ADDISON
What? Why?

ME
He thinks I'm...beautiful.

85

ADDISON

HE SAID THAT?

ME

Yes.

ADDISON

You're acting like that's not common knowledge, though. Maybe he was simply stating a fact and not trying to flirt with you or anything.

ME

That is so sweet. I love you, Adds.

ADDISON

See? That was me just stating facts. Not complimenting you. You're easily confused by these things, apparently.

ME

He also said he likes the sound of his name when I say it.

ADDISON

OKAY...UM...

This is giving me flashbacks from when I was Perry's nanny. But still, we can work with this!

Ah, yes. When her deep attraction to Perry made her panic during a family trip with him and his kids. I remember texting her about it last summer, talking her down in a way similar to how she's texting me. Except there's nothing for her to talk me down from, because I'm not panicking. Yes, Bash is extremely attractive himself for a tattooed giant, but that has nothing to do with me. It doesn't affect me *at all*, in fact.

ME

Come to church with me tomorrow morning. We can talk more about this then.

ADDISON

I don't know. Remember what happened last time?

I briefly recall the way Addison's newborn cried on and off the entire service before she and Perry ended up leaving early.

I'm about to text her back, but my mom calls me. I lift the phone to my ear. "Hey, Mom!"

"Hey. How did the paint turn out? You never told me."

A twinge of guilt nicks my stomach. "Sorry. It turned out great!"

She laughs. "Good. Just wanted to make sure you don't need anything else before your father and I leave town."

"You're leaving town?"

"Yes. He's taking me on a *just because* trip. A cruise, actually. Just the two of us."

I frown. "What about Aiden?"

"Zara will be home with him. She's going to take him to school," my mom says. "It's a good thing, too, because I'm sure that boy would miss the rest of his senior year if we'd let him. And before you ask me, I don't know where we're going because it's a surprise."

The joy in my mom's voice does strange things to my heart. Part of me feels happy for her, because she and Dad have always had such a loving, healthy relationship, even after giving birth to me and my siblings. I've definitely envied them more than once. And now is no exception. But along with the envy, there's sadness knowing I'm pushing away the possibility of what she has—a happy marriage and children who love her. By letting Cole taint my view of relationships, I'm pushing away surprise trips to share with the one I love, or fostering children like I once dreamed of, and Christmas mornings filled with those children's laughter as they rip open their gifts. I won't have that note of romantic wanderlust in my voice when I tell people how my husband made me smile. I won't have any of it, because I no longer want it. I *don't*.

"I hope you two have fun, Mom. I, uh, have to get back to work."

"Thanks, sweetie. Don't work too hard, okay?"

If only she knew. "Okay."

When I hang up, I try to focus on the positive. *You have a place of your own to call home, Romilly. You own a thriving pet salon. Or, at least, it will be thriving once Agatha comes back. And best of all, you're not lonely. You're just fine. And no one can break your heart again.*

But then Bash breaks my focus as he emerges from the back and locks eyes with me. He looks like he has a question, but when he takes in the way I'm hunched over at my desk, aggressively rubbing my temples, his expression shifts into concern. "Are you alright?"

"I'm fine."

His frown deepens. "Have you eaten anything today?"

I frown right back. "No. Why?"

"Are you trying to make yourself sick?" He stomps over to the desk I'm still moping at. Rifling through one of the drawers, he pulls out a protein bar and hands it to me. "Here. You should eat something."

"Where did those come from?"

"Eat one, and I'll tell you."

Rolling my eyes, I unwrap the bar and take a bite. Mostly, I do it because my stomach has been screaming at me all morning, but I didn't have time for breakfast because I accidentally overslept.

"More," he urges. He picks up another and unwraps it, like he plans to feed me like a baby once I finish the one I'm working on.

I continue eating until I'm left with only an empty yellow wrapper. "These are really good."

"Thanks." He grins. "They're my favorite."

I resist the urge to laugh. "And you...stuffed a bunch of them up here for later?"

"Yes. They're delicious. And *some people* don't enjoy masochism."

My mouth falls open. "I'm not a masochist!"

"You've been starving yourself all morning. What do you call it?"

I open my mouth to answer, but I come up with nothing. Bash smirks and hands me his other unwrapped protein bar before he walks away.

I convince Addison to come back to church the next morning. She's had a perfectly valid excuse for missing the past four months: her baby hardly being able to get through thirty minutes without shrieking at a high pitch, but I'm hopeful this time will be better.

"Alright, Marina. We're going to practice staying calm today." Addison gently rocks the car seat her daughter is napping in. We're already in our seats near the back of the room. This way, it will be easy for Addison to make a hasty escape if Marina starts wailing during a quiet moment.

Her husband, Perry, is talking to Logan in one of the aisles after dropping his four other kids off at their Sunday school class.

"Have you ever thought about dating Logan?" Addison asks in a hushed tone.

I wrinkle my nose. "Me?"

"Yeah. It's hard to imagine someone more perfect for you, to be honest."

I want to laugh at her suggestion. "No. Logan is like a brother to me. Besides, I don't want to date anyone, Addy. Ever again."

A deep V forms between her brows. "I know things ended badly with Cole, but—"

"I'm happy alone. Trust me. I'd rather have an extra groomer on staff than a man, any day. Maybe then I could take some time off work." The words feel ridiculous as I say them. Because the things I used to dream of, like a husband and children, are what I used to want a surplus of free time for in the first place. Working has become my way of *filling* that void, if anything. Without distractions, the loneliness always creeps in.

She worries her lip, staring past me. And then she squints. "Wait...who is *that*? The blond guy Logan is introducing to Perry?"

I don't even need to look to know who she's talking about, but I peek anyway.

I see him standing there, his relaxed, hulking form, looking bored and mischievous. Those cuffed sleeves of his dress shirt straining against his muscled forearms, forcing my gaze to reluctantly linger on all his tattoos. His smirk. His eyes. His—

"They're coming over here." Addison bounces in her seat. "Hurry and explain before they get too close."

"What makes you think I know him?"

She gives me a withering look. "Oh, I don't know. Maybe the fact that you spend more time at church than at home. You know everyone who steps foot in here."

She has a point. "Fine. His name is Sebastian Black, but he goes by Bash. He's my new dog bather at The Paw Spa."

Her jaw drops. *"That's him?* The one who called you beautiful?" And then a dreamy undertone creeps into her voice. "And he has tattoos?"

"Yes."

"Look at that face. He's so handsome."

I shrug. "He's...decent to look at."

"Ugh, his tortured soul. You would fix everything."

"Okay." I elbow her. "First of all, we have no idea if he even has a tortured soul. Second of all, we're at church. Stop with the match-making."

"Sorry...I'm hardcore failing at thinking straight at the moment. Please try again later."

I laugh. *"Addison."*

"Okay, fine. I'll stop. But just know that he's currently tied for second-place of Most Handsome Man I've Ever Seen."

"You have a list?"

"Of course. Perry is the most handsome. Logan has been second since I met him...but now it's a tie between him and Sebastian."

"Bash," I say. "He goes by Bash."

"Even better."

I don't get to fire a retort at her, because the three men approach us. I can't deny, seeing Bash here, regarding me with playful interest makes my insides stir. *Don't look at me like that*, I want to say. But instead, I return his stare with my most saccharine smile. "Thought church wasn't your thing anymore."

"Guess I found something to make it interesting."

Our mini audience is silent, but I can practically feel the collective amusement of Addison, Perry, and Logan as they process my exchange with Bash.

Perry finally breaks the tension and sits beside Addison. His arm gently slides around her waist as he leans down to smile at Marina. "Hey, sweet girl," he murmurs. "Please stay asleep this time."

We all laugh.

"Do you all have room over here for two more?" Logan asks, eyeing the empty seats next to me.

I gesture to my right for them to sit, even though my stomach flips at the idea of Bash sitting next to me. I half expect Logan to sit between us, but Bash takes the seat next to mine.

As Logan squeezes in on Bash's other side, Bash leans down to whisper in my ear. "Shouldn't you be up there, singing?"

The way his cool, minty breath caresses my cheek makes me want to lean in closer. "Not this week."

"What a shame. You have a beautiful voice."

"Thanks." A bead of warmth appears in my chest at the compliment, but I push it away. The lights dim, and the worship team appears, Hadley leading the set this week. Bash remains silent throughout the service, but he rests his arm between us at one point, and I have a very hard time not noticing all the swirling patterns of his tattoos. For the first time, I'm close enough to see what they are. Well...briefly, without staring. I can't help but notice he has a cross on each forearm, blending with the rest of his ink. This close, it's also impossible to ignore how good he smells, despite the faint cigarette scent masked beneath.

Somehow, Marina makes it through without crying, and with Addison's permission, I lift her out of her car seat while we all make our way to the outdoor seating area after service. I'm overly aware of Bash walking beside me, but I try to ignore him.

"You are the cutest baby I've ever seen," I tell Marina. I gently tap her little nose, and she wiggles, accidentally yanking her bow out of her dark, wavy hair. She has Addison's wide brown eyes and Perry's olive complexion.

"To be fair, Enzo was pretty adorable as a baby," says Perry. "But I'm probably biased."

"I bet Romilly was a stunning baby because she was in so many pageants growing up," says Addison. Somehow, the statement seems directed specifically at Bash. "She's always been pretty, in fact. Beautiful, even."

Perry gives her a funny smile, but I glare at her. I know what she's doing. She's referring to that text I sent her about Bash calling me beautiful.

Bash shoves his hands in his pockets. Looking directly at me, he smiles. "That doesn't surprise me."

I want to run to my car and hide. But years of pageants and philanthropy have taught me how to hide my thoughts and smile like I'm unbothered. "How kind. If you'll excuse me, I'd better get going."

I hand Marina to Perry, and Addison shakes her head

at me like she's disappointed I'm not going to endure any more of her blatant match-making attempts.

As I hasten to the parking lot, the past few minutes replay in my head. It's impossible not to let Addison's implication affect me. Now I'm imagining what it would be like to date Bash, and it's annoying how appealing the idea is to me. Especially since he's the opposite of the kind of guy I'd typically go for—someone safe, reliable, and stable. And even men like that can't be trusted.

But I know the problem isn't Addison, it's that with every interaction I have with Bash, the sturdy brick wall I put up just seems to keep crumbling.

Chapter Nine

BASH

I WATCH Romilly walk to her car from where I'm standing with Logan and the rest of the group. Romilly's friend with the dimples—Addison—says something to me, but I'm barely paying attention. A man is now talking to Romilly in the parking lot, and she's frowning.

My shoulders tense without my permission. I start forward toward them when Logan catches my arm. "Everything alright?"

"Do you think she's okay? Do you know that man?"

"That man?" Perry follows the direction of my gaze. "You mean the pastor?"

I blink. "Oh. That's the pastor?"

Addison covers her mouth with her hand like she's trying not to laugh, and Romilly and the pastor walk toward us. As soon as she's back within my vicinity, I ask her, "What's going on?"

"Nothing." But she bites her lip and stares past me. I may not know her that well, but it's clear she's worried about something. The pastor isn't far behind her, but he's stuck in a conversation with someone else for the moment.

Gently, I place my hands on her shoulders but keep distance between us so she's not uncomfortable. "Tell me."

Romilly meets my gaze, debating.

"You do look stressed," Addison says. I almost forgot she was here.

Romilly bites her lip. "Okay, fine. There's been an emergency with the Sunday school teachers. They need to leave before the next service, so I'm going to stay and help out. I just need to find another volunteer to join me."

Perry tilts his head slightly, lips pressed knowingly into a thin line. "It was my kids, wasn't it? They caused the emergency."

"Sorry, Perry." Romilly winces. "I think Enzo and Abel might be getting sick. They just threw up on the volunteers, who now want to go home and get cleaned up."

Addison's mouth falls open, and Perry runs an exasperated hand down his face. "I'll go get them." Then, turning to Addison, he says, "Will you meet me at the car?"

"Of course." Addison sighs. "See you later, Rom. Sorry you have to stay and help fix this mess." She lifts Marina's car seat and starts walking to her car. Perry heads the opposite direction, toward the main building.

Romilly turns to Logan, placing her hand on his arm gently. An unexpected frenzy of jealousy takes hold of me when she touches him. *Get a grip, Bash. She's your boss, and she's made it clear she's not interested in you.*

"Are you available to help with the kids' class next service?" she asks him.

He winces and checks the time on his phone. "I would if I didn't have to head to work."

"It's okay, I totally understand." She gives him a hug before he leaves, but the disappointment in the way her shoulders are drooping is impossible to miss.

I don't know how anyone turns her down. I can't explain the pull I feel towards her, or how that frown on her face would make me call in sick just to make it disappear. But then again, if I actually called in sick, it would be from my job with *her*.

"I'll do it." The words fly out of my mouth just as the pastor approaches.

Romilly shakes her head. "It's fine, Bash. I can just do it alone." Turning to the pastor, she asks, "Can we make an exception for today, Mason?"

He winces. "Unfortunately, no. We'd still need one more adult. There's a teacher-to-child ratio that has to be followed, so you can't take on all those kids alone."

With a smirk, I cross my arms. "Like I said, I'm available."

The pastor eyes me curiously. "And you are?"

I reach out to shake his hand, using a tone I used to save only for my mother's high-value clients. "Sebastian Black. I couldn't help but overhear your debacle with the childcare this afternoon."

"Mason Campbell. Nice to meet you. I saw your name on the counselor list for our homeschool retreat. But you look familiar." He rubs his graying beard as he regards me. "Wait, you're a fighter, aren't you? I watched your debut fight, and I have to say...you were incredible."

"Why, thank you."

Romilly's eyes widen as she looks back and forth between the two of us. "Bash, you don't have to. *Really*. We'll find someone else."

But Mason laughs. "You got something against this guy?"

"He's my new dog bather," she says. "I—"

Mason arches a brow. "And we've already background checked him. So we're all good there, right?"

"Yes, but—"

"Perfect." He beams at me. "Thanks for the help, Sebastian."

"Call me Bash."

We shake hands once more before he melts back into the rest of the crowd. I don't have much time to reflect on this recent, impulsive decision of mine before Romilly's sweet voice cuts into my subconscious.

"Why would you volunteer to help with Sunday school?"

I turn to face her. That plump mouth is downturned, and her neat brows are arranged into an adorable frown. I gently tap her button nose with my index finger. I can't tell her it's because she's so magnetic, or that I can't seem to leave her alone, and I quite like being around her. So I say something I know will agitate her. "Because you, sweet Romilly, are going to owe me a favor."

Her frown deepens in the cutest way. "A favor? Are you serious?"

"Serious as the plague."

"Let's just get this over with. Follow me." Her tone is deep and strained, but the way she walks back toward the main building would fool anyone into thinking she's on a gentle stroll. She doesn't check behind her to see if I'm following along. She doesn't need to. I'm right on her trail, letting her lead the way to the children's classroom.

This is going to be interesting.

I don't have much experience with kids. I can't even remember the last time I interacted with one. But the idea of Romilly all alone, potentially getting thrown up on by more sick children like Perry's makes my stomach sink.

The classroom is empty when we arrive, and smaller than I expect, with walls painted an intense shade of yellow, one way too bright for little amount of caffeine I've had. The ceiling is low, making the whole space feel slightly claustrophobic, and posters of Bible stories are plastered everywhere. Bright colors and cartoonish figures grin down at me. I don't remember Noah's Ark looking quite so happy at my church back home.

Romilly gets to work on the empty room, arranging the plastic, primary-colored seats in a circle.

"It's far too cheery in here." I wrinkle my nose against the faint smell of crayons and glue in the air, along with something vaguely sweet, like...squashed raisins? It's nauseating.

"I think the word you're looking for is stimulating. Or maybe exciting."

"No, no. I said cheery, but I meant dreadful, actually."

Romilly ignores me, restocking a tiny table in the corner with craft supplies. "You know, I'm actually glad you volunteered. You're way too confident for your own good. This should do wonders for your ego."

"This will be *no problem*," I say. "Sorry to disappoint you." But I'm lying, and deep down, I think Romilly knows it.

As if on cue, young voices drift in from the hall. Romilly opens the door, and the first wave of parents arrive with their miniature humans. My nerves skyrocket.

Romilly checks in each child and eventually hands me

a clipboard to do the same. Once a good ten minutes pass without another kid arriving, I set mine down on the counter and take in the chaos around us.

At least six different conversations are going on at once, all of them in squeaky, high-pitched voices. I shift my weight from one foot to the other, glancing over at Romilly. She's across the room, crouched by a kid who's apparently upset about his drawing. Romilly looks like she belongs here, like this room and these kids were already penciled into her day. It's strange, watching her like this. She's usually so composed, so focused, whether she's having a conversation or even working on her dogs. But here with the kids, there's something even softer about her. Her smile is brighter, her movements more relaxed.

Meanwhile, I'm...well, I'm just hoping I don't break anything. Or anyone.

A few kids crowd around me, looking me up and down. It's like they can sense that I don't belong here, but instead of driving them away, it's made me the target of all their attention.

One boy, maybe five or six, steps closer. He's got a wild mane of brown curls and a streak of blue marker on his face. His shirt is too big, and he looks like the type who would be constantly falling into puddles. He's clutching a toy dragon, and his eyes widen as they lock onto me.

"Do you fight dragons?" he asks, voice full of wonder. "You look like a knight."

I blink down at him. "What?"

The other kids go quiet, like they're interested in my response.

I glance toward Romilly, hoping for some sort of rescue, but she's still helping that kid with the drawing, completely oblivious. Wincing, I answer the kid. "Oh, yeah. I fight dragons all the time, mate."

His eyes widen even more, and a girl next to him gasps. "You do?" she whispers, as if I've just confessed to being some kind of superhero.

I nod slowly. "Yeah. I mean, I don't fight them like—" I struggle for the right words, something that won't get me in trouble with the parents later. "—like hitting them or anything. It's more strategy. You've got to outsmart the dragon."

A girl wearing a princess dress jumps in. "How?"

"Not with swords, obviously. Dragons fight with fire. So, you know, you have to put out the fire before they can spread it."

That earns me a chorus of "oohs," and I try to relax my shoulders. Apparently, that was a good answer.

"But how do you do it?" the boy with the dragon toy presses. He's looking at me like I'm his new favorite person in the world.

"Water, of course. You put out the dragon's fire with water. That's their weakness."

The boy gasps, clutching his toy even tighter. "Like the ocean?"

I nod, catching Romilly's eye as she watches us. There's a tiny smile on her lips that makes me wonder if she's just as amused by my tale as the kids are.

"Yeah, like the ocean," I say, forcing a grin. "Dragons hate the ocean."

"And why not swords?" another kid asks. "I thought all knights use swords."

I raise an eyebrow. "Swords? Nah. That's too messy. Like I said, you've got to *outsmart* the dragon first. Dragons are really stubborn, you know. They think they're so much smarter than everyone else, but they're really just controlling. So you have to make them think they're winning, before you can finally break free." It takes me a moment to realize how low my voice is. I take a steadying breath when my mum and dad's faces come to mind. *Relax, Bash. No need to get so intense about it.*

But the boy nods solemnly, like I've just imparted some ancient wisdom.

Romilly finally walks over, crossing her arms. Her green eyes flash with amusement. "Bash, I didn't realize you were such a dragon expert."

I shoot her a teasing grin. "There's plenty you don't know about me."

Romilly blushes, and her gaze jumps back to the kids. "Alright, everyone, why don't we finish up our drawings before song time?"

There's a chorus of excitement as the kids scramble back to their tables.

"Thank you for your help," she says. "You really didn't have to do this. I could have found someone else, but I'm still really grateful."

"Well, you're not bad company, you know."

She fights a smile with impressive effort. "You mean, you're not sick of me yet? After the week we had at work?"

"No way."

She shrugs a shoulder. "Don't worry. It's only a matter of time."

Romilly saunters off before I can respond. "We'll see," I murmur to myself.

What she doesn't realize is how much each moment I've spent with her is only making me want more. But I know deep down getting sick of her would be better for both of us. Me, because I don't need any distractions right now, and her because I've disappointed everyone else in my life. My parents, when I became a fighter. The church, when I made decisions that labeled me a bad influence. My friends, when their parents told them not to talk to me anymore. The list goes on.

And I'm sure Romilly has a different type of man for herself in mind when it comes down to it. One who's nothing like me. I doubt I could ever live up to the kind of standards she has.

But for some annoying, terribly aggravating reason, there's a part of me that wants to try.

Chapter Ten

ROMILLY

I SMIRK AT BASH. "Let me make you lunch. It's the least I can do for the dragon-slayer." After the way he stepped in, saving me from managing all those kids by myself, I can't help but feel some gratitude. Besides, I bet he's hungry. It's lunch time, and my own stomach is currently rumbling in discomfort.

Those hooded blue eyes jerk to my face with amusement. "If you want to spend more time with me, all you have to do is ask."

"No, it's not that. I'm just grateful for your help. "

He grins. "Well, now I feel you've invited me over out of obligation. How uncomfortable."

A surge of annoyance races through me. *Oh, I'll give you uncomfortable.* "Bash, I'd love to have you over for lunch," I say through my teeth. "You're a delight to be around, and your blatant flirting doesn't affect me one bit."

"See? Was that so hard?" He checks the time on his phone. "I just need to stop at home and then I'll be on my way to entertain you with my wittiness."

I nod, but my stomach somersaults. What was I thinking? What did I just initiate? All our encounters have been strictly business so far. Even our coffee date was about offering him a job. We've never spent time together outside of work or church, so I can't imagine what it will be like to have lunch with him.

Just the two of us. No business involved.

The thought has adrenaline racing in my veins. "Sounds good. I'll text you my address."

My mind spins like it's on fast-forward as I drive home. *What if Jasper scratches him? What if he has food allergies like Addison? What in the world should I make us to eat?*

By the time I park in the driveway at home, I've settled on something, but I text Bash just to make sure.

ME

You aren't allergic to anything other than hard work, are you?

BASH

Sunshine and small children will also do me in. Why? Hiding either of those in your cupboards?

ME

Very funny.

BASH

I'm on my way. Be there in a few minutes.

I try not to smile and fail as I set down my phone. At least he won't go into anaphylactic shock like Addison did last year at the Miss Meadow pageant. Hearing about that whole thing almost gave me a heart attack.

With a sigh, I shift my gaze around to make sure my

place looks as cozy and inviting as possible. I try to see what Bash will see when he gets here—warm light filtering in through heavy curtains, soft rugs in earth tones, and plants on every surface. It smells like vanilla and the sourdough bread I baked last night. Perfect.

God, why am I excited to have lunch with Bash? Are you trying to tell me something? If not, please make this excitement disappear.

Bash, of all men. I can't afford to like him because dating a co-worker would be messy enough. Dating Bash—my only help at work—would be especially messy now that I need to raise my rating. Somehow, I doubt a workplace romance would help things.

"What do you think, Jasper?" I tap his nose as he slinks over, standing on the table even though he's not supposed to. Today, he's wearing a crocheted hat that makes him look like a lion. Most cats would probably play with the tassels and take it off, but Jasper is special. I pet him until he purrs.

And then I hear knocking.

My stomach does that annoying little flip again.

You don't want a man, Romilly. You don't need a man.

I repeat it in my head like a mantra as I walk to the front door and gently creak it open.

He's standing there in a wooly blue scarf and olive green jacket, shoulders shrugged against the chilly afternoon air. Bash's silky blond hair blows around his face, making me want to run my hands through the strands. He's not even inside yet, but his sandalwood scent invades my nostrils.

"Welcome to my cottage." I open the door wider.

"Why, thank you." He walks in and removes his shoes

at the entryway without me even having to ask. Despite his gruffness, there's a refined, classy vibe to him that makes me wonder what his parents are like. "Your home is beautiful, like you," he says.

I blush. "Thank you. Make yourself comfortable. I'm about to make us sandwiches."

"Wait a minute...I must be hallucinating. I just complimented you and you didn't get angry at me."

I clear my throat. "Sorry. I must need water or something."

He laughs and shakes his head. "I'm—uh—going to step outside for a moment. I desperately need to have a smoke."

The look in his eyes makes me feel bad for him. It reminds me of the hunger I see in the eyes of the homeless at the soup kitchen. "The yard is that way." I point, and he heads past the living room to the back door.

I uncover the sourdough loaf I baked last night. Apparently, there's nothing more comforting than fresh bread. At least, according to my mom. And staring down at my masterpiece, I can't help but agree.

Bash's voice cuts through my thoughts from the living room. "Hey there, kitty," he says.

Oh, no. Jasper is going to break him. Biting my lip to keep from laughing, I peer around the kitchen corner to the living room where Bash is now sitting on my sofa beside Jasper. A lollipop stick juts out of his mouth, and he's holding a fidget spinner. Bash sets it down and reaches a tentative hand toward Jasper, probably expecting him to sniff it like a normal pet would.

Instead, Jasper bats at him with his paw and—claws

fully extended—knocks Bash's spinner onto the ground, sending it rolling across the room.

"So that's how it is, huh, you little lion-cat?" Bash mutters under his breath. He gets up and retrieves the toy. He sits back down and rotates it a few times, but Jasper's tail flicks against his arm. Bash gently pushes him away, but Jasper just swipes at Bash's spinner, sending it flying from his hands again.

"Seriously, mate?" He glares at the cat.

A giggle bursts from my lips. "Um, Bash?"

He looks at me from the sofa. His expression is unreadable. "Yes?"

"Is Jasper bothering you? Because I can totally move him to my room."

He gives a half-hearted glare at the cat, who is now lounging as if nothing had happened. "No, no. I think Jasper's just plotting my demise. No need to worry."

"Right. And ruining your smoking session?" I nod at his hands with a puzzled smile.

"Alright, then. If you must know, I've quit smoking, and this... *thing* helps tremendously."

"So, you didn't go outside and smoke just now?"

He shrugs. "I meant to, but then I thought about it." He glares at the spinner in his hand. "Better than wrecking my lungs, right?"

"Oh, absolutely." My chest feels warm and light. Part of me wants to laugh at Bash holding a child's toy with those strong, fighter's hands, but there's something annoyingly attractive about it.

The only sound in the room is Jasper's low purr—probably gloating over the chaos he's caused for Bash.

I put my hands on my hips. "I have to admit, your bad boy look is tarnished in my eyes now."

"You think I'm a bad boy?" A laugh escapes him. "I guess I'm not surprised. Most people I've met assume the same thing."

"No, no. You used to be one, but now I know you like fidget spinners."

"What can I say? They really help."

I try not to smile, but my mouth betrays me. "I'm going to finish up lunch. I hope you're hungry."

"I'm never not hungry, Romilly. It's time you knew." He rises from the couch.

I roll my eyes, walking back to the kitchen.

Bash follows me and glances at the bread waiting on the counter. "How did you learn to bake?"

"My mom taught me. I've been helping her cook family dinners once a week since I was a kid, but it's been a while. My parents are on a cruise right now."

Bash steps aside as I move around the kitchen to gather all the ingredients. When it's time to slice the bread, I hand him a knife. "Go ahead."

He smirks, twirling the knife in his fingers. "What? Do you see a dragon that needs slaying?"

"Just cut the bread, Bash."

"Fine." He places the knife in the center of the loaf, and I reposition his hands at the end. He lets me guide them to the correct place. This close, I can feel his soft breath on my arm. The fine hair along his fingers tickles my palms, and everywhere his skin touches me makes me feel like I'm burning up.

I let go of his hands and clear my throat. "Okay, go ahead and slice."

I watch him slowly create three uneven slices of bread and nudge him with my elbow. "On second thought, maybe I should do it."

He scoffs, though the bread slices are clearly a crumbling mess. "No way, I've got this. I'm practically an expert now."

I shake my head but don't press. Instead, I set the table with our plates and fill the misshapen sandwiches with meats, cheese, and veggies. I also pour us each a bowl of the leftover minestrone soup I made yesterday.

When the table is ready, our steaming bowls and sandwich plates waiting, we sit across from each other at my small wooden table. There's really only enough space for three people to sit comfortably, but when Zara, my parents, and my brother, Aiden, occasionally visit, the five of us somehow manage to squeeze in together. And bumping knees with my family is fine.

Bumping knees with Bash on the other hand...*not* fine.

"Oops, sorry," he says, bringing his feet in so they're not touching mine.

"It's not your fault." I sigh and wrinkle my nose at the piece of furniture. "It's this tiny table. But I don't really have company often, so it wouldn't be smart to splurge on a bigger one."

Bash studies me.

"What?" I try not to fidget under his gaze.

"Have you always been so responsible?"

"I—I don't know. I just don't want to have any regrets, I guess."

"And buying a new table would be something you'd regret?" He gestures to the small, round tabletop. Neither of us has taken a bite yet, and hungry as I am, the way Bash looks at me has my nerves jangling in a way that affects my appetite.

"Yes. Because I'm trying to be smart with money so I don't end up back home with my parents again. I finally just got back on my feet."

"I can't even imagine you moving back home." He lifts his sandwich and takes a bite. A groan rumbles in his throat. "Romilly, this is . . . amazing."

The compliment warms me. "Thanks. Why can't you imagine me moving back home?"

"Because you're good at everything." He says it so simply, like it's a fact instead of an opinion.

"No, I'm not."

"Yes, you are. You succeed at everything you do. It's fascinating to witness."

I scoff. "My last dog grooming business with my sister, Zara, completely failed. We made the mistake of buying the building instead of renting, and the place fell apart. It was too expensive for us to fix, so we both had to move back home."

"But look at you now," he says. "Successful new pet spa full of bloodthirsty beasts who adore you. Helping the needy. Good with kids. Voice like an angel."

I blush furiously. Is that really what he thinks of me?

But my own thoughts happily intercede. *Don't let the compliments get to you, Romilly. Compliments mean nothing. It's all about actions.*

"Trust me, my business is closer to failing again than you think. My rent just went up, and the only groomer left in Meadow Hills won't come back to work with me unless I raise my online rating."

"That shouldn't be hard. Not for you," he says.

If only I felt as certain as he does. I lean closer across the table. "Can I ask you something?"

"I'm an open book."

"What happened with your last job to make you accept a position with me?"

His stormy blue eyes settle onto mine. "Are you sure you want to know? The truth might reinstate me as a *bad boy* in your mind."

"Whatever it is, I doubt it's that big a deal. I already ran a background check on you."

"Alright then." He smiles wider. "My parents are members of high society in Woollahra, and their auction house in Sydney has a crazy amount of prestige. I've assisted them with events now and then. But I hated it. What I really love—what I'm passionate about is fighting."

I nod. "And they're not happy about that, I'm sure."

"Of course not. I'm their biggest embarrassment. Their sweet, charming Sebastian, a fighter? Not a chance." He smiles. "I was supposed to eventually take over the auction houses for them. The one back in Sydney, and the other, over in Portland, so they could retire. But when I told them I had no desire and I wanted to fight instead, that was it for my parents. The last and final straw."

"I'm surprised they're not proud of you...making it like that as a professional fighter? That must have taken a lot of guts," I say.

He smiles. "Thanks. Deep down I think I hoped they would be. But my parents were so furious they canceled my cards and left me here, stranded. My sister, Ingrid, stayed with me, even though my next fight isn't till November. I won't make much from it either, not without a sponsor."

My laughter dries up instantly. "So you've just been... they abandoned you? And they left you with no money at all?"

"Unfortunately."

"And you have no money of your own?"

"Only what I've made working with you. The cash I earned from my debut lasted maybe a week. And Ingrid's salary, plus the money from my pawned watch got us through till I met you."

Empathy surges through me. Yeah, he kinda put himself in this situation, with the rebelling and doing something he knew would upset his parents. But I still feel bad for him because he was just trying to do something he loves.

"Enough about me. Tell me about your family," he says.

"Well..." I bite my lip. "My sister, Zara, is nosy and optimistic. My brother, Aiden, is crazy good at video games. I hardly ever see him because he games so much. And my mom loves cooking and spending time with family. She stayed home to raise us."

"What about your dad?" he asks, eyes glinting with curiosity.

"He's a plumber here in town. Taught me how to unclog a drain at six years old." I smile at the memory.

"You should be thankful," he says. "I'd give anything to talk about my family the way you talk about yours."

Guilt pricks at my heart. "Well, what about your sister? Do you not get along with her either?"

Some of the tension in his expression eases. "Actually, Ingrid and I get along just fine. She's been going on about making brunch for you. Which is ridiculous because she's still learning how to cook."

I blink. I'm sure I must have misheard him. "Did you say she wants to make brunch for...*me?*"

He nods. "As thanks for hiring me."

I laugh, but it comes out unsteady. Has Bash talked about me to her? The thought makes my cheeks feel warm. "When is it?"

"Tuesday. And before you say you have to serve breakfast at men's group, it's been cancelled this week because of a scheduling conflict with one of the leaders."

I laugh. "I know. And I'd love to come." The words come out before I can stop them.

"That's good. Because if you said no, I would have been forced to cash in that favor you owe me for helping this morning."

I giggle. "Thank you again for that, by the way. You were actually pretty great with those kids."

The corner of his mouth lifts, and our gazes lock. Neither of us says anything, but I can feel the weight of his stare like it's touching me. For the briefest moment, I wonder what it would be like to kiss him. And then I force the thought from my mind.

"Thank you for lunch," he says, standing to collect our plates. "I'll clean up and get going. I've taken up your whole afternoon."

The way he speaks makes it easy for me to imagine him in a setting like an upscale auction house, schmoozing clients and greeting them with his charming words. It's probably easy for him to slip into that mask, the one that he knows will please his parents and the people he needs to impress.

And then an idea comes to me.

"Wait a second. What were you saying earlier about sponsors?"

He frowns. "If I don't find one, I won't make much from my next fight."

"And *I* need to raise my rating at the salon to get my old groomer back. Do you see where I'm going with this?" I raise my eyebrows.

Bash's frown only deepens. "That we all have problems?"

"No. I'm trying to say I'll sponsor you if you can help me raise my rating."

"Sponsor me?" Bash crosses arms. "How? I thought your business is close to failing."

"It is. But if Agatha comes back, it would solve everything. I'd make twice what I am now. I could afford to sponsor you, easily."

Bash rubs the back of his neck. "What could I do to bring up your rating that you can't do on your own?"

"I need to be more available, which means taking more dogs every day. And I also need help finishing my grooms faster. I can train you to help me speed things up." I shake my head. "There's no way I could do any of it without your help."

Bash mulls my words over. He doesn't break the stare we have going. For a minute, I think he's going to turn down my offer, but then an understanding smile spreads across his face. "You got yourself a deal."

Chapter Eleven

BASH

I'M LATE FOR WORK.

Of course I am.

After leaving Romilly's yesterday, I ended up at Harbor Strike MMA, the closest decent gym—which, of course, was all the way in Portland. And turns out, the long drive was worth it because the head coach, Greg, recognized me the second I walked in. Apparently, he's seen the viral clip of me against four guys in a parking lot and had also caught my pro debut. So, instead of brushing me off, he offered me a spot right then and there to train alongside the other fighters. I didn't even have to ask.

And this morning, the welcoming scent of the sweat and rubber matting in the gym woke me up in the best way. Even if it was the kind of smell that stuck to my lungs long after leaving. Thankfully, I've been doing plenty of strength training and cardio before now, but grappling and sparring with the other pro fighters had me struggling. And that wouldn't do. I lost track of time, and after three hours, realized how late I was about to be for The Paw Spa.

As I drive home to change, I overthink my lunch with Romilly the same way I did last night. I can't help it. The woman is taking over my mind.

I still can't believe she made those sandwiches. With fresh bread. I don't feel worthy.

I've been wondering if she's the woman of my dreams, but the moment I tasted the meal she effortlessly crafted, my suspicions were confirmed.

Romilly is perfect. She's too good to be true, and definitely too good for me. It's even more evident now that she's willing to sponsor me over something as trivial as helping her rating go up. She hardly knows me, and she already believes in me. Something my own parents aren't even capable of.

Shake it off, Bash. To be in a relationship is to be controlled. Just like how Mum is with Dad. I recall the way they've always bickered, how Mum is always hurling insults and names at Dad whenever he so much as meets with a friend during the week after work. I've seen what a relationship looks like, and I want no part of it.

But when I try to imagine Romilly in my mother's shoes, yelling at me and calling me names, my mind goes blank. She simply doesn't fit that bill. Not with her gentle tone, her kind demeanor, or the way she's always going out of her way to think of others before herself.

Besides, it's impossible to be controlled by someone who wants nothing to do with you. And Romilly obviously has no interest in me. She's made it more than clear.

I park at home and head to my room so I can strip out of my gym clothes and rash guard. Shaking my head to scatter the intrusive thoughts, I shower and dress for work in a hurry. Thankfully, Romilly provided me with a pair of black scrubs to wear to work in case I don't want to ruin my regular clothes. I've never considered wearing them before, but I don't have clean laundry right now, so I put them on. Glancing at the time on my phone, I realize I won't even have time to read a few quick verses on my phone by the lake out back. Not today.

I brush my teeth, splash some water on my face, add a spritz of cologne, and I'm out the door in less than twenty minutes. The drive goes quickly. I ignore my "check engine" light and speed down the tiny, narrow streets of Meadow Hills. It's such a quaint town, one that reminds me of a fairytale, with its cobbled pavement downtown and the baskets of autumn florals hanging outside the windows of passing shops. Even though Romilly's salon isn't on the same street as all the other downtown businesses, it doesn't take long for me to arrive.

I stride from my parked car to the entrance. And freeze.

There's a man outside The Paw Spa, backing Romilly against the side of the building. He's wearing a sweatshirt with holes in it and tattered green trousers. The man's back is facing me, and over his shoulder, Romilly's smile is frozen on her face. To the average person, it might look as if they're having a friendly conversation, but I know better. I've seen that smile before. It's the one she wears when a customer gets upset, or I antagonize her slightly too far, or she gets stuck watching kids last minute at church. At first, I think I'm imagining it, but as I get closer I notice her hands shaking at her sides.

She's afraid.

I've never ran so fast in my life. The moment she sees me approaching, her shoulders loosen. The idea that she's currently distressed enough for the sight of *me* to bring her comfort makes me feel an array of emotions. The most notable of those emotions? Anger at this man, and a surge of possessiveness toward her. It doesn't matter what's going on because all I know is that I'll protect her.

"Is there a problem, mate?" I grit out them moment I'm standing beside her. Now that I'm facing the man, I take in his scraggly beard, the murderous expression on his pale, deeply wrinkled face, and the powerful stench emanating from his body.

"I know you have more money than that," he spits in her direction, ignoring me. Romilly's body tenses beside me, and by instinct, I step in front of her so I'm between her and this man.

"Did you hear me?" I raise my voice. "I asked if there's a problem. You can talk to me now, not her." Turning to her, I say, "Go inside."

"Romilly isn't going anywhere." The man shakes a fist. "Not until she gives me the same amount I've seen her give others."

My final thread of patience snaps. I grab the man by the front of his shirt, ignoring Romilly's sharp inhale beside me. "She's not giving you a dime," I grind out. "Now get out of here, before I hurt you."

"Sebastian," she says softly and touches my arm. "It's alright, just let him go."

I release him, but my gaze remains locked on him. He glares right back at me.

"Like I said before," she continues, "I just need to go inside to see if there's any cash left in the tip jar, so if you'll excuse me—"

My eyes jerk to her face. "Absolutely not. *Romilly*. This man is harassing you. Do not give him any money."

She looks torn, so I take out my wallet and shove a fiver at him. "If I see you here again, you'd better hope she's not here to save you." The words come out low and gravelly.

He tucks the money in his pocket and runs off toward the street.

When I face Romilly again, I take her hand and pull her against me. All I can think about is that I'm glad she's okay and that I don't want her to be scared. And for a moment, she relaxes as I tighten my arms around her. "Are you okay?" I murmur into her hair.

"I'm fine." She pulls away to stare at me wide-eyed. "You didn't have to do that."

"Oh, yes I did," I say. "Because you were practically moments away from giving him the shirt off your back. He could have hurt you. You need to be more careful."

At that, she frowns. "I'm fine. I know how to take care of myself."

"Oh, really? Tell me then, why on earth were you backed into this corner looking as if you've never been more terrified in your life?"

She huffs, turning on her heel toward the salon entrance. "I'm not doing this with you, Bash."

"Doing what?" I'm right on her heel.

"This thing where you pretend to care about me."

Her words stop me in my tracks. She continues to unlock the entrance, and I follow her in. She shuts the door behind us, and I blurt, "I do care about you."

She rolls her eyes. "You know what I mean. I'm grateful that you stepped in, but I don't need you getting all up in my business. I've always done fine handling these kinds of situations on my own."

"Then why were you shaking?"

"Because..." She shrugs. "It's still a little scary."

I frown as it dawns on me that she's referring to this incident like it's happened before. "How many times have you been cornered by a strange man?" The thought makes me so angry, I can't see straight. Romilly is gentle, so kind. The thought of anyone taking advantage of her generosity makes me want to punch a hole through the nearest wall.

"Just let it go, Bash."

"How many times?"

She sighs. "It's happened once or twice. It's just something that comes with volunteering sometimes. But there's no way I'm going to let anyone ruin it for the people who really need help. Guys like him are few and far between."

I clench my jaw. "This isn't right."

"It's really no biggie."

I shake my head. "No biggie? *No biggie?* Romilly, you have no idea what some men are capable of."

My words invoke a strange reaction in her. Something plays behind her eyes, something I can't see. It's as if she completely gets lost in her thoughts for a moment. The openness in her expression dims, like a light being shut off. I know that look, because I've caused it before. Not to her, but other women, past flirtations that barely had a chance to form before I shut them down.

Someone hurt her. Someone broke her heart.

My thoughts are confirmed the moment she says, "Believe me. I know exactly what men are capable of."

"I only meant—"

"And I know I said yesterday that I'd be at your sister's brunch, but I can't make it. I'm sorry."

No. "Wait...please don't cancel. This brunch is a big deal to my sister."

She barely looks at me. "Bash..."

"Please." I take her hand. It's meant to be friendly, comforting, but the moment our fingers come together, a pleasant tingle races through my spine. I swipe my thumb across her palm. *"Please."*

She takes an unsteady breath and looks up at me. She looks like she's fighting for control, like the ease in which she usually wears her polite smile has dissipated.

I can't help but wonder if she feels it too, this connection between us forming, taking root and growing quicker than I can comprehend.

She takes her hand out of mine. "I'll think about it and let you know soon."

I nod, because I have a feeling if I ask again, she'll give me a final no.

We complete the rest of our workday in mostly silence. Romilly is swamped with dogs, thanks to her mission to raise her rating. She barely takes a break from grooming to drink water, let alone eat. I haven't seen her eat a thing, in fact, and after five hours it's alarming.

She sways a bit on her feet as she grooms a large Bernadoodle. It tugs against its restraints as she shaves its underside, pulling her right along with it. I glance around the pet salon. The floors are swept, all the dogs that needed washing are clean, dried, and have gotten their claws trimmed by yours truly.

There's nothing left for me to do, and plenty Romilly still needs to get done. She has four dogs waiting for her in their comfy, assigned kennels. That's another eight hours of work for her, at least. I don't know how she'll accomplish it. But then again...I've doubted her before. Still, I just wish she'd eat something.

And then an idea takes hold of me.

"I'm going to step out for a moment," I say.

She smiles brightly as if she hasn't been on her feet all morning and afternoon. "Of course. Take all the time you need."

If only she followed her own advice.

I make for the reception area and find Romilly's phone face down on the desk. "Please don't have a password," I mutter, unlocking the screen.

Sure enough, I have access to her entire phone the moment I turn it on. *Romilly, luv, you are far too trusting in humanity.*

I find the number in her contacts I'm looking for and send a quick message from my own phone.

ME

What's Romilly's favorite food?

ADDISON

Um...who is this?

ME

It's Bash

Several moments pass before I receive a response.

ADDISON

Sorry, I'm good now. Everything's fine.

Her favorite food is a very specific dish at
my husband's restaurant, Rosemary
Banquet.

I frown.

ME

Where is Rosemary Banquet located?

Addison sends me the address, and I'm already shrugging on my coat, halfway out the door. Thankfully, the restaurant is in Meadow Hills, so I won't be gone long enough to raise suspicion. Hopefully.

Either way, I need Romilly to eat something. And by ordering her favorite food, she'll be less likely to resist.

I arrive at the car park and get out of my Camaro, brushing dog hair off my scrubs. As soon as I open the door to the restaurant, I know I'll be returning. This establishment looks as if it's the type of place I'd frequent in my parents' circle. It's decorated with taste—elegant white linens draped across sturdy wooden tables. Warm lighting emanates from exquisite chandeliers, and a touch of foliage dons the table settings.

I'm definitely underdressed. Worse, actually. I'm covered in dog hair, and I've never been more humiliated. The ironic thing is, the majority of my closet is filled with quality, designer pieces. But the one day I decide to wear scrubs to work and get myself covered in fur, I end up inside the first five star restaurant I've visited in some time.

Do it for Romilly, Bash.

I check my phone again. There's another message from Addison.

ADDISON

I called and ordered the dish. It's on the house and ready for you to pick up! *smiley emoji*

ME

What ever for? I can pay.

ADDISON

Don't worry about it. Just make sure Romilly knows this was your idea.

I frown at the message and force my feet forward. The hostess greets me, and I ask if there's been an order placed for Bash or Romilly.

She beams. "Yes, of course. Mrs. Whitmore called and said you'd be here. I'll be right back." She walks away from her podium, leaving me contemplating why on earth Addison would go to such lengths for me to pick up Romilly's lunch.

The hostess returns with a paper bag containing a takeout box. "I hope she enjoys the meal," she says sweetly, looking up at me through her eyelashes.

I want to laugh. Did Addison tell her specific details? Why is the hostess acting like I'm about to propose or something?

"Thank you," I say, and race back to my car as fast as I can without appearing rude.

By the time I get back to The Paw Spa, no more than thirty minutes have passed. It's a reasonable amount of time for a lunch break, so I doubt Romilly has caught on that I left. I can understand why so many people like small towns. Ease of access and hardly any traffic are some of the many perks.

I carry the bag straight to her station, set it down on the table, and take hold of the Australian Shepherd's restraints that she's working on.

"Bash, what—"

"You need to eat," I tell her. "Now. I'll take the Aussie to his kennel while you do so."

She looks at the bag on her station and then back at me. "Where did this come from?"

"I went and got you lunch."

She blinks. "You...went all the way to Rosemary Banquet?"

"All the way? You act as if it was far." I laugh. "But yes. Now go."

"But Bash...I don't understand."

I lift the bag and place it directly in her hands, my gaze zeroing in on her. "You need to eat. It's been almost six hours, and you haven't eaten a thing, and you've barely had any water. You're working yourself too hard. And before you say you need to work faster to raise your rating, taking a simple lunch break isn't going to prevent you from doing that."

She's speechless. She just stares at me with wide green eyes, her lips slightly parted like she didn't even realize she hasn't eaten all day. "I guess I could take a ten minute break," she says.

"You'd better take longer than that." Placing my hands on her shoulders, I ignore the parade that flurries through my stomach from touching her so casually, and I spin her around and gently scoot her off toward the reception area where she normally eats.

Normally, when she's *not* overworking herself like a crazy person.

Chapter Twelve

ROMILLY

I CAN'T BELIEVE what I see when I open the box. It's my favorite food in all the land—Rosemary Banquet's signature roast chicken and cranberry pecan salad. There's even a wedge of Camembert cheese on the side, my favorite because of its mild flavor and creamy texture.

I can't believe he did this.

In all the time I spent dating Cole, he never got a single food order of mine correct, let alone did anything this thoughtful for me.

Be smart, Romilly. Keep your head on straight. Resist his charms.

But the lecture I give myself doesn't work. I try to stop the feelings from surging up inside me, but I can't. A flutter rises in my stomach for Bash, accompanied by gratitude and disbelief. I don't know how to stop it, to shove it back down, no matter how badly I want to.

I think I like him. And not just any kind of like...but a crush.

I have a crush on Bash.

I scarf down my meal. My stomach is cramped and tight because of how long it's been since I last ate. He was right—I am hungry. And I can't believe he was watching me closely enough to know how long it had been since I last ate.

I try to push thoughts of him away as I satisfy my hunger, but I just keep imagining the way his demanding gaze captured my attention, his insistence that I take a break. His concern this morning when he stepped in between me and the homeless man is practically burned into my brain. I'll never forget how quickly he went from the playful, unbothered Bash to murderously defensive for me.

I've never felt so protected. He made me feel safe.

It was...hot.

Come on, Romilly. Where is that fierce independence you've been clinging so tightly to? But the words Jake spoke a few weeks ago at rehearsal before church ring through my head as well.

You can have a man, too. You're allowed to do something for yourself.

Can I? Am I willing to let go of the trust issues Cole so graciously left me with when he wordlessly abandoned me and then later revealed he was seeing someone else the entire time we were together? If I couldn't see through his act during that year together, how am I supposed to ever trust another man and believe he's who he says he is? Maybe it's myself I don't trust because I wasn't able to see through Cole's lies.

Still, Bash feels different somehow.

Even though he's probably the most handsome and

flirtatious man I've ever met, I can't help but feel like there's more to him.

I pick up my phone from where it's resting on the front desk. Nibbling delicately on the cheese, I send Addison a message.

ME

You'll never guess what just happened.

ADDISON

What?!

ME

Bash brought me lunch from Perry's restaurant and it just so happened to be my favorite dish.

ADDISON

HOW THOUGHTFUL

MARRY THAT MAN

I roll my eyes. I know for a fact she had something to do with this. I don't even have to ask, and I won't because she won't tell me anyway. But it still makes me smile.

ME

Not all of us get to have the epic love story you and Perry do. Sorry Adds.

ADDISON

Says who? I'm fully invested in the situationship you two have going on.

ME

There is no situationship. There's nothing between me and Bash

ADDISON

Then why were his eyes glued to your face that day at church? And you kept looking at him, too. There was no hiding those stares, Rom.

ME

I'm getting back to work now.

ADDISON

You know the saddest part of your stubbornness? You're keeping a good woman from someone out there. I feel bad for the man who's missing out on your amazing-ness

A tiny knot forms in my throat as I read her last message. Not because of the compliment, even though it feels so good to know she thinks I'm amazing. But the idea that I've become so hardened to anything close to falling in love—and all because of Cole—makes my heart ache.

He doesn't get to influence this much of who I've become. He doesn't deserve that power.

Maybe, just maybe, I could lower some of my internal walls just an inch, but no more. Closing my eyes, I silently pray, *God, if it's your will, please help me do this for the right person and no one else.*

I take a steadying breath as I clean up my lunch mess. When I head back to my station, Bash is organizing my tools. My scissors are neatly arranged on my tray, and he's oiling my favorite pair of clippers.

"You don't have to do that."

His gaze cuts to mine. "I know."

There they are again, those annoying butterflies making me feel giddy and lightheaded as they swarm my insides. Why does he have to be so sweet? And that voice, so deep and calming. And those arms...

Bash looks me over. "Enjoy your meal? You look a little better."

"How did you know what to order me?" If Addison won't admit it, maybe he will. "Like, not only do I love that restaurant, but that dish is my favorite of all time. Are you stalking me or something?"

"Stalking you? Come on." A massive smile appears on his face. "I'm just glad you liked it. And speaking of food, have you decided to come to my sister's brunch yet?"

Not this again. It's not that I don't want to go. It's that I *do*. Me wanting to go is the reason I shouldn't. "I'm still thinking about it. I really need to get back to work, though. There's still so much..."

"I know. Tell me how I can help."

I normally wouldn't have a bather help with any grooming work, but since I overbooked myself to help my rating and he agreed to help me with this, I show him how to trim the remaining canines' body outlines, paws, and tails with my tools. I outline exactly what to do on each dog. Hopefully he doesn't mess up, because that would probably make my rating worse, and his help will definitely save me a few hours of work.

We get into the groove, working harder than ever and barely speaking to each other. As much as I never wanted to rely on anyone, even a dog bather, I can't deny there's no way I'd be able to do any of this without him.

Still, even with Bash's hands on deck, eight p.m. approaches, and we still aren't finished.

I'm starting to see double.

My hands feel like they belong to someone else as they

move, snipping and shaving each dog's fur to perfection. A dull ache begins in my shoulder blades, and my lower back has been on fire since lunchtime. I step back from Coco, the Maltipoo I'm working on, and release a shaky breath.

"Romilly." Bash's hand grazes my back. That simple touch makes my heart thunder in my chest. "Perhaps we should reschedule the rest. I'm sure the owners will understand."

"But...that's so unprofessional. And the whole point of this was to please them." My throat burns with unshed tears. I can't believe I let this happen. I've taken on more than I can handle in the past, but never to this level. The knowledge that I might have to send some of these dogs home unfinished makes panic and anxiety twist in my chest.

"You're going to work yourself into the ground." Bash's normally casual tone is laced with concern again, just like it was this morning. "Please. You're all work."

"I kind of have to be right now." I mean for it to sound sharp, but I'm so drained, it comes out a low murmur.

"Come. Sit for a moment." He tethers Coco and guides me to the waiting area at the front of The Paw Spa.

I sit.

Resting my muscles feels unreal. Too good to be true.

I cover my face with my hands in defeat. I hate that Bash is seeing me like this. I'm supposed to be the responsible one. His boss. His future sponsor.

"I'm going to call the remaining pet parents and reschedule them," Bash says. There's no wiggle room in his tone, no space for negotiation. This is happening.

I failed.

I swallow back my tears. "Okay."

He crosses the room to the front desk and picks up the phone. Four dogs is a lot to reschedule, even if it doesn't sound like it. I die a little inside with each call he makes, even though it seems to be going well. Maybe *that* has something to do with the way he's laying his accent on thick and calling everyone "love."

I stand up, feeling the need to do something. "I'm going to clean up so we can go home."

Bash nods, the phone pressed between his shoulder and ear as he types on the computer.

As I vacuum up the giant wads of fur covering the ground and put our tools away, Bash makes trips from the kennels to the entrance to return each dog to their parents as they arrive. My cheeks burn with shame. I can't face any of them right now. There's no way.

When I'm done cleaning, I sit on the ground and let a few tears finally escape. *This isn't you, Romilly. You can do better. You have no choice.*

"Are you...*crying?*"

My gaze snaps up to see Bash standing a few feet away with his brows pulled together. He walks over and extends his hand to pull me up.

I take it and get to my feet. "I'm just frustrated. I can't believe I messed up like this."

"It's not your fault. It happens." He says it so nonchalantly.

"Not to me."

He offers me a crooked smile. "Do you want solutions, or comfort right now?"

Solutions, I think to myself. But the word won't come out. Tears clog my throat, so I just shake my head.

Hesitating, he gently pulls me into the circle of his

arms. The moment it happens, a calm washes over me. His steady heart thuds against my right ear, and I sniffle back the remaining tears. I never realized how hard his chest was until this morning when he hugged me the first time, or how having my face pressed against it would still my current of anxious thoughts.

He releases me too soon. I'm still lost in the hug and the way it felt when he says, "Let me drive you home."

"I can drive myself."

"I know you can. But you're clearly exhausted and upset, and I'd feel better if you let me take you home."

I nod, because I simply don't have it in me to put up a fight right now and still be polite about it. "Okay." My tone is stiff because things feel too close between us after that hug. And I need some distance, because right now, it's getting hard to think straight.

Chapter Thirteen

BASH

IT'S POURING OUTSIDE. Romilly ducks into my car and buckles herself in. I want to laugh at the way she hastily avoids the rain because, for once, her clothes are wet from the dogs we worked on. A combination of her subtle lavender scent and the fruity smelling dog products from the day swirls in the air around us. "This is just a ploy to get me to trust you, isn't it?" She smiles as she says it, so I'm sure it's supposed to be a joke, but for some reason, it doesn't sit right. Maybe because her smile looks so tired and defeated.

"Does that happen to you a lot?"

"No." She laughs. "Well, actually, just once, but it doesn't matter."

I frown, hoping if I stay silent she'll continue. Elaborate. She does.

"I had an ex named Cole. He really was the sweetest guy. The whole package, honestly."

A knot of jealousy forms in my gut at hearing her say "the whole package." I have no idea what that means to her, but I doubt it's anything close to someone like me—a privileged rebel who likes to fight people.

"He used to go out of town a lot for work," she continues, "and one day he never came back and stopped returning my calls. Everything was going great between us. We didn't get in a fight or anything, but he just...left." She says it so pleasantly, as if we're discussing her favorite animal. "He eventually reached back out and admitted he'd been seeing another woman out of town the entire time, so that explained all the trips." A small laugh. "And the not coming back."

My thoughts cloud over as I imagine what she's saying. How worried she must have been when he never came back, never returned her calls. How confused she must have felt, and eventually, how angry. It explains so much about her. "He let you down," I mutter. "That excuse for a man destroyed your trust, didn't he?"

She's silent. I risk a glance at her, but she's staring out the window. I return to the road. "Romilly...I can't even begin to explain how angry that makes me. That someone could do that to you. You're so kind, and intelligent, and lovely."

Way to say too much, Bash. You're going to scare her away.

But I feel her gaze shift to my face. "Thank you."

There's a clear tension in the air between us as I drive. Neither of us speaks for a long moment. The only sound is the raindrops pelting against the windshield, and Romilly tapping her fingers against the car door as if she's deep in thought. "What about you? Any heartbreakers leave their mark on you?" With a slight eye-roll, she grins at me.

"As someone who's spent a great deal of life avoiding

long-term relationships, I'm afraid not." The statement should make me feel smug, but it makes me feel uneasy, as if Romilly's going to judge me now.

But she sighs. "I totally get it. I sometimes wish I'd done the same, to be honest."

A deep sense of comfort settles over me. Being around her makes me feel at ease in a way I never have. I enjoy her presence.

There's still a tiny part of my brain that whispers, *no, Bash. You're tired of being controlled, and love will only tie you down.*

But it's not as if I'm going to fall in love with Romilly. Dating her doesn't guarantee that. And I can't deny it anymore—I want to date her. For the first time in my life, I actually want to see where a deep, meaningful connection might take me. But only because it's *her*. No one else has ever made me want to try so badly.

I glance at her. "Romilly, I—"

A loud crash against the hood of the car makes me slam on my brakes.

What in the world?

My body pushes hard into my seatbelt as the tires screech against the wet asphalt. As the car lurches sideways, my temple smacks the doorframe with a sharp crack that leaves my vision flashing white.

My heart races like I've run a marathon while I frantically process what's happening.

We're the only car on the road, and a giant tree branch has crashed onto the hood. The windshield is thankfully still clear, but one end of the branch must have skidded its way up because there's a hairline crack traveling upward from the bottom of the glass.

For a heartbeat, all I hear is the engine ticking and my own pulse roaring in my ears. Panic claws its way up my throat as I turn to Romilly. Her eyes are wide, hands out in front of her as if to brace herself, and she's breathing heavily.

I unbuckle and reach for her. "Are you all right?" Taking hold of her face, I bring her gaze to mine so I can inspect her eyes. As a fighter, I've had enough concussions to know what to look for, but it's a little hard to focus with her face in my hands.

She pulls away and nods. "I'm fine, Bash. But you have a cut on your head."

I turn to the dash, holding up my hands. "Why on earth didn't the airbags deploy?"

"Who knows?"

I stare her down. "Are you sure you don't feel dizzy? Are you bruised anywhere?"

Romilly places her hands on my shoulders and squeezes. "I'm fine. I promise." She giggles. "It's just a fallen branch, and thankfully it's spindly. Your windshield looks a little cracked. But it's not shattered or anything, see? It could have been way worse."

I take a deep breath to calm myself. "I-I shouldn't have taken my eyes off the road. I put us both in danger. I'm sorry."

"It's fine. We're okay." Romilly's face softens as she stares at me, the humor melting away. I'm not sure what she sees, but whatever it is must be notable, because her hands inch toward my face from where they were resting on my shoulders. I don't dare move a muscle as her gaze searches mine. I thought it was hard to focus while touching her cheeks, but to have her palms against my own feels like a dream.

Romilly stiffens and bites her lip.

She must be uncomfortable with how close we are right now. I'm about to back up and give her space, but then she looks at my mouth and blushes.

Does she...want me to kiss her?

Romilly leans in closer, and her lashes sweep down in a slow blink.

My pulse races as I pull her closer. For the briefest moment, our breaths mingle. Her lips are only inches from mine, but then she swallows hard and says, "We should probably get out of the middle of the road so there are no more accidents today."

I clear my throat. "Yeah, you're right." But as I get out of the car and lift the wet, fallen branch from the windshield, I can't make the disappointment fade.

We almost kissed. But she stopped it.

I try to think about something else the whole way to her place. When we arrive, she opens the passenger door to get out. "I'll see you tomorrow?"

"There's no work tomorrow."

"No." She smirks. "But from what I hear, your sister is making brunch, so you can count me in." And then she closes the door and struts to her front door without a backward glance.

I grin as I stare after her and watch her get in before I drive away.

She's coming. Romilly is coming to brunch in the morning.

Ingrid will be thrilled.

And maybe I wasn't imagining it. Maybe Romilly likes me more than I thought.

"Is it too late for you to call her and cancel?" Bright red spots appear on Ingrid's pale cheeks, perfectly matching her copper hair.

"Will you just relax?" I shake my head at her. "You were excited only a moment ago."

She stares at me like I'm swing-dancing in a hospital. "That was before you told me what an amazing cook she is."

I don't know why she's so worried. The country potatoes Ingrid made this morning would put anyone's to shame. And I can't deny how impressed I was, watching her simultaneously whip up a delicious looking egg scramble while whistling a tune of blissful contentment.

But then I went and said, like an idiot, "It reminds me of the sourdough Romilly baked at her cottage."

"Sourdough?" Ingrid turned to face me, her spatula frozen in hand. "She bakes? How old is her starter?"

"I don't know what that means, but she's an even better chef than ours back home."

"She's better than Berta?" It was then that Ingrid gnawed on her lip and exited the kitchen. When she returned, she begged me to cancel, just like she is now.

"I'm going to embarrass myself," Ingrid mutters from behind her hands, which are currently covering her face. I don't know what I was thinking. I'm in over my head."

"Trust me, she's nothing like the people back home. She's kind and gracious. You have nothing to worry about."

In fact, if Romilly is the person I think she is, she'll be just as flattering about Ingrid's cooking whether she pulls off the meal or burns it to a crisp.

"Yeah, right. Just tell her I'm sick or something."

I scrub a hand over my face. I can't send Romilly away. Not after the effort it took to get her here in the first place. No way.

And then she texts me.

ROMILLY

I'm outside! Coming to the door.

"Sorry, sis. She's already here," I tell Ingrid. "Please don't ruin this for me."

"Good heavens." She smiles a pinched, saccharine smirk. "I make no promises. And if she so much as alludes to this meal being amateur, I'll show her the door before she has a chance to unfold her napkin."

I want to strangle her. Never mind her opinions of the snooty, judgmental crowd our parents surrounded us with. This is Romilly she's talking about. My sister has no idea how she behaves. "You're going to eat your words," I mutter as I walk past her to the door where she's waiting. "The woman is practically Grace Kelly reincarnated."

Ingrid lifts her orange juice glass, toasting, and then downs the contents. I'm grateful when she paces to the kitchen to finish up the food, because I don't want her to witness how anxious I'm about to get. Anxious, because Romilly is on the other side of the door.

I open it in a single, wide movement. "You're here," I say, breathless. "Hi."

A trace of pink creeps onto her cheeks. "I'm here. Hi."

We stand there for a moment, staring at one another.

There's a thick tension between us, that same tension from the car last night. My eyes trail along her body, and I tense up. She's wearing a white, long-sleeved romper that's tight on the legs but flares out at the bottom near her ankles. When she removes her leather jacket, my gaze lingers on her slightly exposed shoulders, but only for a second. Only long enough to make my mouth run dry.

Romilly smiles and gives a little wave. She's probably worried for my sanity. I'm just standing in the doorway like a moron, thinking only of the way her outfit hugs her body. Of how the white material makes her deep skin glow. Of how she looks like an angel.

"You must be Romilly," Ingrid says from behind me. "Welcome to brunch."

Romilly grins and sashays past me like I don't exist, into the foyer where Ingrid is waiting. She hands my sister a potted plant. When on earth did she get a potted plant? Has she been holding it all along?

"It's so nice to meet you," she says. "Ingrid, right?"

She nods. "I'm Bash's sister, unfortunately."

Romilly laughs. The delicate sound travels all the way to my toes.

Ingrid shows Romilly to the dining area, where she has the food displayed on white platters. The good napkins are out, freshly pressed and run through the antique brass holders my mum only saves for special occasions.

And whether or not either of them realizes it, this is definitely a special occasion. Because I have never, not once, brought a woman home. Not a girlfriend, not a date, not a female friend. Not once.

But there's no reason to tell Romilly that. It would completely freak her out or force her to remind me we work together. She'd insist that she'd mistakenly given me the wrong idea. Probably send me a handwritten apology note through the post, or something equally ridiculous.

"Have a seat, everyone," Ingrid says. "The food is hot. I won't have us eat it any other way."

"You made this?" Romilly's eyes widen in wonder. "This meal looks like it belongs in a magazine." There's no denying the sincerity in her tone.

The compliment strikes my sister, quite visibly, right in the heart. "Thank you."

I settle into a seat across from Romilly, and Ingrid sits beside me. Romilly is facing the window framing the lake, and when she sees it, she says, "Wow. What I wouldn't give for a view like that at my place."

"I love it out there," I tell her.

"I can see why."

Ingrid takes a bite. The way her feet tap under the table makes me think she's still nervous about Romilly's opinion. "So tell me," she says around a mouthful of food. "Why would you hire a wayward soul like Sebastian to work with you at your pet salon?"

"Um..." Romilly laughs, but her gaze dips down. "He seemed ready to work and easy to train."

I arch an eyebrow at her. "Lies do not look good on you." But now *I'm* lying, because she looks stunning no matter what she's doing.

"I'm—I'm not lying."

"She's lying," I tell Ingrid. "She hired me because I'm irresistible, of course. She can't get enough of my presence."

Romilly rolls her eyes at me. "Believe me, I had enough

of you the moment you first spoke to me." But her cheeks look flushed as her eyes bore into mine.

"Ha! I like you." Ingrid points her fork in Romilly's direction. "And here I was, worried you'd fallen victim to Bash's charms, just like the others."

A little V appears between Romilly's eyes. "The others?"

"Everyone back home had a crush on Bash. It got so bad, there were rumors at our church about him being a player, even though it's not true."

I glare daggers at my sister. The rumors didn't bother me *that* much, but that doesn't mean I want Romilly to know about them.

"It's probably because he's so charming," Romilly says. "It's hard for me to believe those rumors aren't true, too."

Charming? She thinks I'm charming? I arch an eyebrow. "Was that a compliment or an insult? I can't tell."

But she just shrugs with a teasing smirk.

"Tell me some embarrassing things Bash has done at work," Ingrid insists.

I grimace. "Why must I be the topic of conversation? Really. Let me tell you something about Romilly, Innie."

Ingrid ignores me. "Has he told you how he landed us in this mess?"

"Yes," I say. "I've told her. It's old news, really."

"You should have seen Mum and Dad," Ingrid says. "They went ballistic over his contract with Munera. Cut Sebastian off entirely, so I figured, might as well join him."

Romilly's gaze lands on Ingrid. "To be honest, I'm surprised they let you stay behind."

"Let me?" She laughs. "What were they going to do? Call the police?"

"Ingrid is incredibly spoiled," I explain to Romilly, ruffling my sister's hair.

Ingrid glares at me. "Look who's talking." Even though she likes to pretend otherwise, I can tell she cares about me in a way our parents don't.

Romilly smiles at my sister, like she, too, can see through Ingrid's act. "That was really nice of you."

"I figured it would be entertaining. Watching him struggle."

Romilly laughs.

Ingrid lifts the lid off the platter of the freshly-baked breakfast potato wedges, and the three of us really dig in then, eating in silence for a few minutes. Romilly and Ingrid talk about their favorite recipes, and I can tell Ingrid eats up every word. When we're finished they clear the table together. A warm feeling envelopes my chest at seeing them bond. I shouldn't be surprised. It would be impossible for Ingrid not to like Romilly, but then again, my sister has a knack for disliking people.

"I'm off to work now," Ingrid announces. "It was a pleasure to meet you, Romilly. Please keep my brother in his place while I'm gone."

After she leaves, Romilly grins at me. "She's great."

"Yeah, when she's not scolding me for existing." But I say it with a smile on my lips. "Thank you for coming today. It meant a lot to Ingrid. She's been dying to show off her new cooking skills, and you hiring me was the perfect excuse."

Romilly shifts on her feet. "I should probably get going."

I can't deny how badly I want her to stay. Her leaving right now feels much too soon. I know I'm in trouble because it seems no matter how much time I spend with her, I only want more. I really need to get a hold on myself and remember all the reasons I should leave her alone. "Are you busy today?"

She shakes her head. "Nope. It's my designated day of rest. I take one every week."

"Let's go do something fun."

She arches an eyebrow. "What's your definition of fun, Bash?"

"We could rob a bank. Set a hospital on fire." When she laughs, I nudge her shoulder with mine. "See? I got you to smile. I can't be that bad."

She tries to stop smiling and completely fails, that adorable grin lighting up her entire face. "Nothing dangerous?"

"No promises."

"Fine." She shakes her head like she can't believe she's agreeing to this. "Let's go."

Chapter Fourteen

ROMILLY

"ARE you ever going to fix your car?" I ask, gesturing toward the warning lights on the dashboard as we get in.

"Too expensive, but that won't be a problem soon, will it, sponsor?"

I laugh. "Not if my rating goes up, it won't. But I wouldn't hold your breath after what happened yesterday."

Bash's gaze softens, but he doesn't say anything. He probably knows nothing he says could comfort me about that mess. And I'm too scared to look at my reviews to see if anyone mentioned me rescheduling them after their dogs had already been waiting at my salon for hours.

"Stop fretting," he says. "You're riding with Sebastian Black. Which means only fun and wildly irresponsible ideas are allowed from here on out."

I snort. "Right."

I'm probably going to regret this later. Letting Bash surprise me with a "good time" can't be a wise idea. I should probably make him pull over and let me out now while we're still downtown. That way I could get a maple lavender latte and text Addison to come meet me. We could sit outside Old Joe's and sip our drinks, watching orange and yellow leaves fall and get crunched under the feet of those walking by. It sounds like the perfect autumn afternoon. I know I should do it.

But deep inside...I want to keep spending time with Bash. And that scares me.

"At least give me a hint about where we're going," I say.

"Not a chance, pumpkin."

"Are we going to be indoors or outdoors? What if I'm not dressed nice enough?"

He glances at me before turning back to the road but just laughs to himself.

"Give me a hint, Sebastian."

He grins. "No."

My mouth falls open. "Why not? I mean, this romper *is* an Iris Lily, so it's one of a kind, but still. What if it's not right for what we're doing?"

"I have no idea what an Iris Lily is."

"It's my favorite boutique."

He chuckles. And then after a semi-long pause, says, "You always look nice, Romilly. No... *nice* isn't the right word. Beautiful might be, but even that seems insignificant."

I don't know what to say to that. My first reaction is to laugh, because he must be teasing or baiting me. But when he doesn't follow his question with an explanation, I get angry. "How can you say that to me?"

He shrugs. "It would have taken more effort not to say it."

"We work together. I'm your boss. I've told you that's inappropriate."

"Like the thoughts I get when I look at you." His gaze lands right on my face, and he smirks. He actually smirks. Like it's no big deal what he just said. I can't believe him.

"You're terrible."

"Why?" His smirk is replaced by a full grin now.

"I'll say it again. We. Work. Together."

Bash's smile widens. "That's it?"

"And because it's unnecessary. I don't need to know what you think of me."

"What if I need to know what you think of me?"

"I'll tell you. But you won't like it."

He laughs loudly.

The car takes a narrow road that leads to the outskirts of Meadow Hills. We wind past a row of weathered picket fences, old barns with faded red paint, and maple trees that explode in a riot of gold and scarlet on either side of the road. Hay bales sit on a front porch we pass, decorated with pumpkins and a scarecrow wearing a flannel shirt. A group of kids on bikes zoom by in matching knit beanies. I roll my window down just in time to hear their laughter trailing behind them like ribbons.

I squint at Bash. "Is this the part where you murder me and toss my body into the woods?"

"Oh, Romilly...how I wish I could have kept you around longer."

I flick his shoulder. "No, but really. Where are we going? The only thing past here is Sunset Ranch."

He turns to me with an annoyed expression. "You just had to ruin all the fun, didn't you?"

"We're going to the farm?"

"Yes. You guessed it, you fun-killer."

I laugh. "You see, this is what I mean about being

150

dressed for the occasion. I'm just glad I chose boots instead of flats."

Bash parks in the dirt lot outside the entrance to the farm. Then he turns to me and looks me over. He tucks a piece of my hair behind my ear. It makes my stomach whirl with butterflies. So does the way he's looking at me.

"You're perfect, as always." The words are a low murmur, different from the teasing tone he used when he said I give him inappropriate thoughts.

Part of me wonders if—like so many others—all he sees when he looks at me is my appearance. I know I've been hard at work with shutting his flirtations down, so I can't blame him if that's the case. Still, it disappoints me that it might be true.

But then I remember what he told me while driving me home last night.

You're so kind, and intelligent, and lovely.

I can't help it. I blush.

Bash gets out of the car and comes around to open my door for me. It should make me want to roll my eyes, but instead, I feel slightly giddy.

Especially when he takes my hand to help me out and then doesn't let go.

He gives me a challenging grin, like he's waiting for me to say something, or pull my hand out of his, but I don't. I tell myself I'm holding his hand to challenge him right back and make him think he can't get to me.

But the truth is that I like this way too much. Holding his hand makes my heart thump unevenly, and the pit of my stomach dance.

He leads us to the entrance of Sunset Ranch and buys

all-day tickets. Curiosity burns inside me at what could possibly keep us here all day.

Together.

The wind picks up, finding its way into the opening of my leather jacket and making goosebumps spread across my arms. I take my hand out of Bash's to zip it up, and his eyes trace the movement.

"You're cold," he says, removing his jacket and the scarf from around his neck.

"No, it's alright. I'll just zip this up."

"Don't be silly." He hands me his jacket and wraps his heavy, maroon scarf around my neck himself. Instantly, his scent swarms my nostrils. It's not that his scent is too strong or overpowering or anything. It's the opposite, actually. I can't get enough of it, and when he's not looking, I lift the scarf to my nose and inhale deeply, letting my heart react to the spicy citrus and sandalwood smell of Bash.

When I glance up, we're standing in line to ride a hot air balloon. My eyes widen. "Um...have you done this before?"

He grins. "Many times. But I get the feeling you haven't."

"Nope. Can't say I make a point to randomly ride hot air balloons."

"Well, then you're clearly missing out."

I just stare at him, frozen in place.

"You're not afraid of heights, are you?" He looks amused, lips pulled up in a teasing smile.

"Of course not. Heights are fun!" I try to sound upbeat, but my voice wavers. "I'm fine."

He laughs, throwing his arm around my shoulders. Leaning in close to my face, he whispers, "Truth be told, I was terrified the first time my mum dragged me onto one of these. She's a bit of a thrill seeker, and I was nothing but a pansy the entire time. But I promise you're going to have fun."

I can't help it. I smile. Being here with him *is* exciting, and the thrill of what we're about to do makes me feel jumpy in a good way. "You're right. We're doing this."

"That's my girl."

"I'm not your girl." But the inviting grin that invades his expression when I say it makes him magnetic. Not to mention, his face is still right up close to mine.

Desire pools inside me, making me want to lean in closer. By instinct, I blurt, "You should smile more. It looks so nice on you." And then I realize how that sounded. I scramble to clarify. "Not that you don't always look nice. You're very handsome. But your smile is..." I trail off, feeling extremely foolish. My entire face burns with embarrassment.

But he just smirks, like I handed him a basket of gold. "And here I thought you found me repulsive."

"Very funny."

Layla Owens, the teenage daughter of the family who owns the farm, is managing the balloon line. She signals us forward, and I notice the balloon up close for the first time. The vibrant reds and golds of its fabric stretch upward into a massive dome, contrasting with the blue afternoon sky.

I take in the basket hanging below. It's larger than I expected, woven from thick wicker, with high edges that will probably make me feel less exposed. But still, my stomach churns at the thought of stepping inside. The faint roar of the propane burner igniting overhead sends a shiver down my spine.

It's our turn next.

With shaky limbs, I let Bash and Layla help me into the basket of the balloon. She explains the safety protocols for riding before checking our basket and shutting us in.

The pilot is a friend of my dad's named Mr. Gerald, and most people in town know him as the stoic, elderly man who spends his mornings ignoring society at Buttercup Bakery with a cup of black coffee and a copy of *The Meadow Bee*. Mr. Gerald gives us a nod as he tests the burner, sending a blast of heat upward. The balloon lurches slightly, and I grip the edge of the basket, my heart pounding.

Mr. Gerald turns to us. "Hello, Romilly, and hello to you, young man. I'll be flying with you today." He goes over some basic safety protocols before tipping his hat to us and turning back to the burner.

"I sincerely hope there are parachutes on this thing," I mutter, and as soon as the balloon rises into the air, I let out a nervous squeal.

Bash chuckles. "You're adorable when you're frightened, you know."

"Stop flirting with me." I may sound convincing, but I can't deny I like it. No matter what I say, I don't want him to stop.

The ground falls away beneath us, the farm shrinking into a patchwork of pumpkins, hay bales, and cornfields. Beyond it, rolling hills stretch out into a fiery sea of autumn foliage. The air feels cooler up here, crisp and carrying the faint scent of leaves and earth. It's breathtaking, but the growing distance between me and the ground is enough to make my knees tremble. I cling tighter to the basket's edge, trying to focus on anything other than how far we're climbing.

But as we get higher, panic grows like a massive wave inside me. I look to Mr. Gerald, expecting him to be panicking, but he continues to ignore me and Bash, completely focused on operating the balloon.

And then the basket jerks as a gust of wind hits us.

No, no, no.

By instinct, I grab onto Bash. I grip his sweater in iron-tight fists and try to steady my breathing. Bash must be surprised, because it takes him a moment to stop laughing and put his massive arms around me. He pulls me against him tight enough for me to feel the warmth of his skin through his clothes. The contrast between his body heat and the chilly autumn air makes me shiver.

"Okay, I'm trying not to be a baby right now, but I'm scared," I say. Admitting it makes me want to cry, not at all helping my mission to not be a baby. "Ugh. I hate that I'm scared right now."

Bash rubs his hand across my back in soothing circles. "It's all right, I promise." His voice is a low murmur, tickling my ear. It's annoying how safe I feel wrapped in his strong arms like this. Even though we're miles above ground in a teetering basket with no one but Mr. Gerald to steer us, I've never felt more secure.

And then the basket jerks again. I force down a sob. I think I might faint. "Can you distract me?" I ask.

"How?"

I squeeze my eyes shut. "I don't know. Anything. Please."

He's silent for a moment. I peek up at him, not expecting his gaze to connect with mine. His bright blue eyes take me in, searching my face. "I could always kiss you. I've been told the feel of my lips is *quite* distracting."

I laugh nervously. "What?"

"I bet it would work."

"And I bet it wouldn't."

He arches a brow, a slow smile spreading across his lips. "Is that a challenge?"

"No." I lower my voice. "I'm not kissing you with my dad's friend a foot away." But part of me has wondered what it would be like to kiss him, and the idea of doing it right now is more nerve-wracking than tumbling out of this balloon basket.

"Fine. Come here." Bash reaches for my face, leaning in close.

"What are you doing?"

"Shh. Let me distract you. I won't kiss you, I promise."

I close my eyes, still clinging to him as his nose grazes mine. His soft breath tickles my face, minty and spiced.

My heart thunders as his lips brush across my forehead, not in a kiss but a simple touch. My brain is both desperate for more and fully incredulous at the situation. And then his thumb caresses my cheek. Nerves race through me like wildfire, mingling with desire and spreading through my veins too quickly to control.

It's delightful.

Dizzying.

Dangerous.

I let go of Bash's sweater and bring my hands up to his chest. My knees wobble when his fingers gently comb through my tresses. The sensation feels too good to be true.

"You have the softest hair," he whispers in my ear. His

thumb traces little comforting circles on the base of my neck.

And then the basket we're standing in tilts too much for my liking. Bash grabs onto me to keep me from stumbling. He shoots Mr. Gerald a glare, but the elderly man remains oblivious.

Below us, the farm comes back into view as the balloon begins to return to the ground. Mr. Gerald adjusts the burners, releasing bursts of heat to control the speed of our descent. Bash keeps his arms loosely around me, his touch casual now, as if that embrace didn't just flip my entire world upside down. The landing is smoother than I expect, the basket brushing against a soft patch of hay before coming to a stop. The ground crew hurries to steady it, waving us forward as Mr. Gerald lowers the balloon's envelope. As soon as we land, Mr. Gerald regards me with a nod and a twinkle in his eye, like he was paying more attention to the way I was holding onto Bash than I thought. At least I didn't kiss him. My face burns when I imagine Mr. Gerald reporting the details of this event back to my dad at one of their poker nights.

"That wasn't so bad, was it?" Bash teases, his grin crooked and maddeningly charming as he helps me step out.

I give him a look. "Says the guy who didn't spend half the ride panicking."

He smirks. "At least I distracted you."

Thinking about the soothing way he touched me causes another round of butterflies to flutter through my veins like they don't have a care in the world. "Okay, fine. Your tactics may have worked."

He arches an eyebrow. "What kind of first date would this be if I let you die of fear?"

"First date? Who said anything about this being a date?"

"I did." He takes my hand again and swings it between us. "Just now."

I don't know how he does it. He's so irresistible, even for me. And that's exactly the problem. I'm having a hard time keeping my head intact, the more time I spend with him. And the worst part is...right now I don't even care. "What are we doing next?"

"I thought you'd never ask."

Our hands loosely connect as we wander past the farm's pumpkin patch, where rows of orange globes catch the late-afternoon light like little suns. The air smells faintly of hay and cider, and a breeze picks up through the tall cornstalks we approach.

Bash stops us at the entrance of the "haunted corn maze" the Owens family, who live on the ranch, put on every year.

I take a step back. "No. Absolutely not. I don't do haunted things."

Bash's mouth falls open in amusement. "You can't possibly believe this nonsense of a maze is actually haunted."

"I don't, but that doesn't mean I'm going in."

"Romilly, you're exploring this maze with me. You must."

"It's not happening." I cross my arms.

"I insist."

"No way, Bash."

He looks like he's having trouble not laughing. That's fine. He can laugh all he wants.

"I'm easily spooked, okay?"

That does it. The laughter escapes his mouth for a split second before he reins it back in. "Teenagers put this thing together. You do know that, right? And God is way bigger than anything that could hurt you."

"I know that."

"Besides, you'll have a professional fighter at your side. So, I'll ask again. Will you please do me the honor of exploring this pathetic and possibly very haunted corn maze with me?"

He extends his hand.

Lord...please protect me in there. Send me every angel you can spare. I sigh. "I hope your dragon-slaying skills are also cross-compatible with ghost-busting."

Chapter Fifteen

BASH

SHE ACTUALLY TAKES my hand in agreement to enter the maze. I feel like I've just been handed the winning lottery numbers.

As I lead Romilly through the entrance, I rack my brain for ways to make her feel more at ease. I *did* nearly scare her to death with that hot air balloon ride. Not my brightest idea, but it led to her trusting me enough to hold her close and protect her, so it was a win in my book.

I can't stop thinking about the way her body relaxed as my arms wrapped around her, how she rested her hands on my chest, or how it felt like I'd gotten sucked into a timeless vortex of pure bliss.

Lining the maze entrance is a pair of cheerful orange string lights, their warm glow bouncing off the cornstalks, creating golden shadows. The air smells like hay, earth, and the sweetness of cider from the tiny, nearby festival booths. As we step into the labyrinth with walls of cornstalks towering above us, the faint crackle of dried leaves crunches underfoot.

I can't believe the farm is advertising this maze as haunted. It's way too cute to qualify, as if the person who decorated it happens to be as detesting as Romilly about such things.

Romilly's hand tightens around mine as the first prop in the maze comes into view. It's a weathered scarecrow. The burlap head is tilted unnervingly to one side, and one of its straw-stuffed arms droops like it's waving at us. A real crow perched on its shoulder flaps its wings and caws, making Romilly jump. I can't help but stifle a laugh. If this is enough to make her nervous, I already feel bad for convincing her to do this with me.

"Did you know the owners of the farm go to Harvest Valley Church?" she asks.

"I didn't. But it seems like all of Meadow Hills attends your congregation, so that doesn't surprise me."

She exhales a laugh. "All of Meadow Hills. Except you, right?"

"Well, I'm only here temporarily." Saying that out loud makes my chest ache, but I ignore it. "Still...I can't really claim that anymore, can I?" We turn a corner, where a section of the maze narrows, and a hanging skeleton swings gently in the breeze. The dim lights strung through this area make the hollow sockets of its eyes look like they're watching us. "Not since you sucked me in with that pretty singing voice of yours."

She blushes. "Thanks. But I hope—I mean I'd like to believe I'm not the reason you've been continuing to go. I'd like to believe God has more to do with it."

"Romilly..." If only she knew the way I've wrestled with not going to church, hoping God wouldn't be disappointed in me as long as I continued to deepen my relationship with Him.

"I'm sorry," she says quickly. "We don't have to talk about this if it makes you uncomfortable." The cornstalks rustle in the wind, their dry leaves brushing against each other with a sound like whispers. Romilly pulls closer to me, her hand clutching mine more tightly.

"No, it's all right. When I said church wasn't my thing anymore, it was because of my church back home. *Your* church is nothing like mine." I swallow, trying to decide where to start. "I've honestly been so scared that avoiding church in general has disappointed God, and I've prayed about it a lot. I don't know if I've told you this, but my parents love to pressure me. I never live up to their expectations, and they always try to get me to look a certain way to their church friends, so I don't embarrass them because everyone there is crazy judgmental. When I got my first tattoo, none of my friends were allowed to talk to me anymore. And when I started smoking, which I admit was a huge mistake, there was only more judgment. Never compassion." My heart thuds as I rehash one of the many old wounds I still haven't recovered from.

"Oh, wow," she says, her voice laced with understanding and compassion. "I'm so sorry that happened. And during all that, did you ever blame God for what you went through?"

I consider her question carefully. *Did I?* "I think I might have at one point, but not anymore. I know now that's not how God intended the church to be. It's taken a lot to show me there are rotten people in every category of humanity, but also plenty of good people in those same categories. Including your Harvest Valley lot. And blaming an entire group for the actions of a few might not be fair." I laugh sarcastically. "In fact, it might be equally as judgy."

When I turn to look at her, she's staring back at me with an odd expression. "Well, I'm glad you changed your mind."

We've stopped walking, and I can't help but fully face her, lean in closer. "Well, a huge part of that has been you. You're nothing like the judgy people I'm used to, who treat religion as a status and a way to control people when it's supposed to be a gift. A place of community. You're kind and understanding and so, so generous. I'm convinced if love were a person, it would be you."

Romilly's lips part. "Bash..."

"I'm sorry. Was that too much?"

She shakes her head, searching my face. Her lips press together in a faint, soft smile. "Those are very pretty words."

"I meant every one of them."

She places her hands on my cheeks and pulls my face closer to hers. The distant sound of laughter from the festival fades as I focus entirely on her. The earthy scent of the maze mixed with the faint floral notes of her perfume wraps around me. My chest hammers like I'm fourteen, like this is my first interaction with a beautiful woman.

And this isn't just any beautiful woman.

This is Romilly.

The most beautiful soul I've ever met.

When she gently presses her lips to mine, a warmth spreads through me, like curling up under a blanket on a cold night. A tenderness for her makes me pull her closer so I can wrap my arms around her. My chest swells with something unfamiliar—some unnamed emotion that makes me feel desperate and crazed, lightheaded and elated.

Infatuation, I tell myself. *Genuine friendship at best. Because she's my boss and I'm leaving after my next fight. Getting attached to her is a bad idea because whatever's happening between us can't last.*

But no matter what I tell myself, it's clear I have feelings for her. What those feelings are, I'm not sure, but what I *do* know is I can't deny them anymore.

Kissing her feels like breathing for the first time. And now that I've done it, I fear it's become essential to my survival.

Romilly breaks away.

"Maybe we should sit down," she says.

"Why?"

"Because kissing you makes me feel weak. And because it doesn't seem like we're getting out of here any time soon."

I grin. "Are you finally accepting that this maze isn't really haunted?"

"I'm coming around to the idea."

I laugh and pointlessly dust off a bale of hay for her to sit on. The hay crackles under my hand, faintly prickling my skin. It might get her clothes dirty, so I remove the light sweater I'm wearing over my undershirt and drape it over the hay for her to sit on.

"Bash, no. You're going to get cold. I already took your jacket."

"I'll be fine. Sit." The chill in the air doesn't faze me; I'm burning up just being near her. "*Sit.*" I pull her down to sit beside me.

She takes out her phone, opening the camera and pointing it at our faces.

"What are you doing?"

"Taking a picture with you. That way if anything happens to us, there will be evidence."

I bark out a laugh. "Evidence of what? The fact that you faced your fear of mazes?"

She rolls her eyes but beams. "Fine. I may or may not be having fun, and I'd like to remember this day. Now, smile."

I offer the camera a close-mouthed grin, leaning my face close to hers. Even in photos, Romilly's beauty is absolutely radiant. Her eyes glow against her dark skin, and her jet black hair looks thick and shiny as a satin curtain.

She tucks her phone away, and we stay seated for a while, just talking. To my surprise, not a single person comes through the maze.

As she speaks, I can't help but notice Romilly has a way of making even the smallest details feel significant, like how she's convinced that Jasper, her grumpy little cat, has a secret soft spot for anyone who sneaks him people food, or how she used to want to be a foster parent.

"That was something I wanted when I didn't have to work so much. But I'm way too busy now," she says. "I wouldn't even adopt a dog with my current schedule, but thankfully, Jasper doesn't mind his solitude."

Her eyes light up as she talks about her favorite things about autumn—carving pumpkins with her sister, the smell of cider with orange slices and cinnamon simmering on the stove, and the way Jasper attacks every stranger he meets, but lets her dress him up in any outfit she likes. She even admits her lavender smell comes from the essential oils she puts in her early-morning baths.

I can't stop watching her.

She gestures as she speaks, and every now and then, she tilts her head in a curious way, as if she's rediscovering the joy in her own memories while sharing them. Her laughter is soft and infectious, tugging a smile to my face.

It's early evening by the time we finally get back up and wander through the maze again. The dimming sunlight filters through the corn stalks, painting them in shades of amber and honey, while their long shadows stretch across the ground. The cool breeze rustles the leaves, making them whisper secrets only the autumn air seems to know.

Romilly points at a shape in the clouds, visible through breaks in the corn. "That looks so much like a bear eating an ice cream cone."

"I don't see it," I tease, squinting up. "It's obviously a dragon holding a sword."

"You and dragons. You just want everything to be cooler than it is."

"Oh, absolutely."

She rolls her eyes but smiles.

A message on my phone from Max comes through.

MAX

Check out this post from Munera.

I click the link and see my face on a graphic next to Connor Stronghold's. The text underneath says: The Prince VS. The Powerhouse. Who are you betting on?

With a sigh, I put my phone away. I don't even want to read the comments on something like this. It will only get under my skin. And right now, I'd rather stay present with Romilly than discover whether or not my parents are the only ones who don't believe I can win.

By the time we stumble out of the maze's exit, it feels like we've emerged from a dream, but the sound of children laughing, mixed with the distant sound of a tractor, feels like a snap back to reality. The rest of the farm sprawls ahead of us, glowing against the orange and pink hues of the evening sky.

Sunset Ranch definitely lives up to its name.

"See? I told you we'd make it out." I dust a bit of hay off my jeans.

"I'm still not convinced you didn't get us lost on purpose."

"Me? Never." I try to sound earnest, but I absolutely dragged out our time just to stay close to her a little longer. Our journey through the maze almost feels transformative. I don't know what to do with my new feelings for her. And I definitely don't want to say goodbye yet, even though we've now spent the entire day together.

I know she must be hungry by now. I myself am starving, as usual, so I order us each a bowl of chili and a pumpkin spice latte from the food truck parked only yards away. It's delicious and warm, and Romilly gobbles her food down for once, but we finish eating much too soon.

Come on, Bash. One more activity to win more time with her. "Do one more thing with me. And then I'll take you home."

She raises an eyebrow. "What are you scheming now?"

"Apple picking." I nod toward the nearby orchard. Baskets are already waiting between the rows of trees, and a few other people are collecting the fruit with laughter.

"Apple picking? Are you secretly a Hallmark movie protagonist?"

"Secretly?" I feign offense. "Come on. Let's make it a competition. Who can find the largest, reddest apple in ten minutes?"

She narrows her eyes. "Alright. But don't get upset when I destroy you."

"Oh, it's on." Already, I'm moving toward the orchard. I pluck one off the nearest tree and hold it up. "This one is going to be the winner. Mark my words."

Romilly shakes her head. "Too small, too green, and too weirdly shaped." She tosses several apples into her own basket. They look a thousand times better than the one I just picked, so I swipe one of hers from her basket as soon as she turns around.

But she catches me instantly, and her mouth falls open. "Cheater!"

"Strategist," I correct, grinning as I jog backward down the row to escape her playful wrath.

By the time the sun dips lower on the horizon, our baskets are brimming, and I've somehow managed to lose the competition by a landslide.

"As promised, I destroyed you." Romilly holds up her basket. Her hair is adorably mussed. Twigs and hay stick out of the tangles, and there's even a smudge of dirt across her cheek.

"I let you win." I lean against a tree and cross my arms.

"Sure you did. I'm going to have to make cider, or pie, or something. There's no way I can eat all these apples before they go bad."

I watch her inspect each one with such focus. I can't help but smile because of how seriously she takes it.

We walk to my car. Once inside, I crank up the heater for her. She immediately places her hands in front of the vents.

"When can I take you out again?" The words slip out without my permission.

She sends me a sideways glance. "*Bash.*"

"*Romilly.*"

She bites her lip. "I don't know."

"You want to go out with me again, don't you?"

She sighs, trying not to smile. "I'm not sure. This feels official. Are you asking to be my boyfriend now?"

"If I asked, what would you say?"

"Probably no. You don't seem like the commitment type."

"Allow me to prove you wrong."

Romilly laughs. "Bash..."

"How about just a date, then?"

A torturous, long moment passes before she responds under her breath. "I can't."

"You can't?"

"*I can't.* I'm sorry, but I can't go on another date with you."

I try not to let it be obvious how disappointed I am inside. *Keep it cool, Bash.* "Why not?"

"What happens after your next fight? I'm supposed to replace you at work, and you'll be living somewhere else."

A bead of dread forms in my chest, because she's right. I have no idea what my life will be like then, and it would be unfair of me to string her along, knowing I won't even be here long-term. Romilly deserves someone who will stick around. Who will help provide for her and be a steady thing in her life.

"I have my business here," she continues in a soft voice. "My family. My friends. Meadow Hills is my home, and I don't do long-distance relationships. Not after..." She swallows. "Not after my one."

I nod because I get it. With my stomach in knots, I capture her hand and bring it to my mouth for a kiss. It's hard to remember why I was so against relationships whenever I'm with her. The scariest part isn't the idea of being tied down anymore—it's how much I want her to be mine. I can't deny there's a part of me that doesn't only want to win my next fight to prove to my parents I can do it, but also to help her. With real money coming in, I could make sure she'd never have to worry about losing her business again.

And I want her to want me back. I wish I could convince her I'm worth it by promising her a possible future with me. But how can I do such a thing when I don't even know if I have a good one?

If I lose that fight, I'll have nothing—no money, no sponsors, and no choice but to go back to my parents. I won't be the kind of man I'd want to be for Romilly.

One who could support *her*, not the other way around.

October

Chapter Sixteen

ROMILLY

ZARA'S KNEES bounce as I drive. She's getting more and more impatient by the minute, knowing I'm withholding information from her that she's only moments from discovering.

"I still don't see why you can't just tell me first," she says.

"Addison is my best friend."

"I'm your *sister*."

"True." I laugh. "But that's why it's only fair I tell you both at the same time. I'd never hear the end of it from either of you, otherwise."

That seems to placate her. She shifts her priorities from bouncing her knees to cracking her knuckles.

Addison's three-story house comes into view as I pull into the driveway. It really is an immaculate place. And now that it's officially October, the dark wood and gray stone exterior looks even more cool and moody among the tall pines and vibrant, autumn leaves surrounding it. I still remember the first time I visited Addison here, when she started nannying for Perry before they got together. I took one look at her flushed cheeks that day and watched her stumble over her words when she talked about Perry and knew she was a goner.

When she answers the door, she beams at me and Zara like she didn't know we were coming. A dimple pops in her cheek as she motions us to come in. "Marina just went down for a nap, and the kids are still at school, so I'm currently a free woman."

"We'd better make the most of your time then." I flash a grin. "But I have to admit, I'm disappointed I don't get to see all your little munchkins today."

"Sorry." She sets a plate of freshly-baked cookies in front of us and picks up a steaming kettle to pour me and Zara a mug of tea. Handing one to me, she sighs. "It's always weird when I have time to myself now."

I take the tea from her and have a small sip, settling onto a stool at the kitchen island.

Zara glances around us. "Where's Perry?"

"He's doing a restaurant visit, so it's just the three of us." She smiles, lifting her own mug in the air. "What's new with you two?"

I bite my lip. "Um...well—"

"Romilly has a secret, and she refuses to tell either of us first so she brought me here so she could tell us at the exact same time." Zara barely breathes as she spouts the sentence.

"I don't have a *secret*. I need advice."

Addison's mouth falls open. "Did something happen with Bash? Spill!"

"We...may or may not have gone on a date last week." I launch into the story of our time at the farm while Addison and Zara listen. My sister gets a dreamy, faraway look in her eyes. Addison's lips set in a soft smile, and she even twirls a thick curly strand of hair around her finger. When I'm done, they're both speechless.

Addison finally breaks the silence. "I can't believe you kissed him. Are you two officially together now?"

"It was just a peck. And of course not. He asked me on another date, but I had to say no."

Zara gasps. "What? You said no?"

I nod.

She sighs. "I need to see a picture of this guy. I'm a much better judge of character than you are."

Addison giggles. "A picture isn't going to do him justice. Trust me."

But I show them both the photo we took in the corn maze. It's definitely not my first time gazing at it since it was taken, but my heart still reacts to seeing Bash's handsome face. His deep blue eyes stare into the camera with the same intensity as real life. The way we're leaning toward each other in the photo makes me blush. I can't seem to meet Addison's or Zara's gazes when they glance up at me.

"I think I forgot how to speak," says Zara.

Addison bites her lip. "I was wrong. This pic totally does him justice."

My sister nods. "It's giving refined, crazy-boy. Old money with a dark side."

"Okay. Putting the phone away now." I shut off the screen and slide my phone into the tiny black bag on my shoulder. I can't deny how hard I'm blushing, especially now that they're studying me so obviously.

Zara frowns. "Wow. Look at you. You really like him, don't you?"

I cover my face with my hands. "I don't know. I'm still processing the fact that we work together, and I went on that date with him. And *kissed* him."

"I mean..." Addison shrugs. "I worked for Perry when I met him, and things turned out pretty amazing. Just saying."

I bite my lip as her words sink in. "I know, and that's the problem. I...I *do* like him, but I'm trying so hard not to. Dating Cole last year felt so safe. I thought for sure he was the kind of guy I could rely on not to do anything shady, and he turned out to be the biggest red flag I've ever met. It bothers me how off my radar was about him." I'm filled with turmoil at the mere memory, but I continue. "And dating Bash would feel so much more risky. He's an MMA fighter who isn't even in Meadow Hills long-term. He's going to leave eventually, and I'm staying here. So I'm a thousand times more nervous about him than I was with Cole. I know it's not fair of me to compare them, but it feels like getting burned last year left a permanent mark on me or something. One I don't know how to erase."

They both listen to me in silence, and eventually, Addison reaches over and squeezes my hand. "I get it. Trust me."

"Yeah," says Zara. "But, sis...you can't blame every guy for the mistakes of one. Cole was the bottom of the barrel. And it was nothing you did wrong. You're literally amazing."

"She's right," says Addison. "And I've thought a lot about what happened to you and Cole, you know. Just because he was able to up and leave you after a year doesn't mean Bash would. But first, you'd have to give him a chance if you ever want to find out. Who knows? He might even decide to stay in Meadow Hills."

Even though she says it so nonchalantly, the words pierce straight through me because it's what I'm secretly hoping for deep down.

But what if my feelings for him get stronger and he doesn't stay?

The thought just makes me want to protect my heart from getting shattered a second time. I shake my head. "I'm doing fine alone. I don't need anyone else, so I don't know why I'm suddenly so worried about getting left again. What's wrong with me?"

Addison bites her lip. "Maybe because until Cole, you've never really had a taste of that kind of heartbreak. You've won practically every pageant you've entered. I can't think of anyone who doesn't like you. You succeed at everything you do, Rom."

"But not Cole," I say.

Addison nods. "Not Cole. He was, like, your first taste of rejection, ever."

Zara laughs. "Welcome to the real world. We have cookies, at least." She takes a bite of the one she's holding and washes it down with her tea.

I roll my eyes, but I can't deny they're right. "So you're both saying I just need to get over it?"

"Come on. Remember what Mom and Dad taught us. You need to have more faith, sis. Ask God to show you what He wants for you, and then trust Him," says Zara.

176

Addison nods. "Yep. I know it's hard to move past trust issues, and all it takes is one loser to burn that hole in your heart. But you can do it with God on your side."

They're so right.

I'm sorry, Lord. Where has my faith been? I do trust you.

What Cole did really affected me, but they're right. It's time to move past it. I'm just grateful I have Addison and Zara to remind me to have faith when I start to doubt instead. I should probably call my parents to hear their thoughts too, now that they're back from their trip.

I used to be the one handing advice out to everyone, like meals at the soup kitchen. Now, I'm eating up every crumb of wisdom they have to spill for me.

I just hope I can find a way to make a trail from each little crumb to return to when I inevitably get lost again.

There's breakfast waiting for me at work the next morning. The scent of pumpkin spice lattes and warm muffins wraps around me like a hug as soon as I walk in. I eye the stack of muffins, set of thermoses, and cup of to-go coffee on the front desk with suspicion. Since our date, Bash has been extra attentive to how many meal breaks I have or haven't been taking. "What's all this?"

"Breakfast. Did you know you've barely eaten all week? I've had enough." He picks up a muffin and hands it to me. "Here."

I stifle a laugh. "You're not responsible for feeding me, you know."

"I am when I see you take no breaks every day to

nourish your body. I get that you're overbooking yourself to help your rating, but you still need to eat." Before I can respond, he grabs one of the thermoses, pressing it firmly into my hands. The metal container feels warm against my palms. "Protein. You need this, too."

I twist open the lid to the stainless steel container and find freshly scrambled eggs inside. Steam curls up, carrying a buttery aroma that makes my stomach growl. "Did Ingrid make these for me?"

"No. I did." He grins proudly.

My mouth falls open. "You scrambled?"

"I scrambled." He hands me a plastic fork. "Now eat. Every last bite, alright, pumpkin?"

I moan around a mouthful of the eggs, the richness melting on my tongue. The taste is a perfect balance of salt and cream. It's like comfort itself. "Bash...these are really good. I can't believe you made them."

"I'm a man of many talents." He taps my nose before he heads to the back to start working on the first and only dog waiting so far.

As I watch him walk away, the image of his broad back burns into my mind. A smile tugs at my lips as I finish eating everything he brought—the eggs, the muffins, and the pumpkin spice latte. Heat spreads through me that has nothing to do with the food. I can't deny how nice it is to start the day with a full stomach for once. I usually don't have time for all this.

See Romilly? It's not such a bad thing to let others help you, sometimes.

My day gets even brighter when I get to work on Paige's dog, Betty Lou. But my thoughts are in a daze as I trim Betty's nails, clean her ears, and even brush her teeth because it's hard not to dwell on the negative reviews I've gotten. I always try to do my best at work. And though I understand Agatha's hesitation to come back and work with me, I wish she could see how seriously I've been taking my business after that failure last year.

I even dropped out of the Miss Meadow pageant to focus on it, which I'd done every year until then. And I was twenty-six, so it was my last opportunity to compete before I aged out, but I gave it up, anyway.

When Paige comes to get Betty Lou, I'm still ruminating on my business when I realize I forgot to put Betty's complimentary bow on.

Maybe I can still catch them.

I rush out of the salon, ignoring Bash's questioning gaze as I make for the exit. "I'll be right back. Stay with the dogs," I call behind me.

Paige is just loading Betty Lou into her car when I reach her.

"Wait!"

Paige spins around. She's so graceful as she does it, like she's demonstrating a ballet move. "What's wrong?"

I hold out a pink bow, panting. "I forgot to put this on Betty's collar. I'm sorry."

She takes it, grinning. "No problem. Thanks."

"I can't believe I forgot," I continue. "My mind has just been all over the place, with the rent getting raised and whatnot."

Paige's brows draw together in concern. She tucks a strand of her short, chocolate-brown hair behind her ear. "Your rent got raised?"

I nod. I probably shouldn't be telling her this because it's unprofessional, and that's the last thing I need to be labeled. But I really like her, and I've felt so comfortable around Paige since meeting her at the pageant last year, when I came to pass on the crown I won the year before.

"What can you do?" Paige asks. She looks so genuinely worried for me, it makes me love her even more. "Can Agatha come back?"

I sigh. "Trust me. I've practically begged her. But my rating is too low to tempt her."

"Ah." Paige nods and taps her chin. She stares at the sky for a moment before her expression brightens. "A low rating might not tempt her...but what about a small-business feature from *The Meadow Bee*?"

I frown. "What? But Elena Ferrera only features the best small businesses in town."

She grins. "Exactly."

"I would never get featured," I tell her. "Not with a three-star rating."

Paige waves away my worries. "You wouldn't, unless you happened to know the best friend of Elena herself. And you're looking right at her."

My mouth falls open. Though I know of Elena, I haven't interacted with her much because we have different friends and haven't had a chance to cross paths often. I didn't even know Paige until last year for the same reason, so I had no idea Elena was her best friend. "You..." My voice comes out wobbly. "You would do that for me?"

"Of course." She scrunches her nose like it's no big deal, causing the sea of freckles on her nose to ripple. "I mean, I'll definitely talk to Elena. I don't know if there will be strings she has to pull, but it's worth a shot."

I wrap her in a giant hug. "You're the best!"

She laughs. "Anything for you."

I watch her drive away before heading back into the salon. Though I know there's a possibility Elena won't cover my business, it means so much to me that Paige is willing to try to help me.

Bash cocks his head at me when I return. "Everything good?"

"Better than good." I fill him in on my conversation with Paige.

When I finish, he crosses his arms, and a smirk graces his lips. "Do you see what I mean now about you succeeding at everything you do? It's becoming annoying at this point."

I roll my eyes. "Well, it hasn't happened yet. There's still a chance it won't."

"It will. Trust me."

I shrug. "We'll see."

As the workday progresses, the only thing that distracts me from my excitement about Elena is when I catch sight of Bash staring at me more than once. It's not subtle. His gaze is like a magnet, pulling at me even when I'm trying to focus. Each time my eyes shift in his direction, his head doesn't turn away like I expect. Instead, he holds my gaze for a beat longer than necessary, making my face burn hotter than a campfire before he turns back to the dog he's working on.

When I try to calm a new, angry schnauzer in the tub, the dog twists and jerks, soaking the front of my shirt with soapy water.

I almost give up before Bash comes up next to me. "Need some help?" Without waiting for an answer, his strong arms brush mine as he takes charge, holding the dog still with ease so I can finish washing him. "There, now.

You're alright" he murmurs to the dog. But his deep voice is so close to my ear, butterflies swarm my stomach.

Our hands touch as he passes me a towel, and when he leaves me with the dog, it's hard to focus again. It makes me wonder what work will be like when I'm forced to replace him.

A lot less distracting, that's for sure.

But with Bash, the workdays always pass faster than usual, and today is no exception. Still, by the end of it, I'm just as exhausted as always.

"Don't forget," I say as we're locking up, "we're closed all next week."

Bash smirks. "How could I forget about Autumn retreat? You underestimate me."

I laugh. Though closing my shop for a week makes me nervous, I agreed to go before my finances took a nosedive. And I'm trying to have faith that God has a plan and will provide if it's His will for me to keep my place open. "I just can't believe it's time already," I say. "I feel like hardly any time has passed since I first offered you the job."

"I tend to have that effect on people."

I roll my eyes. "By the way, I got our cabin assignments from Hayden. I'm rooming with Hadley, and you got paired up with Logan."

His answering grin is blinding. "Logan? Logan Henry?"

"The one and only."

His jaw flexes. "I really need to get my car fixed. I know it's been hanging in there, but I don't know if it can handle the trip this time."

I wince. "Yeah, that's true. I can drive us both, if you want."

"Are you sure? I might convince you to do something crazy and spontaneous before we get to camp."

I laugh. "Trust me. You're not *that* convincing."

He arches a brow, amusement lighting up his eyes. "That's what you think."

Chapter Seventeen

BASH

I ADD in double training sessions until it's time to leave for camp, because I don't know if I'll have the opportunity to train while I'm there. Thankfully, since signing up for Harbor Strike MMA, I've been training six early mornings a week before work—regular workouts on top of sparring and jujitsu.

And today, I finally feel more confident with my sparring.

Each blow my opponent lands is easy to withstand, but I can't deny I need to work on landing faster punches.

After sparring, I do an hour each of grappling, drills, and weight lifting before heading home, where I spend some time by the lake out back to read the Bible on my phone. I sit out there, reading on the deck until Romilly lets me know she's almost here to pick me up for camp.

I make my way to the driveway, and a text from Logan comes through.

LOGAN

hey, man. I heard we're rooming together
at camp!

ME

I know. Get ready to spar with me in your
spare time.

LOGAN

stop tempting me. I can't afford to get
injured before my surfing competition
and you know it. This is my chance to
leave limo driving in the dust and I'd be a
fool to squander it.

ME

Fine.

LOGAN

I will take you snowboarding this winter,
though. I'm itching to see what you're
made of.

ME

Not fair. You're making me compete with
you in your element, but you won't spar
with me.

LOGAN

pick a less brutal sport and you're on.

I chuckle as I shove my phone in my pocket. Who am I
to steer the guy away from his dream to make it big? I'm
currently doing the same thing. And I can't deny it stings
knowing I'll be gone before winter hits, so I won't get the
chance to snowboard with Logan, anyway.

When Romilly picks me up, my spirits lift signifi-
cantly. "Hey," I say.

"Hi." A little blush covers her cheeks as she smiles at
me. I put my bags in her trunk and get in the passenger

seat. Her car smells like flowers, and there's a blues song quietly playing.

"You ready for camp?" she asks.

"I was born ready."

She giggles. "I think you're forgetting we're working with teenagers."

"And I think you're forgetting I once was a teenager."

Knowing I'll get to spend two hours in the car with her makes adrenaline race in my veins. And as we drive, the amber and gold foliage grows more dense as her car climbs the winding road nestled in the hills.

It's impossible to imagine leaving Meadow Hills when I think of her. Logan doesn't make it easy either. But at least they'll have each other. Part of me is surprised they never dated. Or...did they?

And then the more I imagine it, the more I want to know. As Romilly drives us toward Cranberry Pines Campground, I debate whether to voice my thoughts.

And then I can no longer contain myself.

"How did you meet Logan?"

"I met him at church. We were friendly acquaintances for a long time, but when Addison and Perry got together, we became even closer because Logan and Perry are best friends, like me and Addison."

"How...sweet."

She glances at me briefly. "Why?"

"No reason."

She studies my face, takes in my crossed arms and the way my jaw is unintentionally clenched.

And then she smiles. "Wait a minute. Are you... jealous?"

"Of course not."

"You *are*. You're jealous."

"That's ridiculous."

She giggles. The sweet sound travels straight to my toes. "I mean, he is really hot."

My stomach coils at her admission, and the urge to punch something becomes so intense it makes me dizzy. "Okay, fine. I'm jealous." The words sound strained because they're so hard to admit.

Romilly bites her lip to keep from laughing. "You have no reason to be jealous, Bash. Logan is like another sibling to me. And...you're really hot, too."

My brain stops working. I feel like a mechanical device whose factory reset button just got pressed. I know I'm good-looking, of course I do. But hearing it from Romilly feels surreal. Not just because she's beautiful in a way that makes me forget my name, but because she's...*her*. She hasn't given me an inch since the moment I decided I wanted a mile. Somehow, this feels like a win.

A massive win.

"Thank you." I can't mask the triumph from my tone. Not this time.

"Don't go getting a big head, now."

"Oh, it's far too late for that."

And then my sense of triumph is ruined when my dad texts me.

DAD

Your mum says you're coming home next month. It will be good to have you back, son.

ME

I'm not coming back unless I lose my fight. Sorry.

187

DAD

You know we're not letting you stay at
the lake house even if you win, right?

ME

yes. I'm well aware. I'll be out of there
regardless.

DAD

It's not too late to call the whole fighting
thing off and just come home. Running
the auction house is a much more
respectable choice.

I don't respond, because his words only make me sad and angry. Sure, running the auction houses would be respectable. But doing that is his choice. And after making it this far, the last thing I want to do is quit.

I'm a grown man. It's my life. For once, I need to make my own decisions.

We arrive at the woods before sunset. Cranberry Pines Campground is speckled with teenagers emerging from the set of vans idling ahead of us. The cabins are nestled among the bright and colorful Maple trees, and right in the center is a fire pit already lit with a crackling flame.

Romilly parks us near the vans and shuts off the engine. She stretches her arms and makes a soft groaning sound. I can't help but stare at her as she does it because her eyes are closed and she typically looks put-together, but right now she's so pretty in a rumpled, messy way.

I glance away before she can notice me staring.

"Ready to get checked in?" She asks.

"Yeah, let's do it."

We get out of the car and head toward a wood-paneled building near the cabins. Excited voices ring in the air around us as we find the youth pastor from Harvest Valley standing out front with a pen and clipboard.

When he sees us, he smiles. "Hey, Sebastian and Romilly."

"Nice to see you, Hayden," she says.

Hayden scans the list. "Alright, so I have Bash in Cabin A with Logan and Romilly in Cabin C. Does that sound right?"

Romilly frowns. "With Hadley, right?"

Hayden winces. "Actually, Hadley just called and she's sick, so she's not coming anymore. There are six girls in your cabin, but if anyone can handle it alone, it's you."

She nods, but I ask Hayden, "Isn't there anyone else she can share a cabin with in case she needs help?"

Hayden looks surprised by my question, but consults his list once more. And then he shakes his head. "No. Everyone else is already partnered up."

"Of course they are," I mutter.

"It's fine, Bash." Her hand brushes across my arm. "Let's put our things in the cabin."

Of course she's fine with it. But I'm not. It's not fair that she's the only one who has to work alone on this trip, so I silently vow to help her as much as I can while we're here.

I follow her back to the car. She opens the trunk, but before she can remove our bags, I grab them all with ease, slinging the four duffel bags over my shoulders, two in each hand.

She stares at my arms. My chest. My feet. Anything but my eyes. "Do you need help?"

"No."

She swallows. Nods. Am I imagining the way her gaze lingers on me?

Romilly speed-walks toward the cabins. I follow behind with her bags. When we're both in the cabin, I set her bags on the floor. All the bunkbeds are empty, save for their uncovered mattresses. Romilly sits delicately on a random bottom bunk and exhales happily.

I shake my head. "How are you this optimistic? I can't believe you have to be in here with no other adults."

"I'll be *fine*."

If I didn't know her so well, I'd think she means it. But I recognize the tone of her voice immediately, the one that indicates she's putting on a brave face and trying to make the best of the situation.

She does care.

I shake my head. "The whole thing is so unfair."

"Look, I'm honored you're so offended for me, but now I'm starting to think you're worried I can't handle it."

"Of course I know you can handle it. But six girls is a lot for one person." I sit down beside her. "I'll be here to help you, don't worry."

"Bash." She bites her lip. "You have your own group to manage. Don't worry about me."

I open my mouth to answer, but someone else's voice cuts into the room.

"About time you two got here," says Logan. "You're missing all the fun."

Romilly blinks a few times like she's trying to clear her head. "What?"

He grins. "We're about to start our first Bible study, and then there's going to be an apple-picking contest after."

I immediately remember picking apples with Romilly, weeks ago on our date. She must too, because she glances at me and blushes before turning back to Logan. "Okay. We're coming."

Logan nods and then glances between us. "Everything okay?"

"Everything is fine," says Romilly.

"Her partner is sick so she's a solo counselor," I tell him.

Logan winces. "Ouch. Sorry, Romilly."

"I told her I'd help as much as you can spare me," I say.

Logan nods. "Oh, yeah. Don't worry, Rom. I can handle most of the activities without Bash. We can share him."

Romilly sighs, but her posture slightly relaxes. "Okay... thank you."

"Of course. I'll see you all out there." He nods at me before walking out of the cabin.

"Shall we?" I hold out my hand to Romilly.

To my surprise, she takes it.

Chapter Eighteen

ROMILLY

THE NEXT MORNING, one of the girls has to shake me awake for the sunrise hike. It's bad enough being the only adult in this cabin. It's worse that one of the girls—Dev— had to wake me up instead of the other way around.

I peek through my lashes to see Dev grinning down at me. Behind her, the five other girls are trying not to laugh as they peek at me from over her shoulder. Dev leans down and whispers in my ear, "Morning, sunshine."

I frown and open one eye. "What time is it?"

"Six-thirty."

I groan. I don't know how I slept so late. I'm usually up much earlier than this, but all the exhaustion from over- working myself lately must finally be catching up with me.

I muster up my remaining energy and get everyone lined up outside Cabin C.

Bash and Logan are already outside their cabin across the campground, and when Bash sees me, he says some- thing to Logan before reaching my side.

"Where can we get some coffee around here?" he mumbles.

"In the mess hall after the hike."

His eyes widen. "After? Did you just say *after*?"

I laugh. "I know. It should be illegal."

"Yes. That's absolutely criminal." He removes a lollipop from his pocket and pops it into his mouth. "I'm going to partner with you for the hike. Logan already approved."

I can't deny my relief. "Thank you."

I motion for my group of six to follow us. I have Dev, Cami, Angelina, Vi, Heidi, and Taylor in our cabin, and they're all squinting against the cool sunlight barely visible in the dawn. Still, the air feels amazing and cool—one of the many perks to camping during autumn like this. And the way the leaves are about to crunch under our sneakers and boots as we hike? It's an experience like no other.

"How long is the hike?" Cami asks.

I smile. "It shouldn't take longer than an hour."

They all stare at me numbly, Bash included.

I laugh. "Oh, come on, everyone. It will be fun." Especially now that Bash will be at my side, just in case. Though I don't want him to find out, my mood is already ten times better now that I know I'll have his help.

We lead the way. The trail is located past the fire pit, and we begin our uphill trot just as the rest of the groups disappear onto the trail. Logan is leading his group in the distance behind the rest of the counselors, so we fall into step last in line.

"Thank goodness it's not hot out," Bash mutters at my side. "Otherwise this would be miserable."

"Miserable is a strong word."

"So is fun, but you used it to describe this hike, didn't you?" He gently pokes my side.

I roll my eyes. "You'd think this would be nothing for you, with all the training you put yourself through for your fights."

"I've told you I'm allergic to sunlight. I'd rather be punched in the face any day."

I can't help but giggle at the way he says it, like he's letting me in on a secret. He's so cute. It's *annoying*.

Angelina peeps up behind us. "Are you two dating or something? What's with all the flirting and whispering?"

My cheeks burn. I spin around to walk backwards so I can face them and notice Taylor and Heidi grinning at Angelina's statement. Dev, Cami, and Vi, thankfully, remain composed.

"We're not dating," I tell them. "Bash is my friend."

"Can he be my friend, too?" Angelina whispers under her breath, earning a hushed laugh from Taylor.

Heidi whispers something else I don't catch, but Bash's grin grows, which only irritates me further.

I shoot him a glare. "Don't encourage them."

"Encourage what?" he says innocently, brushing a leaf off my shoulder like he has every right to touch me. "You're very popular with the youth, pumpkin."

"Don't call me that in front of them."

"Why? Afraid it'll catch on?" His voice is low and teasing, only for me to hear.

I turn back around quickly, trying not to let the girls see the way my face is burning. The trail narrows into a winding incline, tree roots crisscrossing the path like hidden booby traps. I guide the teens carefully around them. "Watch your step, everyone."

But just as I round a bend in the path, my boot catches on a twisted root hidden beneath a pile of damp leaves. My ankle twists sharply to the side, and pain shoots up my leg as I tumble forward.

"Ow—" I almost land on my hands and knees, but Bash steadies me before it happens.

"I'm fine," I grit out, trying to pull away, but as soon as my foot touches the ground, the throbbing makes me hiss.

Bash doesn't let go. "You're not fine. Sit down before you make it worse."

I reluctantly lower myself onto a nearby log. The girls circle around, distress written all over their faces.

"Keep going," I tell them, trying to sound casual. "I'll catch up in a few minutes."

"No way," Vi says, frowning.

"Logan's group isn't too far ahead of us. I can still hear them. Can you all go get him together?" Bash asks before I can protest. "Tell him what happened and see if he'll turn around. I'll stay here with Romilly."

Angelina and Taylor give me a sly look, but thankfully say nothing before they all continue up the trail.

Once it's just the two of us, Bash crouches in front of me, gently cradling my ankle in his hands. "You always do this," he murmurs.

"Do what?"

"Pretend you're fine when you're clearly not."

"I'm used to powering through." I shrug. "There's not usually anyone around to catch me."

He looks up at me then, his brows drawn together as his gaze slices through me. "Well, I'm here now."

I don't know how to respond to that, so I look away. I try to focus on the way the morning light filters through the amber leaves, or the way the breeze carries the faint scent of pine and smoke. Anything but the pain in my ankle.

"Let's check out the damage." He rests my foot in his lap with surprising care. His fingers are warm against my chilled skin as he slowly unlaces my boot. The confident but gentle way he touches me sends tingles racing up my leg.

"You really did a number on yourself." He brushes some leaves from my knee. "I should've carried you from the start."

I roll my eyes even as my cheeks flush. "You're impossible."

"Maybe." He smirks and looks up at me. "But you're smiling."

I try to fight it, but he's right. I am.

He slips off the boot and carefully examines my ankle. "It's not broken, but it's definitely not safe for you to walk on."

"Since when are you an expert on broken bones?"

"I've broken plenty myself, pumpkin. Trust me."

Bash stands and, without warning, scoops me into his arms.

"Sebastian!" I protest, wrapping an arm around his neck for balance.

"Do you really think I'm going to let you hobble your way down this trail?" he says, already walking.

"I could lean on you," I mutter.

"You could, technically. But this way, I get to carry you through the woods like a rugged, lumberjack hero. Let me have this."

Despite myself, I laugh. Besides, the girls should be back by now and carrying me will probably get us to them faster. Knots form in my stomach at the thought of something happening to them.

As Bash carries me through the trees, the wind rustles the leaves above us until they fall like soft, golden rain. And even though I'm off my foot, the throbbing in my ankle continues. "I can't believe you've had worse injuries than this and still want to be a fighter."

He chuckles. "It's not so bad once you get used to it."

"Do you ever think about what you want in life, like, other than fighting?"

He hums. "Getting deep on me, are you?"

I smirk. "Why? Are you afraid to get deep with me?"

"Of course not." Bash hums as he thinks. "Other than fighting, I used to think I wanted freedom from expectations. From my parents. From anything that tied me down. But now I think I just want something real. Something that isn't for show."

His words lodge somewhere in my chest. For a moment, I'm so caught up in his eyes, I don't realize he's stopped walking until I hear voices up ahead.

Logan and the kids emerge from a bend in the trail, their faces etched with worry.

"Are you okay?" Logan calls from a few feet away, jogging over with his own group trailing behind.

"She twisted her ankle. We're taking it slow," Bash says, but he doesn't put me down.

Logan eyes us both with amusement but thankfully doesn't ask questions. Vi nudges Cami and whispers something that makes her giggle.

"We got a little lost. Sorry to leave you two alone so long," Angelina says with a wide grin, looking not sorry at all.

I bury my face in Bash's shoulder. "They wanted us to be alone together. They probably think we're secretly in love."

He chuckles softly. "Don't let them get to you. They're just trying to see you flustered."

The group gathers around us. Logan takes the lead as we make our way back to camp.

And in Bash's arms, surrounded by dropping leaves, I try desperately not to fall even harder for him and prove the girls right.

Thankfully, all it takes is some ice and a few hours of sitting for my ankle to feel a little better. Bash insists I should keep resting it, but I glare at him. "I'm not wasting this entire retreat over a twisted ankle."

"Of course you're not. We've only been here one day. Besides, it's almost chapel time, and then dinner." He scans the itinerary, which was printed out and given to each counselor. My group is having their hour of free time, and I can't deny I'm grateful, because it's giving me even more time to rest my foot after the hiking catastrophe. The sound of excited voices and laughter drifts into the cabin where Bash and I have spent the entire afternoon. He's done nothing but bring me ice for my ankle every time it melts and make sure I'm comfortable.

It's infuriating.

Because every touch, every glance he sends my way makes my heart twist in my chest, and it's getting harder to ignore.

"I need to stretch," I say. "I'm tired of sitting."

He frowns at me. "Your ankle—"

"It feels much better now." I stand, ignoring the pain when I shift my weight onto my left foot. "See?"

He eyes me with suspicion. And then I fall right back down.

"I think you should sit here as long as possible," he says. "I can stay with you if you want."

"You don't need to do that. I'll be fine."

He sighs, but grins as he sits beside me. "Come on. Admit it. You'd be miserable without me."

"Either way, I better get used to it, since you're not staying in Meadow Hills."

His grin fades. He's silent for a long moment before he asks, "Does that upset you?"

My heart hammers. "No. Why would it?"

"I don't know. I guess I thought it was part of the reason you won't be my girlfriend."

His words remind me of what I keep trying to forget—that he wants to be my boyfriend. That he likes me and possibly cares about me as much as I care about him.

What happened with Cole isn't even my reason for fighting my feelings anymore. Now, it's mostly about maintaining a level of professionalism at my workplace, something I need to do if I want my business to succeed. But more than that, I don't want the long-distance thing. But more than that, I don't want to ask him to stay. If he wants to be with me as much as he lets on, I want him to choose to stay all on his own.

"Where do you think you'll go?" I ask him, instead of responding to what he said.

"I guess I thought I'd be going back to Australia, but

I'm a dual citizen, so I could technically go anywhere I want."

I look at him. "And where do you want to be?"

He runs a hand over the back of his neck. "I just want a place not tied to my parents. Unfortunately, the lake house I'm in right now is theirs, and staying there would feel like another avenue for them to control me. Just something for them to hold over my head whenever they want."

"That's too bad." I nudge his shoulder with mine. "Because it's a beautiful place. Too bad you can't buy it from them or something."

He arches a brow. "Ah...so you *do* want me to stay in Meadow Hills."

I hide a smile. "Either way."

Bash hesitates before gently brushing a piece of my hair away from my eyes. My heart gallops in response. "You know, it's okay to want things, even when they're scary."

"I know that."

"Do you?" He smiles faintly. "What do you want that scares you, Romilly?"

You, I want to say. *I want you so bad it hurts.* But instead, I say, "You first."

He finally drops the hand lingering at my face. "I want someone who feels like home. I've never had that."

My throat burns at his words because of the way he's looking at me. Because he said *someone who feels like home*, and not *something*.

Is he talking about me? I don't dare let myself think it, not with everything so up in the air between us. Still, I unintentionally lean closer to him. My head feels dizzy from his proximity.

My next words escape in a whisper. "Bash...I really don't count on people easily anymore. But if it means anything to you, you're someone I'm starting to trust."

"It does mean something to me. It means a lot."

I glance up at him, and for a split second, I consider closing the distance between us. Abandoning all my fears and simply exploring his mouth with mine, exploring the emotions bubbling up inside me.

Exploring what it would be like to let myself fall, really fall, for once.

But I nod and pull away.

Because if today has taught me anything, it's that falling almost always hurts.

Chapter Nineteen

BASH

AFTER CHAPEL TIME AND DINNER, everyone gathers around the bonfire to make s'mores for dessert. As Romilly plops down next to Logan, across the fire from me, her words from earlier echo in my head.

She's starting to trust me.

I'm a little convinced I imagined the whole thing. Hearing her say that felt better than winning my debut match.

Logan claps his hands together to get our attention. "It's time for bonfire wins. In case you're new here, I'll explain what that is so you know it's not as scary as it sounds." A few chuckles come from the teens around the fire. "Bonfire wins are just a time where we can share a prayer God has answered recently, or a way He has been working in your life, lately."

At first, no one says anything, but Angelina pipes up. "My mom was sick recently with Pneumonia and my whole family has been praying for her. She's finally doing a lot better."

Applause rings around the fire.

A boy in my group named Greg smiles. "I got my driver's license last month. And believe me...I prayed for it. A lot."

We don't stop until all the kids have gone. A few of them bring up prayers that haven't been answered yet, and we all bow our heads to pray for their requests. I can't deny the sense of community and kinship present around the bonfire. I've always thought of church as a building full of judgment. But Harvest Valley has proven me wrong in the past, and it's doing it again right now. This is warm and comforting, and it's not even taking place inside a building.

When we're finished praying for the kids, I offer one of my own, silently.

Lord, is this the kind of church you want for me? Are you trying to show me what I could belong to if I stay?

Because, I have to admit, Harvest Valley feels less like a building and more like a family than it did when I arrived.

The sun has fully set by the time Hayden passes out the marshmallows, graham crackers, and bars of chocolate. Sticks with marshmallows speared onto the ends find their way to the fire, and the flames turn everyone's faces orange and gold.

Romilly makes her way over to me. She hands me a foam cup of hot cider before sitting beside me with her own. The log we're sharing is small enough that our knees touch, and I'm painfully aware of it.

When I look at her, I notice her staring at my forearms before blushing and glancing away. And then a little shiver races through her, so I take off my jacket and wrap it around her shoulders.

Vi smirks at us. "How romantic."

"Stop it," says Romilly with wide eyes.

But Vi only smiles.

Taylor makes her way over and rubs her hands together. "Me and the other girls are about to play truth or dare. Romilly, you and Bash should join us."

Romilly winces. "Truth or dare? Really?"

Taylor nods. "Yep. Come on."

Romilly shakes her head. "No, sorry."

Taylor turns her gaze upon me next.

"Absolutely not."

But Heidi skips over to us, clapping her hands. "Romilly and Bash, you're not getting out of it. You have to play!"

The two of us try to protest, but it's no use. Logan rubs his hands together with a wide grin on his lips. "Come on, guys. Don't be cowards."

"You're just as bad as them," Romilly tells him.

"Yes, but you already knew that."

Romilly sighs. "We're counselors. It's really not appropriate."

But then a circle is formed, and the questions begin whether we like it or not.

Upon request, Ryan eats a burnt marshmallow with zero hesitation. Fernanda dares Logan to sing a show tune at full volume, which he does with insane skill. Greg reveals he cried during the end of Toy Story 3, earning a round of supportive nods and one fist bump from me.

"Romilly," Dev says, her voice sing-song. "Truth or dare?"

She shakes her head. "Truth."

Dev's grin turns villainous. "Who's the last person you thought about kissing?"

Her face flames. Across the fire, Logan raises an eyebrow like he's daring her to say it.

"Pass," Romilly says. "And let's avoid questions like that. Keep it innocent, girls."

Dev snickers. "Fine."

"She totally was going to say Bash," Cami whispers to Heidi.

"I was not!"

I stretch my arms back behind me. "I mean, I wouldn't blame her."

She kicks dirt in my direction with her good leg.

"Go on, Romilly," says Logan. "You have to tell us."

"You're setting a terrible example right now, Logan."

"I'm following the rules. *You* are not." Logan shoots me a smile, like we're on the same team.

"Your turn," she says sweetly to Dev. "Truth or dare?"

"Dare."

She smirks. "I dare you to serenade the group with a dramatic rendition of 'I Will Always Love You.' Bonus points if you use a stick as a microphone."

Without missing a beat, Dev stands and picks up a marshmallow skewer. She stares directly at her and launches into a loud and breathy performance. By the end, the kids are doubled over, and Romilly is crying into my jacket from laughter.

The game eventually winds down, and the fire fades. There's an ache in my stomach from laughing so hard. It's not something I'm used to but I like it. A lot.

I stand to get another marshmallow, and Logan meets

me at the table. "It seems like you two are getting more cozy." Logan's eyebrows dance suggestively, but he thankfully keeps his voice low enough so it's barely audible over the crackling fire.

I sigh. "Be honest with me, mate. Do you have a thing for her?"

Logan's goofy expression slips away instantly. "For *Romilly?*"

I nod.

"Nah. She's like my sister. I mean, she's beautiful and all, and I'd do anything for her. But it's not like that between us."

"Right."

His eyes sparkle with mischief. "But I'm guessing it *is* that way between you two?"

I rub a hand down the back of my neck, and my gaze finds Romilly without my permission. "It's like that for me, but not her."

He laughs. "Believe me, I doubt that."

"Thanks for the vote."

"Hey, I could be wrong." He nudges me with his shoulder. "And if she doesn't feel the same, don't let it get to you."

He walks back to the fire pit.

"Too late," I mutter.

I walk Romilly back to her cabin early so she can rest her ankle.

She drops onto her bunk with a dramatic sigh. "Finally.

Peace, quiet, and no giggling girls whispering about our chemistry."

"Sorry to disappoint you, but they'll be back soon." I shove my hands into my pockets and flash a grin. "You tired?"

"Exhausted. And mildly traumatized by the fact that Greg dared Logan to lick a tree."

I smirk. "Don't forget how you dared Cami to let you do her eyebrows blindfolded."

"She looked amazing."

"She looked like she'd been attacked by a feral brow marker."

Romilly giggles. "You're just jealous no one asked you to do their eyebrows."

I lean against the wall across from her. "That must be it. My deepest regret in life, right there."

A twitch of a smile graces her lips. "You play too much."

"I'm a delight," I correct.

"Annoying."

"Charming." I push off the wall and step closer. "And you think so, too. Otherwise, you would have never refused to admit who you last thought about kissing."

"Admitting anything would have been inappropriate."

"Fair enough." I lean down until our faces are level. "But if you want me to kiss you, all you need to do is say the word."

She stares at my mouth, making her cheeks flush. She sits up straighter on the bunk. "We can't do this, Bash. I told you that back at the farm."

Frustration boils inside me. "So just to be clear, all of

this—" I motion between us. "—this tension is just my imagination?"

She crosses her arms. "Don't make this harder than it needs to be."

"Romilly...if I stayed in Meadow Hills, would you want to be with me?"

She closes her eyes. Exhales. When she opens them again, it's like she's taking off a mask. Her gaze sweeps over me with clear, unfiltered desire.

It sets my entire body on fire.

"I can't answer that. You have to make that choice regardless of what I want." It's nothing more than a mumble, but it's laced with all the same things I'm feeling and trying to fight.

But I don't have a chance to process her words because the campers begin filtering in.

Romilly jerks her gaze away from mine like she just woke up from a trance.

I rise from the bed, swallowing the ache in my throat.

"Ohhh, it's warm in here," Angelina says, tossing her sweater onto the nearest bunk. "Things always seem to heat up between you two."

"Actually," I mutter, heading for the door, "they feel pretty cold to me, at the moment."

Romilly shoots me a sharp look. I shoot her one right back.

Somehow, the teens don't notice. Cami is already recounting a dramatic retelling of her truth-or-dare moment like she's auditioning for a play, and Dev passes out stickers she's been collecting for the other girls to see.

As I head back to Cabin A, I can't stop thinking about what Romilly said.

You have to make that choice regardless of what I want.

Yeah, I do. And if I had my way, I'd stay right here and never leave her. But if she doesn't want me back, the last thing I want to do is stay in a town so small, I'll be forced to watch her be with someone else right in my face.

But at the same time, I almost don't care how much of her I get. As long as I get her.

Chapter Twenty

ROMILLY

I DON'T WANT to do the kayaking activity. I really don't. Not only is it cold outside, but my hair is freshly washed and straightened for the week, so possibly tipping over and plummeting into the lake is the last way I want to spend my morning. But it's on our schedule for today, and as the only counselor in my group, I have no choice.

The sun is warm on my skin. It's the kind of autumn day that makes me forget winter is coming. Orange and red leaves float lazily down from the trees lining the lake's edge, dotting the surface like little boats of their own. They mingle with the actual boats already holding two teens each. Everyone is partnered up, and when Heidi and Taylor—the last two in my cabin—take the oars and push off in their own boat, I'm the odd one out.

And now, here I am, standing at the edge of the lake, blinking at the two-person kayak I'm supposed to somehow navigate alone.

Logan nudges me with his shoulder. "Bash is going to

be your partner. You're going to need his help more than I will."

Hope blossoms in my chest. "Are you sure?"

"Oh, yeah. The water is my domain. I got this."

Bash grins as he walks up beside me, pushing up his sleeves like we're about to compete in the Olympics. "Ready to paddle into the sunset with me, pumpkin?"

"I'm ready to get through this as quickly as possible. Preferably dry."

"That's the spirit."

Bash lets me get in first. When I take a step into the front seat, he steadies me by the waist so we don't tip, and then he gets in behind me. The water sloshing against the sides of the kayak is nothing compared to the nerves and butterflies crashing in my stomach. But my excitement quickly transforms into irritation, because we're barely five strokes in before it becomes clear that we are terrible at paddling together.

Bash rows too aggressively, like he's trying to beat the water into submission.

"Easy. We're not in the ring right now. Calm down."

"What do you mean? I'm doing an excellent job," he says.

Maybe he is, but my rowing is so weak in comparison that we spin in a circle, drawing the attention and laughter of several teens as they paddle past us. Pretty soon, we're the last ones drifting away from the shore.

"You're not following my rhythm," I say.

"I didn't realize this was a rhythm-based activity."

"Stop muscling it. Paddle lightly."

He scoffs. "I don't know how to paddle lightly. Have you seen my arms?"

"Unfortunately."

He eases up slightly.

And then we tip. One sharp lurch of the kayak and we're in the water.

The lake is icy, as expected, and shockingly quiet beneath the surface. When I come up sputtering, Bash is already laughing.

I glare at him. "You did that on purpose!"

"Me? Never." He floats effortlessly, his black sweater drenched and clinging to him in a way that makes it hard to form coherent thoughts. "I mean, I didn't *not* see it coming."

"Bash!"

He grins. "I'm sorry."

Everyone else is so far ahead of us by now. Even Logan has caught up with the rest of our groups.

We swim toward the nearest section of shoreline. By the time we drag ourselves onto the grassy bank, my pulse is racing for a reason that has nothing to do with cold.

We're alone.

"You're maddening." I spin away from him and stomp deeper into the trees. Of course, *of course,* I'd end up completely soaked after partnering with him. It's bad enough that I was trying to avoid getting wet in the first place. It's even worse that I can't fully be angry at him because his contagious smirk is making it hard for me not to start laughing right along with him.

As he follows me, another low chuckle escapes him, making me spin to face him. I take in the water dripping from his hair and the leaf stuck to his shoulder. I reach for it without thinking, and when I brush it away, my hand lingers.

Mistake.

The tension blooms instantly. Bash's storming gaze collides with mine, sending a thunderclap of feeling through my veins.

"You should stop doing that," I whisper.

He doesn't move. "Doing what?"

"Looking at me like that."

"I'm not looking at you any kind of way."

"Yes, you are."

He shifts closer. Heat rolls off him despite how cold the lake was.

"Romilly," he says, his voice low and tantalizing. "Why do you keep pretending you don't want this?"

I try to look away, but his hand gently brings my face back to him.

"You're just...you're everything I swore I wouldn't fall for."

He looks stricken by my answer. Something sharpens in his gaze like he's seeing clearly for the first time. "And what's that?"

"You're way too charming. You're overprotective and constantly concerned about my appetite. You make it hard for me to stay serious and professional because you turn everything into a joke. You make me want to break all the rules, and you can't even slice sourdough bread." I try to find more reasons but come up empty. And I can't deny the ones I just gave him are hardly marks against him. If anything, they only draw me into him even more.

Neither of us speaks.

And then I kiss him.

Or maybe he kisses me.

Either way, our mouths find each other in a rush of

heat and desperation and want. His hands are on my waist, on my back. Bash pulls me closer, and the way his fingers slide against my soaking, skin-tight clothes give me goose-bumps. My fingers twist in his shirt to tug him toward me, but I'm simultaneously trying to make sense of the chaos inside me.

His mouth finds mine again with no hesitation this time. His hands slide into my hair, fisting gently at the base of my neck as he deepens the kiss. His lips move with a kind of hunger that steals the air from my lungs. It's slow at first—velvety, coaxing—but it builds fast, like a flame against firewood.

When his tongue brushes against mine, my knees go weak. I gasp softly against his mouth, gripping his arms like I'm afraid I might fall again, even though he's the one who's doing all the unraveling.

Bash's mouth captures mine over and over like he's memorizing it, like he's making up for all the times we've come close but pulled away.

The world disappears. I'm hyper-aware of everything, like how his chest is pressed tight to mine, and how one of his hands slides down my spine, slow and reverent, like he's mapping out something sacred. The other stays tangled in my hair, holding me in place as if he can't bear to let me go.

Heat coils low in my stomach and spreads outward, making me feel dizzy, drunk on him. When he pulls back for air, I chase his mouth—because I need more, because this feels too good, too much, and yet not enough.

He groans softly. "You drive me insane, you know that?"

"Likewise."

His thumb strokes along the edge of my jaw. My lips

are still tingling, my whole body practically humming, and his eyes...oh, his eyes. They look like they've just seen heaven. Or maybe like he's staring right at it.

And I hate that I'm about to ruin it.

It's too much. Too good. Too dangerous. He still hasn't decided he's staying. If he really wanted to, he would have told me by now, but he hasn't. That's as good as a no in my book.

And now, it's going to hurt so much worse when he leaves.

"Romilly—"

"Don't." I hold up a trembling hand. "If you care about me at all...just let me go." *And Lord, if he's not for me, help me let go of him, too.*

Bash frowns. "What on earth are you talking about?"

I hug my arms across my chest. "We want different things, Bash. I want someone I can count on, and you're not even staying in Meadow Hills because you want freedom."

Bash cradles my face in his palms. "All I want is *you.* I'll stay. I promise." His eyes look feral. Desperate. They tug at my heart.

But the truth rings in my ears. *He's only agreeing to stay for you. If you let him, he's going to regret it or resent you for it. If he really wanted to be with you, he should have decided to stay on his own before you mentioned it.*

It's all the things I know I should tell him, but to do so would be admitting way too much.

"No. We're not right for each other," I tell him. "We're much better off as friends."

Bash's brows knit together, but he doesn't argue. He doesn't try to kiss me again. He just swallows and steps away from me, but I still feel his touch like it's branded onto me.

My eyes sting. I wish he'd yell. I wish he'd call me dramatic or stubborn or difficult. But he just looks at me with those wild blue eyes.

"I want to be a lot more than your friend. And I don't think I can let you go," he admits, voice thick.

My heart cracks.

"But I can give you space. If that's what you need."

I nod, even though it feels like someone just pulled the sun from the sky. And when he finally steps away, everything in me aches to chase after him. But I don't.

Chapter Twenty-One

BASH

THE REST OF THE WEEK, I keep my distance, just like I said I would. But it's not easy. Not when I see Romilly coming outside her cabin each morning, looking so beautiful in an otherworldly, angelic way. But not just beautiful. Sad. I want to discover what's on her mind, but I promised to give her space.

Still, it takes every ounce of strength I've got not to reach for her as she brushes past me in the mess hall or circles the chapel with her Bible and a purposeful expression. Especially since our kiss in the woods is still burned into my brain.

It's been three days since, and all I want is to pull her right back against me and devour her. But she rejected me, even after I told her I'd stay in Meadow Hills. I thought it would make her happy, but it only pushed her away. It's a good thing I didn't tell her how badly I want to make her little town my new home, how much it already feels like home, or just how much of my heart is with her. It would have made things worse.

And now, I want a cigarette for the first time in ages.
Lord, help me.

I've started training every morning to work out my frustrations. Thanks to the prodding and reminders from my agent, Max, my fight is only four weeks away. So, each morning before sunrise, I head into the woods with a jump rope, resistance bands, and enough tension in my body to snap a tree in half. The crisp, cold air stings my lungs as I shadowbox beneath a canopy of amber and fire-colored leaves. I grunt through push-ups in the dirt, slam my gloved fists into the trunk of a tree, and try not to think about her.

But I always do.

Romilly, with her soft laugh and stubborn streak.

Romilly, with her guarded eyes and the way she looks at me like I might just be dangerous enough to ruin her.

And maybe I am.

We barely speak the rest of the week. When we do, it's polite. Careful. Surface-level. She thanks me when I hand her a ladle in the kitchen. Nods when I offer to carry supplies for her. Smiles a faint, flickering thing that never reaches her eyes.

It kills me.

Because after that kiss—after the way she melted in my arms like she was made to fit there—I was sure we were on the same page. But I should have known better. And I should have remembered the walls she's built were there for a reason.

I really need to stop trying to knock them down. I need to just...wait.

One of the few wise things my mother once told me

comes to mind. *Sebastian, trying to rush a woman is like trying to force a fruit to ripen.* She said it to me while my dad was trying to rush her to get ready one morning so they wouldn't be late, but still. I think the sentiment applies in this case just the same.

I train. I help the other camp counselors. I pretend to enjoy when the campers ask me if I'm really "Bash the Smasher," a name that recently started circulating social media with my fight approaching. I hike, chop wood, stoke the fire at night, and sit across the bonfire from her with my heart in my throat.

The next morning, I get up an hour before wake-up time and find a log to sit on. I'm so deep in thought, I don't even notice when Logan comes up behind me.

"You look like a man who needs to punch something," he says, arms crossed, his breath fogging in the crisp morning air.

I narrow my eyes at him. "What makes you think that?"

"Hm, I don't know. Maybe the fact that you're currently sitting on a log by the empty campfires with your face resting on your fists."

"I'm fine," I grunt, pushing myself off the log and rolling my neck until it pops. "And I'm about to go train anyway."

"You've been brooding like a rejected Disney prince for two days straight," he says.

"Yeah, well, I don't know the correct way to respond when I've been rejected after kissing Romilly."

Logan pauses, wincing. "Ouch...okay, I know I wasn't down before, but if you need to tackle someone, I'm game."

I side-eye him. "You're volunteering to be my punching bag? What about your surfing competition?"

"Hey, I've got brothers. I'm used to getting beat up emotionally and physically. Plus, I know you won't actually kill me because then you'd have to attend all the extra activities you keep avoiding so we're not short a counselor."

Tempting.

"And look. I brought these." Logan tosses me a pair of makeshift sparring mitts he must have brought from his cabin.

"What in the world, mate? Did you anticipate this moment or something?"

"You moping and needing to punch something? Always." He shoots me a cocky grin. "Come on, Smasher. Let it out."

"You sure about this?"

"No, but I had two cups of coffee and a piece of banana bread this morning, so I feel invincible."

I laugh, despite myself. "Okay. But I'm not going easy."

"Wouldn't dream of it."

We grab some pads from my bag in the cabin and head straight for the woods. Since it's early in the morning, we have some time before camp activities begin for the day. Logan insists we warm up first, and by the time we're on our second set of push-ups in the clearing near the trailhead, both our sweatshirts are drenched in sweat. The sharp breath I inhale carries the scent of the damp leaves clinging to the air around us.

"You ready?" Logan asks.

"Let's do this."

We square off. I throw a few light jabs at the pads to start.

"You're holding those wrong," I tell him.

"Says the guy who's currently monologuing between punches."

I hit harder.

Logan staggers back, then recovers. "Okay, wow. Your feelings for Romilly are doing wonders for your upper body strength."

"Shut up."

"Just saying. If you two ever actually kiss again, I might have to start wearing tougher stuff to these sessions."

I hit the mitts harder, ignoring the way my jaw clenches.

Logan whistles. "Oh yeah, that's the sound of a man scorned."

"She's not—" I cut myself off with a jab-cross-hook combo. "I'm just giving her space."

Logan lowers the pads, breathless. "You've been giving her so much space I'm starting to wonder if she's on another continent."

I glare. He shrugs.

"I'm just saying, maybe she's pushing you away because she's scared, not because she doesn't feel anything."

I throw one last punch for good measure. "Maybe."

"Or maybe," he adds with a smirk, "you're both hopelessly gone for each other but too stubborn to admit it."

"I liked you better when you were letting me hit you."

"Don't worry," he says, picking up the mitts. "I'll shut up now. But fair warning, if you keep looking at her like she's the moon and stars, one of the kids is going to start writing poetry about it."

I roll my eyes. "Get back in position."

He grins. "Yes, coach."

And by the time we're finished, I feel much better. I hate it, because that means Logan was right about me needing to punch something. And of course, I'll never tell him.

But he *was* right.

Two days later, it's finally time to pack up and leave. The kids have a dazed look in their eyes from all the fun, and even the trees seem to rustle a little more softly, like they're mourning the end of our time together.

When I see Romilly loading her luggage into the trunk, I approach her. Nerves swim in my stomach because I haven't spoken much to her since our kiss. But I manage to say to her, "I was thinking about riding back with Logan. If you'd prefer it."

As if by instinct, she bites her lip. She meets my gaze like it's painful for her. "That's probably a good idea." And then she stares at the ground. "See you at work tomorrow?"

I nod. "Of course."

When I grab my things and stuff my duffel bag into the trunk of Logan's SUV, he shoots me a wince. "Ouch, man."

"Stop it." I stand by the open door, watching as Romilly gives a lingering hug to each of her campers. She laughs at something Taylor says, brushing a piece of hair behind her ear, and I feel that ache in my chest all over again.

***

I'm standing at the front door of the lake house when my mother texts me.

MUM

Have you been ignoring my messages, Sebastian?

ME

Which messages?

MUM

The ones asking if you'll be attending the gala this Tuesday in Portland with us? After all, you're already there.

Frowning, I scroll up to see what she's talking about. Indeed, there are at least three texts I somehow missed about a gala.

Dread pools in my stomach. If I believed she was asking me to attend out of kindness, or even convenience, I might consider it. But I know for a fact this is her way of trying to rope me back into my old life. Mum has never asked me to come to their annual autumn gala before.

Even though I feel pressured by her right now, guilt slices through me as I reply.

ME

Sorry.

MUM

Well, then, expect a visit from me and your father at some point while we're there. This is getting ridiculous.

ME

Should I find somewhere else to stay while you're in town? I'm guessing you'll want the lake house to yourself.

MUM

No. There's a beautiful hotel in Portland I've been itching for an excuse to stay at.

I sigh and tuck my phone in my pocket.

I'm going to see my parents.

It's been so long.

A mix of emotions present themselves—anxiety, sadness, and even a little excitement. Because even if we don't see eye to eye, they're still my parents, and I love them.

But I'm guessing after they see me, they won't go back to Australia without me. Not easily, at least.

Ingrid waves at me when I come through the front door. She's flipping a grilled cheese at the stove that makes my stomach rumble. *She's really gotten good at the cooking thing.* "About time you showed your face around here," she says.

"Nice to see you too, sis."

"Yes, well, I have to admit it's been lonely. Having the house to myself has made me realize you technically count as company."

I laugh. But it fades too soon, and Ingrid must notice.

She narrows her eyes at me. "What is it?"

"What is what?"

"That look on your face. I think it might be defeat, but I've never seen it on you, so I can't be sure."

"It is *not* defeat."

Ingrid's eyes widen as she points a finger at me. "It's defeat!"

I sigh.

"Tell me what's happened."

I launch into the story of my time at camp with Romilly. Though I know it will cause Ingrid to gag dramatically, I don't exclude the bit about that searing kiss between us after the kayak dumped us into the water. When I get to the part about Romilly needing space, Ingrid frowns thoughtfully. She rubs her spatula back and forth under her chin without seeming to realize it.

"Poor thing. She's just afraid," she says simply.

I hold my palms out. "How do I show her she doesn't need to be?"

"Well, stop giving her space, for one. You're basically giving up, and that's exactly what she's worried will happen when things get serious between you two."

I arch an eyebrow. "When?"

"Yes. *When.* I've never seen you so hung up on anyone before, so things are clearly already serious for you."

I grunt in response. "So you're saying I need to go back to smothering her?"

She snorts. "Believe me, you weren't smothering her. Otherwise she wouldn't be freaking out. Whatever you were doing before was working. Just keep doing it."

I mull over her words. It sounds simple enough, but the problem is I'm not even sure what I was doing to begin with. I haven't been playing any game. What's happening between me and Romilly is genuine. And I think that's why it's so hard for me to see things from a distance like Ingrid can.

"Thanks, Innie." I muss up her red curls like I know she hates.

"Stop it."

"I mean it."

She sighs. "Don't mention it. And if you think it will help, I'll bake something. You could invite her over again."

I grin at her. "It sounds to me as if you like Romilly."

She shrugs. "Well, I can't afford to shop for clothes. So, why not sister-in-laws?"

Her words stir something inside me. Not the sister-in-law part, but the bit about not having enough money. I rub my hand across the back of my neck. "That reminds me. I've been thinking that maybe you should go back home soon."

Ingrid pauses her stirring at the stove. When she faces me, there's a mixture of shock, confusion, and hurt playing across her features. "What in the world for?"

"I have a job now. And I'm going to be fighting again soon, so I'll be fine on my own. There's no need for you to work so hard for my sake."

She studies her food. "I really don't mind working all that much. I actually quite like it."

But I know it's a lie. She hates working more than she hates smiling. "I...I'm staying in Meadow Hills. Like, permanently." Saying it aloud makes it more real. And despite where I stand with Romilly right now, it feels good knowing I'm ready to stay and, God willing, fight for her.

She raises her eyebrows. "What about Mum and Dad?"

"They're coming to town for the autumn gala, and they're planning to come visit. You should go back with them because they want us out of here next month, anyway."

She narrows her eyes. "What about you?"

"I'm not going back. I'm going to get my own place here."

She sighs. "I have to admit, I thought you'd eventually go back to Australia, if not back with our parents. But...I'm happy for you. I think this is a good decision."

I smile. "So, you'll go back home?"

"I'll *think* about it."

"Good." I grin at her. I can't deny it relieves me to know she's closer to mending things with our parents, even if I haven't yet. "In the meantime, tell me about this loaf you're considering baking."

Chapter Twenty-Two

ROMILLY

MONDAY MORNING GREETS me with a level of grogginess no amount of coffee can fix. After a week of chapel sessions, campfire smoke, and sleeping a few cabins away from Bash, walking back into the familiar scent of The Paw Spa feels surreal.

I'm halfway through wiping down the reception counter when the bell jingles.

"Morning, pumpkin."

I don't have to turn to know it's him. That voice already lives in the back of my brain, taunting me when I least expect it.

"You're not late," I say, glancing at the clock. "I'm shocked."

"I finished training a little early this morning, so I figured I'd wow you on our first day back." He saunters in, tucking his keys in his pocket. "But I can leave and return in twenty minutes if that's what you're into."

"No. Let's just get to work."

The morning commences quicker than I expect.

Clients drop off their dogs one after another, and Bash moves through the workday like we never left. He's all muscle and ease as he shampoos a wiggly Goldendoodle in the back. I try not to stare. I fail.

"Have you eaten?" he asks, toweling off his arms after finishing with an elderly cocker spaniel.

"No. I didn't have time this morning."

"Just as I assumed." He shakes his head and disappears into the break room without explanation. When he returns moments later, he's holding a takeout bag. "Time for a break."

I blink. "You brought me lunch?"

He shrugs. "I figured if I fed you something decent, you might stop glaring at me like I kicked your cat."

"If you kicked Jasper, you wouldn't be alive for me to glare at."

"Let's keep it that way. I don't want him to murder me in my sleep."

Despite myself, I laugh. He grins at me like he's just won a gold medal. That smile makes my chest somersault. This is the most we've spoken to each other since we kissed, and annoying as it is, I can't deny how good it feels. It's almost like our conversation in the woods never happened. He's back to being his charming self instead of distancing himself like he did at the end of our time at camp.

"What happened to giving me space?"

"Yeah. About that." A smirk tugs at his lips as he crosses his arms and leans against the wall. "Not gonna happen. Sorry."

I gape at him. "Bash..."

"I'm staying in Meadow Hills whether you like it or not, so you might as well get used to it."

Our gazes connect. A warm, happy feeling envelops me, spreading through my veins. *He's staying. He's really staying.*

"What if you lose your fight?"

He shrugs, still grinning. "Eh. There's always the next one. Now, come on. Let's eat."

We sit side by side at the front desk with the food between us. Bash ordered us each a roasted chicken wrap, tomato soup, and buttery cheese toast from Old Joe's Diner. I know he's probably waiting for me to address where I stand with him now that he's proclaimed he's staying. And I want to. But I can't help but worry it's all talk. What if he changes his mind? I'd be devastated.

Lord, what do I do? Should I let him in? Or wait things out a little longer to see if he keeps his word?

"Thank you for lunch," I say, dipping my toast into the soup. "This is really good."

"Of course." He leans back in his chair and smirks. "And besides, if I don't make sure you eat, you probably never will again."

I nudge him. "Are you sure all this isn't just an excuse to tease me? If I didn't know any better, I'd say it's almost like you missed our little tiffs."

He smirks at my reaction, but there's something gentle behind his eyes. "Of course I missed you. It's not that hard to believe."

I open my mouth to argue, to brush it off, but the words don't come. Not when he's looking at me with those soft eyes, completely at odds with the rest of his hard exterior.

"But if you really hate my presence as much as you

pretend to, I can go." He grins and tears off a piece of his toast before popping it into his mouth.

"No, no. You brought soup. That's the best peace offering I could have asked for." I can't stop the smile tugging at my lips.

He leans in just enough to lower his voice. "Then I'll bring soup every day."

My heart stumbles in my chest.

Lord, it's getting too hard to ignore my feelings for him.

When we're finished eating, we both get back to work. Having a full tummy makes me feel stronger as I groom each dog. I really should take Bash's advice and think my meals through better. But it's also so cute the way he keeps taking it into his own hands.

Night finally arrives, and Bash leans against my car after work, dangling my keys in front of me like bait. "You're coming to my house tomorrow. We have the day off. And before you say tomorrow is the men's breakfast, Logan told me it got cancelled while the church recoups from the autumn retreat."

I cross my arms. I already knew that, of course, but I can't deny I'm surprised he's been following along, too. The corners of my mouth lift, but I keep my voice steady. "And if I say no?"

"You can't." He rattles the keys right in front of me like a reminder. "Because Ingrid made an apple cinnamon loaf and I have your keys."

"Hmm. I can always sleep here. The dog kennels look so comfy to me. Who needs to go home?"

"Yes, but then I'd be forced to do the same, unfortunately. I can't possibly leave you here alone. Someone might come harass you for your tips. And worse, you'd probably hand them all over." He scrunches his nose at me. "So either we both sleep in the kennels tonight, or you come over and eat breakfast with me in the morning."

The thought of seeing him again tomorrow makes my palms sweat with anticipation. "You're seriously not sick of me yet? We just spent all week together."

He blinks at me like I just spoke another language. The softest frown creases his brow, and when he speaks, his voice is a low murmur. "If anything, I only want more." At first, I think he's joking, but his eyes bore right into mine with anything but humor. My heart expands in my chest as he takes a step toward me, cradling my face in his warm hands. "Now get in the car before you catch a cold." He rubs his thumb back and forth across my cheek.

I nod, but I'm trapped in his stare, so I don't move. I can't. Not when his gaze is doing unspeakable things to my resolve.

This feels too real, too raw.

I'm not prepared.

And then he breaks away to open the door to my own car for me. I slide in behind the wheel, gently taking the keys when he hands them to me.

"Goodnight, pumpkin."

His voice is soft. Fond. It wraps around me like a blanket. Makes me shiver like a cool gust of wind.

It hits me then just how much I care about him. I already knew I did, but not *this* much.

No matter how much I push him away, he just keeps coming back. It's the kind of dedication I've always craved yet found it so hard to believe in this past year after what Cole did.

But here Bash is, proving me wrong. Since I've known him, he's never let me down the way I thought he would.

He cares about me, and I...I care about him. That's all it is, Romilly. There's no way—no way—this is love.

I repeat the words in my head the whole way home. And as I slip into bed, I pray for clarity, for understanding about me and Bash, because none of this was supposed to happen. I wasn't supposed to feel this way about him. Not about anyone—but especially, not him.

I pray more than once, putting everything I have into it.

But when the answer doesn't come right away, I'm left more confused than before.

Chapter Twenty-Three

BASH

"I CAN'T BELIEVE the day you picked to invite her back is one I have to work." Ingrid pouts and crosses her arms across her black waitress uniform. And here I thought you were starting to become considerate."

"I am considerate. I considered that Romilly might enjoy the treat you made, didn't I? And it's also her only day off this week. I think she'd work all seven if God didn't command a day of rest."

Ingrid huffs, snatching her keys off the counter. I sink back into my chair at the table, opening my phone to a text from my agent.

MAX

Have you seen the comments on Munera's latest post? No one thinks you can beat Connor Stronghold next week.

ME

thank you for the confidence boost, mate

MAX

> As your friend and agent, it's my duty to
> keep the fire lit underneath you.
> Otherwise you might start slacking.

As much as I hate to admit it, he's right. I do need to focus. I've been so obsessed with Romilly I haven't been giving training the attention it deserves.

"Bye," says Ingrid before walking out the front door.

"Bye," I mutter, opening the post on social media Max is referring to. I expand the comment section, seeing several that make me clench my fists around my phone.

```
FightFan24:
    I bet Bash the Smasher will be too
worried about ruining that pretty
face to get his hands dirty.

grappling.junkie:
    I heard he's from high society...
what the heck is he doing in the
ring?

spar_ton:
    Just because he won his debut
match doesn't mean he can stand a
chance against this guy.
```

Adrenaline races through me. *I need a smoke.* But I press my hands against my temples to calm myself. *God, help me.*

Reaching for my fidget spinner, I try to ignore the pressure I'm experiencing.

Deep breaths, Bash. You've got this. You're going to prove to your parents this wasn't all for nothing and you're not the embarrassment they think you are, and—

A soft knock sounds on the front door. I freeze. *Romilly is here.*

I was excited to see her, but now I feel like a mess. I catch sight of myself in the mirror hanging on the entry corridor and wince. My hair is chaotic. The white shirt and grey sweatpants I'm wearing felt like pajamas only moments ago—perfectly appropriate for breakfast. But now, they make me feel rumpled and underdressed.

Another knock. I open the door.

Romilly smiles from the other side in a pink sweater and black leggings. Her hair is in a loose braid, draped over the front of her shoulder. Seeing her does something to calm my racing heart, and when I swallow hard, her brows draw together in concern. "Are you okay?"

How does she know already? Is it that obvious, or does she just know me that well? "I'm fine. Come in." I step aside so she can enter, my hand finding her lower back without my permission as she crosses the threshold.

I expect to touch her sweater, but my hand meets warm skin because the garment is cropped. My entire body feels like it's been singed as her soft skin slides against my fingertips, so I jerk my hand away.

When we're in the kitchen and she sets her bag on the counter, she glares at me. "I know something's wrong. Tell me."

"So bossy, pumpkin. We're not at work, you know."

She crosses her arms, but her mouth twitches like she wants to smile. "First of all, you're right. That was bossy, and I apologize. Second, I—"

"I know, I know. You're not my pumpkin."

"Actually, I was going to say I can tell something's wrong and I'm willing to listen."

Of course she is. Because no one can resist doing a good deed like Romilly.

"Sit, and at least let me get you some loaf before I start unloading all my problems onto you." I pull out a chair for her, and a blush covers her cheeks as she sits.

"Thank you."

I serve us both a slice and pour coffee into mugs, adding cream and one stevia leaf sweetener pack into hers, just the way she likes.

I watch to make sure she takes a bite. I know we aren't at work, but who knows if she'll actually nourish her body anyway? I have her pattern memorized—take care of everyone else first and Romilly last. And if it were up to her, this morning would be no exception.

We eat in silence. Soon, I'm on my third slice before she's even halfway through her first, and as she chews, a faraway look enters her eye.

"I'd love to know what's going through your mind." I pop another bite into my mouth as I gaze at her from across the table. Even here, in her simple pink sweater and black leggings, she manages to look beautiful. Romilly somehow owns every space she's in. It's like the world bends to accommodate her rather than the other way around.

She smirks. "I was just wondering if you eat everything sweet you encounter in one bite or in two."

I lean back, crossing my arms over my chest with mock offense. "Romilly, do I look like the kind of man who doesn't savor his carbs?"

"Yes."

"Well, for your information, I take at least three bites per slice. I'm practically a gentleman about it."

A laugh bubbles out of her. "I didn't know you could be a gentleman about anything."

"You should feel special that I shared with you," I say, leaning in a bit closer. "I don't do that for anyone, you know."

She rolls her eyes. "It all makes sense now when you complain about me not eating enough. Look at your standard for *enough*."

"Exactly. And for your information, you only seem to eat enough when I feed you myself."

She fails to stop the smile tugging at her lips. "You're annoying."

"And yet, here you are. Sharing this loaf with me." My voice drops. "Spending time with me."

The warmth in her gaze catches me off guard, like she's peeling back a layer I didn't know I was hiding behind. And then she looks away, pretending to focus on her coffee cup. "You're surprisingly easy to tolerate these days, I guess."

"Oh, come on. Admit it. You want to be with me. You like me." My words come out wobbly, the playful edge I was going for lost under the weight of my racing heartbeat. Partly because *like* isn't the word I want from her—not at all. It's not enough for how I feel about her, at least. Not for the way every moment with her consumes me. Not for the amount of space she takes up in my thoughts.

"I can tell you're trying to distract me, you know. So you won't have to talk about what's bothering you."

My stomach flips. I wasn't trying to distract her. She's the one who distracted me, but the reminder makes my dread return. I lean back in my chair. "As you know, my next fight is approaching."

She nods. "It's two weeks away."

"Right. Well, it seems no one thinks I'll win."

She tilts her head at me. "What do you mean?"

I slide out of my chair and sit right next to her so I can show her the comments. This close, I can smell that delicious lavender on her skin again. It steals my thoughts away the same way it did on the hot air balloon when she was wrapped in my arms.

Focus, Bash.

I clear my throat, handing her my phone with Munera's social media page pulled up. "Take a look." I press my hands to my temples again. "Read the comments."

She's silent as she does. I can't bear to look, watch her expression change when she finds out no one, absolutely no one, has any faith in me. In my ability to win this or make something of myself.

It's my parents all over again.

Suddenly, Romilly's hand is on my shoulder. "Bash, these comments don't mean anything."

"They mean *everything*."

She shakes her head. "They don't. Not at all."

"How can you say that?"

"Because these people don't know you. They've never even met you. They haven't seen the drive, the determination I have in you since the day we crossed paths. You're smart. You're brave. You're—" she swallows as her gaze sweeps my arms, my shoulders, "—you're strong. Important. And usually much too confident."

"Confidence *is* my specialty." I smirk, but it falters

away as my eyes search hers, trying to memorize this moment and the way she's looking at me. "Would you... would you maybe want to come, Romilly? Just to support me. You can say no, and please don't feel pressured to—"

"I'll be there," she says simply. "Of course I will."

My heart catapults right into my ribcage. "You will? It's in Boston. We could drive there together. "

She nods. "Okay."

"What about the dogs?"

Her expression brightens. "Paige got back to me this morning. Elena is going to cover The Paw Spa in *The Meadow Bee*. Which means I'm one step closer to getting Agatha back, if all goes well, so I'll reschedule the dogs for your fight. It won't be the first time I've let down my pet parents, right?" She winces, and I know she's remembering the same thing I am—the night she overbooked herself and cried when I called the remaining clients to come back on different days.

"Congratulations on the feature. But I know you still don't want to let your customers down, so I won't be upset if you stay here."

She frowns like I'm not making sense. "But it would be so much worse to let you down."

My stomach flips. The feeling in my chest is now too warm, too bubbly to endure. With unspoken, forbidden words practically on my lips, I lean toward her, taking her face in my hands.

She bites her lip, brows drawing together like she's nervous. Like she might not want me to kiss her. "I'll, uh, be right back. I need to use the restroom." She escapes my grip and goes down the hall before I can utter another word.

Lord, am I smothering her, or is she just afraid? If it's the latter, please show her I'm not going to hurt her if you want us together. I'm about to ask Him to give me confidence for my fight too, when a key unlocks the front door.

I frown. *Now, who could that be? Ingrid is at work.*

My brain scrambles to process why on earth the door is unlocking, and then I'm on my feet in an instant.

The door opens. Mum struts right into the kitchen, Dad following meekly on her heels. When she sees me standing by the table, her gaze zeroes in on me.

It's like being smacked in the face. My parents aren't supposed to be here for hours, but here they are, before the gala instead of after.

Seeing my mother glare at me with those icy blue eyes feels like a reprimand. She would look just like Ingrid with her red hair, if it weren't for the compassion absent from her expression. Her natural air of dominance is a lot to take in after being away for so long. And Dad only glances at me before checking the time on his designer watch. He's dressed to the nines as usual, donning a fitted blazer, dress shoes, and expensive slacks. His greying hair is neatly combed in preparation for today's gala.

My mother offers me a strained smile by way of greeting. "Hello, Sebastian. There's still time to come to the event with us, so we thought we'd stop by and see if you had a change of heart."

I stare at her, completely caught off guard until she snaps her fingers at me impatiently. "Did you hear me?"

"Mother...I'm not—"

"Let's go." She taps her foot. "You must know how tired I've gotten of this little game. I want you to work the gala. And then I want you to come home."

My words come out strained. "Why? So you can control me again?" I try to make eye contact with Dad, hoping by some miracle he'll actually defend me, but he just stares at the ground.

"If you're referring to how I feel about you fighting professionally, none of that's changed. You can't expect me to support that kind of lifestyle, Sebastian. Especially not after all the training we've given you within our line of work." She takes a deep breath, pressing her fingertips to her temples and closing her eyes. "Please. I have a terrible migraine, so don't keep me waiting."

"Sorry. I'm not going anywhere."

She pretends I haven't spoken. "You never used that check I sent, so I know you need money, and I'll pay you for today if you come."

"I have a temporary job. I'm fine. And I'll be doing even better after my fight."

Mum's face reddens, but before she can fire her next retort, Romilly emerges from the bathroom. She takes in the three of us, confusion crossing her face, and then she says, "You must be Mr. and Mrs. Black."

Mum's frown lines deepen. "And you are...?"

Romilly blushes, moving toward them with grace and an extended hand. "Romilly Westfall. I'm a friend of Sebastian's."

Dad speaks up for the first time, eyeing Romilly with amusement. "Just a friend?" And then he shoots me a knowing glance that makes rage fill my body. I know what he's thinking. That the rumors all over our church back home are true, and Romilly is just one of many. It doesn't matter how many times I've denied all the talk, despite her being the first woman I've ever been seen with or introduced to them and Ingrid. They never believe me.

"Just a friend," Romilly confirms with a sweet smile. "You've raised such a fine man. Everything good about Bash, I know must be thanks to the two of you."

Mum's pinched face seems to soften a fraction. "Oh... thank you."

"That's very kind, Romilly," says Dad.

She beams. "I can only imagine how proud you must be about his big fight. It's all over social media."

"Ugh," says Mum. "I can't think of anything worse, actually, than my son getting his face punched in."

Romilly places her hand on her chest. "That just shows how much you care about him. How much you love him." She looks at me. "You must be *thankful* to have such loving parents, Sebastian."

As she speaks, I remember something Addison said about Romilly winning pageants in the past. And right now, I can totally see why. She's so convincing and diplomatic.

And then our gazes connect, a silent communication passes between us.

She wants me to play along.

Turning to my parents, I sigh. "I am. I'm thankful you care so much about me. That you want to look out for me. But I've been training so hard, and I have enough skill to avoid getting my face punched in to the lengths you're imagining, Mother."

She deflates a little. "Honey, you have no idea what you've put us through the past four months. Please just give it up."

"I can't." I move toward her. "And I'm sorry."

Tears glisten in my mother's eyes. Dad squeezes her shoulders.

"I suppose I understand why you want to stay so badly." She glances at Romilly with an amused twinkle in her eye.

I nod. "Can you please respect that?"

She exhales loudly. Dramatically. "We'll talk about this more. I have a feeling making you see reason is going to take longer than I have time for right now. But *Ingrid,* on the other hand, needs to come home."

"I'll have a word with her," I say, a wry grin on my lips. "Now, get out of here before you're late for the gala."

Mum crosses her arms. "While we're here, do you need any money?"

"No, thank you. I don't need it." *Or want it,* I almost add, but think better of it.

Mum pulls me into a hug, and then Dad takes his turn right after. "We'll be in touch soon," he says.

They hug Romilly next. It's unusual to see because they don't typically hug strangers. "The four of us need to get lunch this week and catch up," says Mum. "I insist."

Romilly nods. "I'd love to."

We finish saying our goodbyes, and then my parents are out the door.

Romilly turns to face me. "I can't believe you turned down their money. You wouldn't have needed any sponsors. I feel so bad about that, by the way. Not being able to sponsor you, since Agatha hasn't come back yet."

"Hey, don't worry." I tip her chin up with my hand. "I didn't hold up my end of the bargain, either. I didn't help your rating at all. But you did get that interview all on your own."

She shrugs. "Paige did it, not me. And don't change the subject. Their money would have helped you a lot. You could have saved it to move out. Or gotten your car fixed."

"It's still kicking for now. What's a few more weeks? And I will save up to move out. I've already been saving and applying for apartments. Being your bather pays pretty well, so who knows? Maybe I'll stick around a little longer, if you'll let me."

She searches my face like she's seeing me for the first time. With new eyes and possibly a new sense of respect. "Just so you know, you're a much harder worker than I give you credit for."

Her approval means more to me than she knows. But somewhere deep down, I'm still worried everyone else is right about me.

My parents always wanted me to be someone else. Their obedient, well-groomed, polite son. I've never been allowed to try to make something of my MMA passion.

But with Romilly, I'm allowed. I have room to stretch my legs for once, to see how long they actually are. For the first time, I can see myself, and I like what I see. The alarming part is that I didn't expect to find so much of myself when I'm with her.

But still, I might not be good enough. If I don't get sponsors and make it big fighting, I'll be nothing. I can't work at her shop forever, and I won't be able to afford my own place so I can stay here with her like I promised.

But there's still a chance. I can still win, God willing.

I may not be the man she deserves yet, but if I must, I'll die in that ring trying to become him.

November

Chapter Twenty-Four

ROMILLY

THE NEXT TWO weeks seem to pass faster than I can process. Bash's parents get lunch with me and him before they fly home—without Bash, much to their dismay—and hold true to their request that he move out of their lake house after his fight.

By the time the weekend arrives, my own parents are practically kicking my door down for an extremely overdue family gathering.

With everything I've had going on, it's been way too long since I've seen their faces, and I'm ready to fix that.

"I've missed family dinner." Zara sighs the words dreamily as she rests her head on my shoulder.

"That's because you never do any of the cooking," says Mom. "I'd miss it too if everyone else fed me delicious food and all I had to do was show up."

I laugh at the way Zara pouts at our mom's response. "Mom, not everyone has your gift," I say. "You can't expect her to be eager to keep trying when she always burns everything."

Zara turns her glare onto me next. "Okay, I feel attacked. I'm officially going to hang out with Dad and Aiden."

As she stomps off, Mom and I exchange amused laughs. "She's right though. I definitely missed these dinners, too."

Mom smiles. "Now, from you I'll accept that sentiment. You almost do more of the cooking than me. And you wouldn't have to miss us in the first place if you weren't so busy all the time. Going two months without seeing me, your father, and Aiden is unacceptable." She stirs the stew on the stove, rapping the handle of the wooden spoon against the side to remove excess liquid. The salty scent of the meat and vegetables in the pot makes my stomach growl.

I wince. "You're right. I can't believe it's already November. I'm sorry. And I haven't even asked you how your trip was."

"It was just as wonderful as you'd imagine a cruise to the Bahamas to be, sweetie."

I sigh. "I'm happy for you." But as I help make the bread and mix the salad, I can feel my mother's gaze on me.

"Something's different about you," she finally says.

"I don't know what you mean."

She narrows her eyes at me as she searches my face. For a moment, I'm nervous she'll be able to see right through me and find out about Bash, or the fact that I'm about to head to Boston with him tomorrow for his fight.

But before she can ask anything, Dad, Aiden, and Zara enter the dining area, which is attached to the kitchen.

"That smells amazing, honey," Dad says. "Thank you both for cooking."

Aiden barely acknowledges anyone because he's currently immersed in a paid livestream of a mobile game on his phone.

Mom and I set the plates of roasted ham and bowls of stew on the table. My stomach growls again as I plop into my own seat and take Dad's and Zara's hands as we say Grace. When we're finished, I'm more than ready to dig in.

Aiden's eyes gleam as he takes in all the food. "Is it Thanksgiving already?"

Mom laughs. "That would explain why we're actually getting some face time with your sister for once, wouldn't it?"

"Oh, please," I say. "It's not like I've been meaning to stay away so long. I've just been busy with work. I'm trying to make a good impression on my clients, so I've had to overbook myself."

"That and Romilly has been seeing someone," Zara adds.

The remaining three pairs of eyes at the table jerk to my face.

And just like that, my appetite is ruined.

Everyone speaks at once.

Mom: "I knew there was something going on with you!"

Dad: "Then I would like to meet this fellow, Romilly."

Aiden: "What's his name?"

Slowly, I face Zara. She's blushing with shame, like she didn't mean to out me like this. "Was that necessary?" I ask through my teeth.

She shrugs. "What? We're all family. If I don't drag it out of you, you'll never talk to anyone."

"Of course I will. On my own terms, Zara!"

"Yeah, which basically means never."

Mom shushes us. "Stop, you two." Then turning to me, she says gently, "Romilly, tell us about the man you've been seeing."

I take a bite of food to buy me some time before answering. My whole family knows what happened with Cole, so I'm sure this is a big deal to them. After all, I've made it clear I want nothing to do with relationships anymore practically every time I see them.

I finally muster up a sentence for them. "I'm not technically seeing him. Zara is exaggerating."

Zara gasps. "No, I'm not. They kissed. She told me."

I cross my arms. "Kissing doesn't mean dating."

"It should, for you," says Dad. A protectiveness enters his tone. "I don't want random young men thinking they can go around kissing you without commitment."

I sigh. It's pointless to tell them it's not Bash who's avoiding a commitment, but me. In my family's eyes, I can do no wrong. So to keep them from hating Bash before they even meet him—if they even meet him—I tell them exactly what they need to hear. "Okay, fine. We are dating. His name is Sebastian, and he comes from a respectable family. He even goes to Harvest Valley church, and he's a friend of Logan's."

My dad seems to relax at that admission. "Logan? Oh, alright then."

"He sounds wonderful." Mom beams.

Aidan returns to his video game, all interest in my

personal life vanishing now that the promise of drama has disappeared.

And Zara? Well, I choose to ignore her for the remainder of the meal. It's not until I'm outside, about to get in my car at the end of the night that she captures my hand and forces me to face her.

"I told you I'm sorry."

"It's fine, Zara."

"No, it's not. You're mad and I can tell, and I feel really bad."

I sigh. "Would it be so hard to ask me before announcing something like that next time?"

"Believe me, I realize that now. Please forgive me." She hangs her head dramatically. "I wish there was an undo button for life."

My irritation fades, and I can't help but laugh. "Of course I forgive you."

"Thank you."

"And I know just how you're going to make it up to me." She frowns at me in confusion, but I get in my car and say, "I'll text you the details tonight," before shutting the door and driving home.

I sigh as I hang up my phone the next day. My fingers linger on the cool, smooth surface of the screen as I drop it onto my coffee table in the living room. Finally, I've finished rescheduling the last of my pet parents. It's taken all week to get a hold of everyone and find a spot for them. The effort feels like lifting a heavy weight off my chest, but the guilt remains, prickling at the edges of my resolve. My throat tightens as I think of the disappointed tones I've heard all morning.

It's taken a lot of guts on my part.

I'm not used to letting them down, and I've never been driven to before. But the way Bash looked at me when he asked me to come to his fight—it's almost like he'd already accepted I'd say no. The memory of his expression, guarded but tinged with hope, stirs something tender in me. And I can't deny he's really saved my tail with the salon these past few months, so I owe him.

At least, that's what I tell myself.

It's not because you want to go, Romilly, it's because you should. It's the right thing to do.

I tell myself the lie on repeat, because it's the only thing keeping me from backing out.

Next, I call Hadley. She answers almost immediately, her voice warm and familiar on the other end.

"Hey, Rom."

"Hi. Would you be willing to take my set next week for worship at church?"

"Um, sure." An edge of concern creeps into her tone. "Is everything okay? You're not hurt or anything, are you?"

"No, I just won't be able to make it."

She's silent for a beat, and then when she talks again, she almost sounds excited. Eager. "Is this about a guy?"

I shift in my rattan living room chair, the synthetic upholstery creaking beneath me. "Why would you think that?"

"You know the guy that's been hanging around Logan at church? I see him staring at you sometimes during service."

"You're so funny. Thank you again," I say in my most

polite, *you won't be getting any information from me* tone. And then I hang up before she can pry further.

Has she really seen Bash staring at me? The thought makes my stomach flip. And I can't deny the thought of traveling alone with him makes me nervous. Excited. More nervous, though, now that this upcoming fight has served as a reminder that he won't be my bather forever. Even if he does stick around longer than he planned, he'll eventually get tired of washing dogs and want to focus on fighting.

I've known this, of course, but it still hurts to think of him leaving. I know it's silly, but I was starting to get used to having him around, which is exactly what I was worried about.

He's not leaving you, just not working with you forever. And that's okay. He's not another Cole. But the thoughts are as loud as bad feedback on a mic and my brain won't turn down the volume.

As I put up the listing for his job online, I can't shake the feelings of abandonment, and he hasn't even left yet. He can be my bather as long as he wants, but it won't hurt to have another person to help. Especially since there's a chance Agatha still won't come back after Elena writes her article on my business. I checked my ratings again last night, and nothing has changed, so Elena really is my only hope.

I head to my room and glare at my open suitcase on the floor, the corners sagging under the weight of half-folded garments and loose, unorganized toiletries. I need to finish packing. Bash is supposed to be here to pick me up any minute, and I've barely made any progress, because every time I imagine tucking my suitcase into his trunk and driving away with him, my stomach rockets with nerves.

My phone rings, startling me from my thoughts. When I see Bash's name on the screen, those nerves practically triple.

"Hey," I say.

"Hello, pumpkin." A pause. "Are you packed?"

"You could say that." I bite my lip, hoping he won't detect the note of unease.

"What's wrong?"

So much for hoping.

"Nothing is wrong, per se."

"Do I need to come over and help you?" he teases. And then his voice drops after a brief pause. "Are you regretting saying yes to coming?"

Ugh. If he didn't sound so resigned, I'd tell him yes right now. I'd tell him how nervous I am to be alone with him now that I know he's staying in my little town with me. Now that I have no reason left to keep pushing him away.

"I'm fine, Bash. I'll be ready to go in twenty minutes." I hang up the phone.

The knob to my front door turns. Zara comes in, courtesy of her spare key. "And here I thought the favor would be something difficult or inconvenient." She fully enters without my permission, flopping onto my couch and coaxing Jasper to her lap from his spot on the floor. "But all you need me to do is feed and cuddle with the cutest cat in the whole wide world. Is that a bow tie he's wearing? How cute."

"It would help if you watered my plants, too."

"I will," she says. "But I want all the details about your trip with Bash when you get back."

Despite the invasion of privacy, I can't help but crack a

smile. "Thank you for reminding me again why I so badly need to stop telling you things."

"Oh, stop. You love me and you're going to miss me terribly once I move to my dorm." Zara gets off the bed and heads for my closet. "Now, let's find something hot for you to wear on your trip."

I frown. "No, that's not necessary. I've already chosen my outfits."

"Let me guess...flare jeans and several cute tops. Maybe a jumpsuit, and about three to five jackets."

My sister scares me sometimes. I cross my arms. "Fine. What would you suggest?"

Zara leads the way to my room and digs right into my closet, stopping to smirk at me over her shoulder before taking out a dress I hardly ever wear. It's long-sleeved, emerald green, and tight on my body. "This. This is what you're wearing to his fight."

"I'll be too overdressed," I say, though I can't deny the dress does look good on me. It's modest enough to avoid drawing too much attention, but the color brings out my eyes and complements the rich tones in my skin.

Zara sighs. "Haven't you ever been to a fight before?"

"No."

"Exactly. So let me be your guide."

"But I'll be freezing."

"Wear tights, obviously. Wool ones. This is the outfit. You can keep the rest of your regular clothes in that suitcase if you just promise me you'll put this on for the big night."

"Okay," I say, mostly to get her to stop talking about the "big night." Just thinking of Bash in that ring, trading punches, makes my stomach knot with unease. If he gets hurt, I don't know if I can take it.

And that thought alarms me even more.

Zara beams. "It's settled then."

"Yep. Thanks, sis." I try to smile as I pack the dress into my luggage. But the unease in my chest lingers, sharp and heavy.

The twenty minutes I promised Bash when we got off the phone pass way too fast, and before I know it, he's pulling into my driveway.

"Ooh. Let me meet him!" Zara nudges past me to get to his car as he's getting out.

I cross my arms. There's no use stopping this from happening, so I might as well just introduce them. "Bash, this is my sister, Zara. Zara, this is Bash."

They shake hands, and Bash gives her a genuine grin. "Nice to meet you. Romilly talks about you so much, I was starting to feel like we're already friends."

Zara giggles. "Oh, believe me. I've heard a lot about you, too."

At that he arches a brow in my direction. "Oh, have you?"

I blush. "Okay, time to go. We don't want to hit traffic." I hug her. "Thank you again for staying with Jasper."

"Anytime, sis. Anytime." A twinkle enters her eye. "Have fun." Zara waves goodbye from the porch with an annoying smirk on her lips as Bash lifts my suitcase with ease, closing the trunk once it's inside.

And then we're driving away. I risk a glance at him now that it's just the two of us. He's wearing a black hoodie with matching sweats, and his hair is messy in a way that makes me want to run my hands through the strands. I swallow. "Are you nervous?"

"For what?" His eyes connect with mine, awaking my butterfly tenants. "The fight?"

"Yeah."

"No. I'm ready. I've been looking forward to this much too long."

I can't imagine how anyone could possibly look forward to getting hurt, but Bash bounces his knee with impatience, like there's nothing he wants more than to get to Boston and begin his match.

"You look more nervous than I feel," he offers. "Are you alright?" He looks at me again, this time with concern.

Of course I'm not alright, I want to say. *I'm going to have to see you get hurt.* But instead, the corner of my mouth lifts. "Your car isn't going to randomly break down or anything, is it?"

At that he grins. "I'll have you know, I took it to a mechanic yesterday. Got a great deal, too. I promise you're in good hands."

Chapter Twenty-Five

BASH

WE'RE ONLY HALFWAY to Boston when steam begins rising from beneath the hood of my car. It takes me a moment to realize what's happening, because the day is overcast, with a heavy fog clinging to the trees and blurring the edges of the road. The steam blends right in with the thick, damp air, at first indistinguishable from the mist.

But sure enough, it's steam. And there's a lot of it.

"Oh, for heaven's sake," I mutter. "You've got to be kidding me."

Romilly's eyes widen. "Seriously? After you just said your car was good?"

"Oh, believe me. The irony is not lost on me, Romilly."

"I thought you said a mechanic looked at it."

"A very cheap mechanic." I hang my head and pull off to the side of the road to get out. Unlatching the hood, I peer into the maze of metal, tubes, and unknown liquids. If only my dad taught me how to decipher this mess instead of how to overprice items for auction. Anytime I'd expressed an interest in learning, he'd say, "But why go through all that when you can pay someone else to do it?"

Now, I feel like a fool. I may be able to jab my way to victory in the ring, or charm my way through a room full of snobs who'd typically look down on me, but what good is any of that now?

Romilly gets out of the car, the torch from her phone illuminated. She shines the light onto the hood. "It has to be your blown head gasket still," she says, fidgeting with the strand of pearls around her neck. "We'll have to call a tow truck so they can get it to a real mechanic. Hopefully, we'll be back on the road by morning."

"By morning?" My eyes widen. "But...Romilly. My fight is tomorrow."

"I know, but you can't drive it like this. There's no way." She hugs her arms around herself. "We could call someone to pick us up, but then we'd have to leave your car here. We're better off just finding somewhere to stay tonight while we wait."

My shoulders sag. The highway stretches endlessly in both directions, framed by dense woods on either side. The occasional whoosh of a passing car is the only sound breaking the eerie quiet.

Romilly looks up the tow truck company on her phone and dials the number, not wasting any time. I tune her out as she explains our situation.

My gaze snags on a tiny inn within walking distance from the highway exit. Its wooden sign, faintly lit by a flickering lantern, reads *Whispering Pines Inn*. The building is small and rustic, with ivy creeping up its stone exterior and warm light spilling from the windows. "How about there?" I ask when she hangs up.

She glances at the inn and then at me. "Um, sure. The tow truck is going to take your car to a mechanic, and we'll get a call tomorrow when it's done. So that works."

We walk to the inn together, and the gravel shoulder of the road crunches beneath our shoes and rolling luggage as we go. The air is brisk, and the fog seems even thicker off the highway, curling around us like ghostly tendrils.

When we're up close, I can't help but notice the vintage style of the place. The front porch is framed by wooden beams and flower boxes overflowing with colorful pumpkins and hay. A bell rings as I push open the heavy oak door, stepping in after Romilly.

She beams. "Are you kidding me? Bash, this place is so cute."

I look around, trying to see our surroundings through her adorably rose-tinted glasses. The lobby is small but inviting, with a stone fireplace crackling in the corner and leather armchairs arranged around a worn coffee table. The faint scent of pine and something sweet like fresh-baked cookies lingers in the air. It's nothing like the five-star hotels I've stayed at in the past, but it's somehow just as appealing.

A woman stands behind the front desk, her silver-streaked hair tied back in a bun. She looks up with a smile. "Welcome to Whispering Pines Inn. How can I help you?"

I step forward. "We need two rooms for the night, please."

Her smile falters. "Oh dear. I'm afraid we only have one room available for tonight."

I blink at her, sure I must've misheard. "Only one room?"

"Yes. We're usually quiet this time of year, but we've

had a full house since yesterday, thanks to a nearby wedding. It's just the one left, with a queen bed."

Romilly clears her throat beside me, and I glance at her. A fierce blush appears on her cheeks, though whether from the chilly walk or the current predicament, I'm not sure. "That's fine," she says.

I arch a brow, waiting for her to change her mind, but when she doesn't, I sigh and reach for my wallet. "All right, we'll take it."

The woman slides a key across the counter. "Room 4. Up the stairs and to your left."

We make our way to the room in silence. The sound of our footsteps is muffled by the thick green and brown patterned carpet. Our key sticks a little in the lock, but after a moment of jiggling, the door swings open.

The room is so small, it's practically dominated by the bed. I step inside and wrinkle my nose in distaste at the antiquated decor. At least the bed looks sturdy on its wooden frame. The last thing we need is a room as fragile as my car.

But Romilly practically skips through the doorway. She turns on the soft lamplight and sets her purse on the single armchair sitting in the corner next to a little round table. "This is adorably quaint."

"Quaint is one word for it," I mutter, setting the rest of our bags down by the chair. "Don't worry—I'll take the floor."

"That's so sad. I'm sorry we're in this position," she says.

"Don't worry, it's alright. But on a serious note, are you sure you're comfortable with this? Us sharing a room?"

"I mean, it's obviously not my first choice." She sighs. "But we're adults, and I trust you."

Those three words hit me harder than they should. They almost feel like a test coming from her. Though I have no idea what I'm being tested on, I can only hope I don't fail.

Or is this a test from You, Lord? Give me the strength to pass.

She fidgets with her hands. "I'm going to change and brush my teeth." Opening her suitcase on the floor, Romilly retrieves a small, purple bag from it, as well as something burgundy and satin before heading into the bathroom.

I open my bag as well. I imagine Romilly coming out while I'm still undressing and blush like a teenager. Ridiculous. *You're a grown man, Bash. Relax.* But it's hard, because my feelings for her are practically suffocating me, and now she wants me to sleep in this room with her and not touch her and pretend I'm okay being around her without her being mine.

Romilly emerges from the bathroom. Her face is freshly washed, hair in a loose braid, and that satin object she grabbed is now on her body.

It's her set of pajamas.

They're casual, nothing more than a tank top and shorts set, but they're silky and smooth along her body like a river of dark wine, and the shorts stop well above her knees. I've never seen her legs before, but there they are, along with her bare arms and an alarming amount of her neck and collarbone.

I feel like I'm going to die.

"So much better," she sighs. "I'm glad it's so warm in here." Brushing past me, she pulls the quilt back and sits on the edge of the bed. I'm frozen for a beat before I grab a pillow and spare quilt and settle onto the floor.

She peers down at me from the bed. The way she's laying on her stomach with her head resting on the edge of the mattress has our faces perfectly aligned, since I'm still sitting up on the ground. We're much too close. "I feel bad taking the only bed the night before your big fight. Maybe I should take the floor."

"Absolutely not. I'm fine, pumpkin. Don't worry."

Her presence is practically tangible, even with this respectable distance between us. The quiet of the room wraps around us like a blanket, broken only by the faint creak of the old building and the muffled sound of cars outside.

After a few moments, Romilly looks at my lips and blushes. And then her gaze lingers on my arms, my shoulders.

Hope swells up inside me. She's made it clear she doesn't want to date me, but maybe there's a chance she *does* want me romantically as much as I want her. Though it feels impossible, I know I'm not misreading the signals clearly present in her expression.

I scoot even closer to her face, making my voice soft. "I have to admit, I was worried you'd be plotting my demise after failing to get you a separate room."

"Your demise? No," she murmurs. "I'd miss you too much. When you're not being infuriating, that is." She hesitates, then reaches out, letting her fingers brush my arm. The touch is light, tentative, but it sends a bolt of heat straight through me. She's somehow both too close and too far away.

Lord, give me strength. I simply cannot resist this woman.

Before I can stop myself, I tuck a stray strand of hair behind her ear. "I'd miss you too. Even when you're bossing me around."

Our gazes lock, and then her eyes dip down to my mouth once more.

"Do you have any idea how badly I want to kiss you?" I ask.

"*Bash.*"

"Tell me you don't feel the same way. Tell me you don't want me to."

"But..." She swallows hard. "If I told you that, I'd be lying."

And then she pulls me closer by the back of my neck and kisses me. My heart stutters, then picks up in a frantic rhythm, the sound of it pounding loud enough to drown out every rational thought left in my head.

She's going to push me away any second. She's going to get angry or laugh this off as a mistake.

But she doesn't do any of that. She gets off the bed and kneels beside me.

I pull her closer, deepening the kiss, every nerve in my body sparking to life. It's like a dam breaking. My hands move on their own, finding her face, cupping her delicate jaw as though she might vanish if I'm not careful.

Romilly's thumb brushes against my cheek, impossibly soft, and the sensation sends a jolt straight to my heart.

My hands slide down to her waist, pulling her flush against me, and the silkiness of her pajamas and the warmth from her skin pressed to my body sends another wave of heat crashing over me.

The kiss is no longer tentative but filled with something I can't quite name—desire, *yes,* but also longing and something achingly tender. My chest tightens, because what I feel for her is more than lust, or even friendship—it's everything I've been running from. With each passing second our lips are pressed together, it strikes me just how badly I've fallen for her. It's been happening all this time, and not the kind of falling I'm used to. This time, I haven't been falling for lies or superficial beauty. I haven't been falling for an act or a fleeting infatuation.

This is the wrong kind of falling. The kind I've been desperately trying to avoid.

Falling in love.

Every brush of her mouth against mine puts me in a more dangerous position, tangling my heart with hers until I can no longer get away, can no longer deny or suppress the truth.

I love Romilly so much.

And I have no idea if she loves me back.

Our faces remain close together when this kiss ends. All I can think about is how much I wish it wouldn't. The back of my brain screams at me that this is too fast, that I've done it all wrong. I wasn't supposed to be this gone for my boss, but it's too late, and now I can't imagine my life without her.

A future with her flashes before my eyes—Romilly walking down the aisle to meet me at the end. Slipping a ring onto her finger. Helping her at The Paw Spa when she needs it and using my fighting money to make sure she never has to work too hard. Spending years making her laugh, teasing her, and loving her before taking the next step and maybe rescuing a bunch of animals together, or starting a family. Who knows?

One thing is clear though. I want her. I need her. And there's no getting over her now.

There never has been.

Chapter Twenty-Six

ROMILLY

MY HEART SCREAMS at me as I stare up at Bash. His face is still close, and all I want to do is lean back in, feel the press of his lips on mine for the next hour. But that would be dangerous. Actually, things have already gotten dangerous, because no matter how hard I try, fighting my feelings for him isn't working anymore.

I'm trusting you, Lord. I'm giving this a chance.

Bash aligns my gaze to his with his hand by lifting my chin. He taunts me with a half smile. "I really hope you're not regretting that kiss, because your lips are like a dream I never want to wake up from."

My chest expands at his undeniable charm. "You and your smooth words. I have to admit, sometimes when you say stuff like that to me, I get worried you're just trying to play me." I pull away, breaking our eye contact.

The humor vanishes from his voice. "Come on. You have to know I wouldn't do that."

"I want to believe that."

He takes my hand. "Romilly, I've never even wanted a serious relationship before. Not until I met you."

"And you want one now, with me?"

He grins. "Yes. *Very*, very much."

I ignore the storm of flutters that attack me and steady my gaze at him. "Okay, listen, because you need to understand. I want to be with you too, Bash. But I have no intentions of sleeping with you. I'd want us to be married first."

He nods. "Okay."

"Okay?" Hope rises in my chest. I expected him to at least be disappointed.

"Yes. Okay." He gently grazes my cheek with his thumb. "Do you know how good it feels to hear you admit you want to be with me? I feel like I'm flying. But I have to say, it's really hard to keep my thoughts in check when you're sitting here looking this way in your jim-jams."

"Jim-jams?" I cover my laugh with my hand. "That's pretty cute."

"You're pretty cute." He tugs me closer to him. When he speaks again, all traces of humor are gone. "I mean it though. You don't have to worry about me pressuring you or anything like that. I'm in this for the long haul. I just want you."

I can't help but smile. "Do you know how good it feels to hear you say *that*?"

"You should already know," he says. "But I've been so scared of pushing you away by coming on too strong. I haven't told you how much you mean to me Romilly, or how much I love you."

The butterflies in my stomach triple. *He loves me?* It feels too good to be true. I shake my head in disbelief. "No. You're not supposed to do that."

"I know."

"That just makes everything more complicated."

He sighs. "I *know*."

The silence between us stretches. I swallow hard against the burning in my throat, caught between the urge to tell him how much I love him too, how much he means to me. But before I can, he kisses me again. It's such a soft, brief kiss, but it unwinds all my thoughts just the same.

"By the way, if I win, I'm going to help you keep your shop afloat with whatever money I make."

My mouth falls open. "Bash, no. You're going to need that to live on."

"I'll be fine. I'll still be working for you. But even when I'm making enough to stop, I'm going to help you with the dogs when you need it. Even if I'm not working for you officially."

I shake my head. "No. I can't accept any of that."

We both glare at each other in silence for a moment before he speaks again. "This is what happens when Bash falls in love with Romilly. He takes care of her. So you better get used to it."

I sigh. "Can I think about all this? That's a lot to take in."

"Yes." The slow grin that spreads across his lips makes my toes curl. "Think about it all you want."

I giggle. "That doesn't mean I'm saying yes, you know."

"I know. But you will."

I cross my arms. "Don't be so cocky. You don't know that."

"Yes, I do."

"How?"

"Because I won't let you say no, pumpkin. Hate to break it to you."

My entire face burns. I give him one more final kiss before getting back on the bed. I want to say something, anything, to that. But all my words stick in my throat.

He throws one arm over his eyes. "Goodnight."

"Why are you hiding your face?"

"Like I said before, those jim-jams make it really hard to think straight."

I try not to laugh as I sink back against the pillows, staring up at the ceiling. "I, uh, appreciate the effort. Goodnight."

The next morning, I emerge from the bathroom in the emerald dress and wool tights I promised Zara I would wear. I was so tempted to slip on my usual flare jeans and a trendy top, but remembering her excitement made me feel guilty for considering it.

When Bash sees me, he groans and closes his eyes so tight, the lids crinkle. "Are you trying to kill me?"

I laugh. "No. You're trying to kill you in that ring today." My stomach tightens at the thought of him getting hit by his opponent, Connor Stronghold.

Bash takes my hand and tugs me to his chest. Wrapping his thick arms around me, he buries his face in my hair. "The only way I'd die in that ring is from getting too distracted imagining you in this dress."

"I can go change."

"Don't you dare. In fact, don't ever take this dress off again unless it's to get back into those adorable jim-jams."

I giggle. "Okay, *enough* with the jim-jams."

Bash cups my face with his hands. It does things to my heart. "Please don't worry about me today. Because then I'll worry about you."

"Well, don't. Between the two of us, I'll be perfectly unscathed."

"Believe it or not, pumpkin, I intend to leave unscathed, too."

We check out of the inn together and book a driver to take us to the mechanic where his car is waiting. The shop's parking lot smells like oil and rubber, and the morning air carries a crisp bite. I'm still reeling from last night.

Bash told me he loves me. Bash told me he's going to stick around The Paw Spa. Bash told me he wants to use his winnings to help me.

I should have told him I love him, too, but I wasn't ready. I was too scared deep down. Because the last time I told a man I loved him, he left.

God, help me not to be afraid anymore.

The mechanic hands Bash a clipboard to sign. When he's finished, he opens the car door for me, letting his hand linger on the small of my back.

"Thank you."

"Of course."

I slide into my seat, and he gets in, too. Somehow, the tension between us has expanded into something that feels tangible. I know he's thinking about our conversation, our kiss, but I still don't know how to bring it up.

After his fight, Romilly. Just wait until all this is over. Then you can tell him you love him.

The soft rumble of the engine vibrates through the car,

filling the space between us. My gaze drifts to his hands on the steering wheel, the strong, capable way his fingers curl around it, and I swallow hard when his right hand drops down to wind through my left one.

"Did you sleep alright?" he asks in the soft voice I've only ever heard him use with me. As always, it makes my stomach flip.

"Not really."

"Me either. I'm too wired for today." He pulls into the gas station just down the road and cuts the engine. "And I'm in desperate need of caffeine. What would you like?"

"I'm good."

He sighs. "Please name something so I don't have to pick it for you."

"Fine. I'll have a muffin."

That seems to satisfy him. Bash makes for the convenience store, and when he returns, he has two coffees and a paper bag in hand. "They didn't have muffins, but these looked good." He passes me an apple cider donut along with a coffee, and his fingers brush mine briefly. The contact sends heat through me.

"Thanks." I take the cup and pastry. But I already know I'm not going to drink the coffee. He may think he's wired, but imagining him fighting today makes so much anxiety spiral through me, I can't see straight.

When we arrive in Boston, Bash parks at the arena. The lot is already filling up with cars, and the evening air is sharp and cool, carrying the faint smell of coffee and dry leaves.

Bash takes my hand when we step inside. He leans down to murmur in my ear, "It's crowded in there. I don't want us to get separated." He rubs my hand gently, and my body melts in reaction.

The sound of cheers, conversations, and the booming of loud music and announcers swells around us. Bash releases me briefly to check in with his agent and the event organizers. I linger near the edge of the room while I wait. In just a little bit, he'll be fighting. He'll be getting punched, tackled, and kicked. *Hard.*

I try to steady my nerves at the image of it all, but it feels impossible. I'm not even the one stepping into the ring, but it feels like getting punched in the gut knowing Bash might get hurt.

"Hey," Bash says, reappearing at my side. He fidgets with the spinner in his hand, and his jaw is tightly clenched. "I've got to go get ready. You good?"

"Of course. I'll go find my seat. And...you *got* this." I reach out, lightly touching his arm. "Whether or not you win, I'm so proud of you."

"Thank you." His gaze lingers on mine a moment too long, like he wants to say something. "Would you...would you pray for me?"

Something in my chest cracks a little. "Of course. Come here."

Bash shuts his eyes and takes both of my hands in his. I whisper a soft prayer between us, only loud enough for us to hear. I ask God to protect Bash and to give him enough faith to carry him through this fight. And when we break apart, Bash shoulders seem to loosen.

"Thank you."

"You got this. Now, go."

He swallows hard and kisses my forehead before he steps away.

I watch his broad shoulders cut through the crowd as he heads toward the locker rooms. My chest tightens as I lose sight of him, so I go find my seat. It's right up front. I can see the ring perfectly, and the crowd around me is so lively. People are already chanting random names of fighters I don't recognize, and I even hear Bash's name thrown around a few times. I try not to let my nerves for him consume me as I settle into my seat.

I stare at the ring.

This is Bash's world. It's everything he's been looking forward to and training for. It's what he left his parents for and why he allowed himself to be cut off financially. It's a part of him I've only glimpsed from the edges.

Tonight I'll get to see it fully for the first time.

The fights before Bash's pass in a blur. The crowd roars with every hit and every victory, but it's hard for me to focus. One guy gets hit so hard, his eye swells shut. Another loses a tooth. Someone even gets knocked unconscious, and it makes my gut tighten. All I can think about is Bash going through all this when it's his turn.

It's a sport, Romilly. It's no different than a football player getting tackled. He'll be fine.

When it's finally time for Bash's fight, the noise level rises. He steps into the ring, and the sight of him makes my breath catch in my throat. I've seen him in scrubs, in thick jackets and jeans, and even in his pajamas. But there's something about seeing him like this, in his tight, black fighting shorts, with his bare chest exposed along with every tattooed muscle, that unwinds me. My head fogs up as I take him in.

Gone is the gentle, charming Bash who makes me

smile and laugh when we're alone. The one who murmurs softly to me and plays with my hair.

Like this, he looks menacing. His jaw is tightly set in a massive scowl. His muscled arms are crossed in front of him, and his brows are turned downward in a frown. He adjusts his fingerless gloves and nods to his opponent. The fight begins, and for a moment, I forget to breathe.

Bash lands the first punch. The crowd goes wild as he takes Connor down, and the two of them grapple for what seems like forever before Connor breaks free. They're both back on their feet, and Connor lands a kick on Bash that has me painfully twisting my own fingers.

But Bash moves with a precision and speed that's almost impossible to look away from as he strikes back. It's quick and sharp, and his footwork seems so instinctual to him. For a moment, I remember the way he defended me when that homeless man cornered me for money. But I can't help but realize that was the reigned-in, controlled version of what he is right now.

Connor gets Bash into a headlock the announcer calls a Rear Naked Choke. Bash struggles against Connor's arm around his neck and tucks his chin, but his face still gets alarmingly red.

The crowd chants Connor's name. Everyone is on their feet, shouting words I hardly register. Until they do.

Bash is going to lose.

All I can do is watch, my heart pounding in time with every second that passes without him breathing.

Tap, Bash. Just tap. Stop letting him choke you, I think.

And then, *Lord, please help him. Get him out of this.*

I dig my nails into my palms while everyone else shouts. Bash looks like he's about to faint.

I can't watch. I need to leave. Rising from my chair, I make for the exit. I can't watch this go on another minute.

When I'm almost at the exit, the crowd's roar becomes deafening, so I turn around, peeking through one eye.

Bash isn't unconscious. At least, not yet. He gets his hands between his neck and Connor's arm, locked around his neck. Then he steps backward before throwing all his weight forward into a front headlock position and lands several groin strikes on Connor. He shifts his hits to the side of Connor's calf, throwing him off balance, while pulling that arm free and escaping from the chokehold.

The crowd roars as Bash gets back on his feet, free of Connor's grip. He twists Connor's arm—the one that was around his neck—and takes him down, nailing Connor in the face so many times I have to close my eyes.

Bash knocks out Connor Stronghold. And Connor doesn't get back up.

The referee raises Bash's hand in victory, and the crowd erupts. My hands tremble as I clap right along with them. The relief that courses through me makes my knees feel weak.

He did it. He won.

And then a few rows in front of where I'm standing, a commotion breaks out. I tear my gaze away from the ring to see two men arguing. Their voices are sharp and angry, and the people in the seats around them try to edge away.

One of them stumbles, bumping into a woman nearby, and she yells in protest. The commotion makes its way to the aisle, so I try to step out of the way, but one of the men shoves the other and sends him stumbling forward. Before I can react, the guy hurtles into me, knocking me backward. My head smacks the edge of the chair behind me.

Pain explodes in my skull. It's so sharp, it's practically blinding.

The world tilts and spins around me.

I hear shouting, and feel hands trying to steady me, but it's all distant, like I'm underwater. My vision blurs. The edges darken like an old photograph.

The last thing I see before everything fades is the concerned face of a stranger leaning over me, their mouth moving with words I can't hear.

And then...nothing.

Chapter Twenty-Seven

BASH

IN THOSE MOMENTS Connor was choking me out, all I could think was that my parents were right. Everyone who left a mean comment about me on social media was right too.

I can't do it.

But then I caught sight of Romilly's alarmed face, and I knew I couldn't let down the one woman who actually came to support me.

If I lost, all my hard work would be for nothing. The six days a week I spent training in the early hours of the morning before work with Romilly would be wasted. No sponsors would take a chance on me.

This is it, Bash, I thought. *You're finished.*

So I did the only thing left I could.

I prayed. I asked God to give me the strength to win if He wanted me to. And then I somehow hooked my fingers between my neck and Connor's grip.

Now, I look for Romilly's face among the cheers of the crowd as I stand in the center of the ring.

She should still be right up front. Where did she go?

Sweat is dripping down my back, and my muscles are aching from the fight, but I don't care. All I can hear is the thrum of my own pulse in my ears, the roar of the audience, and the aftershock of adrenaline still crackling through my veins.

Victory. I've done it.

Take that, social media.

Even though it's only happened once before, winning is becoming a familiar taste. That, and the metallic tang of blood in my mouth.

I wonder if my parents are watching me now, streaming the fight by some miracle. If they're home in our ornate living room in Woollahra, judging my life choices. If they're even watching at all.

It's not even about money anymore; it's about them accepting me as their son, despite choosing fighting over running their business. Maybe, just maybe, they're proud for once. I know it's a stretch, but I can't help but hope, because here I am proving myself.

I've won a second time.

And it feels good. So good. For now, I'm merely basking in the crowd's cheers, the flashes from the cameras, and the fistful of praise I'm about to get from the press. But I know none of it would matter if it weren't for *her*. And now, I desperately wish she were up here with me, by my side instead of the ring girls.

I want Romilly.

Even though I haven't found her yet, the thought of her watching in the audience makes nerves rattle through my body. It's all I can think about as the announcer's voice crackles through the loudspeakers. "And your winner tonight, the undefeated Bash the Smasher!"

The crowd goes wild, chanting on repeat, "Sebastian Black bashes back!"

I lift my fist and give them the cocky grin I know they'll eat up. But all the while, my gaze darts around the crowd for Romilly.

As a reporter approaches me, I force the grin to remain on my face. He holds the mic out to me, and my body is buzzing. But my mind? It's already halfway to her. I need to find her, but first, I need to get through this post-fight interview.

The interviewer starts by asking, "How does it feel to take home the win tonight?"

"It feels amazing. I'd like to thank Romilly Westfall for supporting me tonight, I'd like to thank my sister, Ingrid, for believing in me, and most of all, I'd like to thank God."

"What's next for you, Bash?"

My gaze scans the audience before I answer. When I still don't see Romilly in the crowd, a nervous knot forms in my chest. I nod absently at the interviewer. "I'll be training hard for my next fight." But inside, all I can think is, *where is she? Where has she gone off to?* The question repeats itself in my head as I finish the rest of the interview, drowning out the buzz of the reporters' questions and the flashes from cameras.

Maybe the fight was too much for her and she left early.

The idea disappoints me, but I know it's possible. And worse is the knowledge that this is only the beginning of my career. Deep down, I've been hoping she'll be here for every step. I want her at every fight, right up front, just like this time.

Every interview, every endorsement, every media coverage I'll get in the coming week are all steps toward being the man I need to be for her. Towards being someone who can offer her more than my parents' money, or an extra set of hands at her pet salon and a risky, long-distance future. I'm going to be here with her, and little by little, show her I'm worthy of her trust, and eventually, *hopefully,* her love. But I can't deny a small part of me will crumble if she decides she hates me fighting as much as my parents do.

My winning set of moves replays on the Jumbotron, but I hardly notice. Because a small crowd in the audience captures my attention. Through the tightly-packed bodies, I catch sight of Romilly's green dress, and then finally, her face.

She's *here.*

And then, just as quickly, my relief shatters.

The sight of the paramedics lifting Romilly onto a stretcher cuts through me like a knife. The world goes still as my blood turns to ice.

I can't breathe.

The stretcher moves through the crowd as the paramedics push it toward the exit. Romilly's head is tilted back, her face ashen, a trail of blood staining the side of her temple.

It feels like the ground has been yanked out from under me.

I don't even hear the words the reporter is still saying into the mic. I don't *care.* She's hurt. Or worse.

No. Don't go there, Bash.

My body moves before my brain can process what's happening. I push past reporters, fans, security, and anyone standing between me and her. I need to get to her, need to know what happened and make sure she's okay. I need to hear her voice, to see her eyes focus on me, to feel her hand in mine.

"Romilly!" Her name tears out of me as soon as I'm at her side. I sound desperate, panicked, even to my own ears.

The paramedics stop pushing when she stirs and gently adjust her position on the stretcher.

As soon as I reach her side, I gently cradle her face in my hands. "What happened? Who did this to you?" I can barely get the words out.

Her eyes flutter open, but it's clear she's not fully with me. Her lips part like she's trying to speak, but nothing comes out. Just a faint breath, a whisper of confusion I can't decipher.

"Talk to me. What happened?" I brush a hand against her face, comforted by the warmth, despite the panic suffocating me. "Please, talk to me."

"There was a fight and she got knocked down," says a paramedic.

Romilly blinks slowly. Her gaze wanders, refusing to focus on anything. I've never seen her like this before, and it terrifies me. Getting choked out feels like nothing compared to this.

"I'm here," I whisper into her hair. "I'm here. I won't leave you." I thread my fingers firmly into hers.

"We need to move her." A paramedic ushers me backward so he can continue pushing the stretcher forward.

I don't let go but speed-walk alongside it, outside to the parking lot. I follow the entire way, holding her hand, until they shut her into the ambulance.

The gasps and murmurs from a few people who notice

me barely even register. I practically black out as I find my car and get inside, following behind on the way to the hospital. It takes me much too long to find a parking spot, and I'm about to give up and leave my car in the middle of the road when I finally find one. Hysteria claws up my throat when I think about what could be happening to Romilly without me there.

I throw myself at the check-in desk. "Romilly Westfall. I'm here to see Romilly Westfall. Right now."

The nurse at the computer widens her eyes at my tone and takes in my appearance. I'm shirtless, still in my fight shorts and gloves, and most likely have blood on my face. The nurse grimaces, but types away to find the room number. When she sees it, her fingers pause and she ticks. "Are you family?"

"No," I grit out. "No, but I'm her boyfriend." The word sounds so stupid. So insignificant, especially at a time like this. I hate it.

"She's on floor B in room 221, but unfortunately you can't go in. It's the trauma unit, so family only."

I think my throat might be closing. I try to swallow the lump that's lodged there.

Family. I'm not family.

"But she's my—" My voice cracks, and I bite it back, swallowing the bitterness in my mouth. "I don't care. I need to be there with her."

The nurse offers me a pitying glance. "I'm sorry. You'll have to wait out here."

But I ignore her. I storm past the desk to go find Romilly's room.

"Sir! Stop. You need to wait out here, like I said."

"I will burn this hospital down before I do that," I tell

her as calmly as possible. As I continue, I register the sound of her calling security. Several armed men approach me, ready to restrain me. The cocky side of me thinks I could take them all. But the more rational side knows I'll be completely useless to Romilly if I try to fight them and end up getting arrested.

I sigh. "Fine. I'll wait out here." I take the nearest seat and rest my face on my fists. Closing my eyes, I do the only thing I can at a time like this.

I silently pray, *Please. Please let her be okay.*

Chapter Twenty-Eight

ROMILLY

A TENSE ACHE in my skull is the first thing I feel when I wake up. It's impossible to ignore—the throb that pulses through every inch of my body, but especially my head. It feels like it's been crushed. Every breath I take sends a wave of dizziness through me. I try to move, but the room tilts too much.

Where am I?

My eyelids flutter open, and for a moment, everything is blurry. The soft beeping of a machine in the background doesn't make sense at first. I blink a few times, trying to make sense of my surroundings.

White walls.

Clean sheets.

The sterile smell.

It hits me all at once. *I'm in a hospital.* I frown as I try to piece it together, but the more I think, the harder it becomes to focus and the worse the throbbing feels.

"Miss?" A soft voice startles me. I turn my head, wincing as my neck protests the movement. A nurse is standing by my bed, a sympathetic look in her eyes as she gently touches my arm. "How are you feeling?"

"I don't know. What happened?"

She smiles gently, but there's something in her eyes that makes me uneasy. "You hit your head during a fight tonight, and now you have a concussion. But thankfully no skull fracturing or bleeding. You've been resting, but we're going to keep an eye on you through the night before we send you home."

That's right. The fight. My head swims with fragmented memories—the lights, the fight among the crowd, and Bash.

Where is he?

"Bash?" I ask, my voice small. I search the room for him, but there's no sign of him. Just me, in this cold hospital bed, surrounded by the scent of antiseptic. "Where's Bash?"

The nurse hesitates, looking down at her clipboard. "I'm sorry, but he wasn't allowed in while we were running your vitals. Family only."

My heart sinks at the thought. "Can he come in now?"

"That should be fine. Oh, and he sent this for you." She hands me a folded piece of paper. "He said you might like this. I'll go get him."

My heart skips a beat as I take the note and unfold it. The scratchy handwriting is familiar, and something inside me softens just from seeing it. When the nurse leaves me alone, I read the note.

Romilly,
I'm sorry I wasn't there when you woke up. I

*wish I could have been, but they wouldn't let me
stay with you. I wanted to be there. I wanted to
hold your hand and tell you everything would be
okay, but I couldn't. I'm waiting for you to wake up,
and I'll be here as long as it takes. I'll never leave
you. I promise. Just rest. I'll be waiting for you.*
    Love,
    Bash

The words make my chest feel light and bubbly. I press the paper to my chest. My hand trembles as the weight of his words settles in. *I'll never leave you. I promise.*

It's simple. But it's everything.

A few tears I didn't know I was holding back slip free. But these aren't tears born from fear or loneliness. They're tears of relief, of hope, and a deep, aching love I'm still trying to understand.

When in the world did Bash become my everything?

Deep down, I've known I love him for a while, but I didn't realize just how much until this moment.

The sound of footsteps pulls me out of my thoughts, and I turn my head. Bash is standing in the doorway, his eyes wild with concern. Not only is he still in his fight shorts and missing a shirt, but there's a bruise forming on his right eye, and his hair is messy and untamed. He walks toward me like he's afraid I'll vanish if he's not careful.

I hold up the note. "You could have just texted me."

He doesn't laugh or smile, just hesitates at the side of the bed, his gaze locked on mine.

I reach out, and without a word, he takes my hand, his fingers trembling as they wrap around mine. His grip is firm, but there's a gentleness to it that makes my heart ache. "Please tell me you're alright."

I squeeze his hand. "I'm fine. My head hurts a little, but I'm sure it will be better tomorrow."

He shakes his head, his eyes glassy. "No. You don't understand. When I saw you in that stretcher after the fight...I thought...I thought you were..." His voice falters. The fear in his eyes is raw and unfiltered. The words hang unfinished between us, but I know what he's trying to say.

"I'm here," I whisper. "And I'm completely fine."

His gaze searches mine. The tension seems to leave his body, just a little. He sits down in the chair beside my bed. "I'm not leaving from this spot until you're out of here."

I frown. "What time is it?"

"Midnight."

"Bash...I'll be okay. You don't have to sleep in that chair."

But he just settles in, ignoring me as if I didn't speak. He makes a show of getting comfortable, or as comfortable as he can in such a small seat.

I rest my head back and close my eyes.

The hours pass, and if the discomfort of the chair is unbearable, he doesn't say so. He doesn't complain. He just stays with me, and I can't deny his presence is a constant comfort. I drift in and out of sleep, but every time I open my eyes, he's there with his hooded gaze, holding my hand.

"You're thinking about something," he murmurs this time. "What's going on inside that beautiful head?"

My throat burns with the threat of tears. It's so stupid. Because even after everything we've been through together, I'm still afraid to admit how I feel about him. Every sweet moment with Cole comes to mind, along with my heartbreak when he up and wordlessly left me. Bash and I have already been through more than Cole and I, and I love Bash so much more than I even liked Cole. So how much more will it hurt if things go badly with him?

I lift my head. My skull practically burns away in the process from searing pain. I try to speak, but as soon as the first tear escapes, his brows draw together. "What is it? Are you hurt?"

I shake my head.

"Come here." He scoots his chair back and stands, sits on the bed beside me, then opens his arms to wrap me in a hug. The warmth from his bare upper body and the citrus smell of him is so comforting, my shoulders relax.

I don't hesitate, because letting him hold me is a thousand times better than letting him see me cry.

"Whatever it is, you can tell me." He murmurs the words into my hair, his voice gentler than I've ever witnessed, and it pierces right into my heart.

"Doesn't this scare you?" I ask.

"Does what scare me?"

"Us?"

I don't expect his next words, but they come out with no hesitation. "I've never been more afraid of anything, pumpkin."

I risk a peek at his face. "You're scared, too?"

"Terrified." His gaze stays steady, like a lighthouse in a storm. "But I'm not going anywhere. I'd never up and leave you the way he did. I'd rather cut my own hand off than ever hurt you. You know that, right?"

The sincerity in his voice makes my chest ache. I swallow back my tears. "You were wrong about what you said before."

"I'm wrong about many things. You might have to narrow this one down."

I giggle. "You were wrong when you said I liked you."

"Oh?" He arches a brow.

I rest my face against his chest. "I don't like you, but I'm afraid I might love you, Bash. Like, way too much."

He's silent for a prolonged moment. All he asks is, "You love me?"

A wobbly smile tugs at my lips. "I love you."

His hand on my back traces circles along my hospital gown as he presses his face against my hair. "I love you, too. I think I've loved you since I tumbled into you while you were holding that pot of soup."

I frown. "But that was the day we met."

"I know. But you were so gracious about the whole thing. You didn't even get mad."

"I could tell it was an accident," I say.

"You see? You're so lovable. I was doomed from the start."

There they are again. Those stupid tears, trickling right down my face. But I can't deny it—hearing him say it feels better than cuddling with Jasper, or a sweet, fluffy dog. It feels better than baking fresh sourdough or winning a dozen pageants. It's better than anything I've ever been through.

I'm about to sprinkle a thousand kisses across his face when Addison bursts into the hospital room. She's breathing heavily like she ran all the way here, and when her gaze lands on me, she exhales loudly. "You're okay!" Her voice is just slightly too loud, but her concern for me is so genuine, a new round of tears enters my eyes.

"I'm okay, Adds. Don't worry."

"Of course I'm worried!" With a low chuckle, Bash moves aside so she can take his chair next to my bed. Addison reaches for my hand and squeezes it. "Do you need anything? What can I get you? Ice, maybe?" Her gaze scans my face like she's looking for battle wounds.

I laugh lightly. "You're such a mom now."

"Oh, stop. This would be me even if I wasn't, and you know it."

She has a point. "True. But I'm fine. I can't believe you're here."

She shrugs. "I saw the fight, and when you didn't text me back, I called Bash. He told me where to find you. Your family is waiting to see you next, since I beat them here. Your mom stopped by your place to pack a bag for you."

"You called my family?" I frown. "You drove all the way to Boston to see if I was okay?"

She looks at me like I'm crazy. "You're my best friend. Of course I did." A pause. "And now that I know you're alright, I'm going to address the very elephant-sized elephant in the room." She looks pointedly between me and Bash.

I blush. "Um, I don't know what you're referring to."

"Don't give me that, Romilly Westfall."

Bash laughs. "Are you referring to my presence? Or something else."

"You two were, like, this close when I came in here," says Addison, holding up two fingers with an inch of air separating them. "So either I interrupted something huge, or—"

"Fine," I say. "Bash and I are...together now." I risk a glance at him. He's staring right back at me with a winning smile on his face.

Addison's eyes widen. "Like, together for reals?"

I nod. "For reals."

"With lots of feels," says Bash.

Addison squeals loudly and claps. I'm surprised she doesn't get up from her chair to do a cartwheel.

Bash examines his nails. "Addison, has anyone ever told you that you're much too cheerful to digest on your own, let alone near Romilly?"

Addison shrugs. "A few times, yeah."

"Don't worry," I tell her. "He secretly loves it."

Bash chuckles and crosses his arms. "I'll give you two some time to catch up and I'll be out there if you need me."

When he's gone, Addison and my family take turns spending time with me. My mom fusses over me like I'm a kid with a broken bone, and I kinda love every second of it. The way she smooths my hair back and kisses my forehead almost makes it feel better.

When it's Zara's turn, she crosses her arms and glares at me with loving affection. "You should have been more careful. I only have one sister."

And it's no surprise when Aiden comes in and shows me his rank on a new video game he's been playing. "But I'm really glad you're okay," he says.

Outside my door, I hear Bash and Addison arguing over who gets to come in next, and apparently Addison wins, because she beams at me and plops into the chair. We talk about her kids, and how her step-daughter Izzy has finally accepted that Addison isn't going anywhere.

"It's such a good feeling," she says, a dreamy look entering her eyes. "Loving someone and knowing they'll never stop loving you back."

At that, I can't help but smile. I'm still not completely

used to the feeling, but even just a taste of it tonight makes my chest feel light and floaty. "Yeah, it really is."

When she and my family leave, Bash comes back in wearing a T-shirt of a teddy bear holding a balloon that could only be from the gift shop. As soon as our faces meet again, that lightness envelops me completely.

"Your family is going to come back tomorrow," he says. "They're checking into a hotel for the night." Glancing down at his feet, he adds, "They're so wonderful. They helped me find the best places in Meadow Hills to rent. Apparently they know someone who's looking for a tenant. You must be grateful to have them."

"That's awesome, and I am." I gently scoot and pat the spot next to me on the bed. "Come on. Sit up here with me."

He smiles. "I'll try, but I might break it."

"Fine by me."

Bash half sits, half hangs off the side of the bed next to me. But he stays there. He wraps his arms around me until I fall asleep again, and even though I wake up a few times, the way I feel wrapped up in him like this brings my body, my soul, my heart, more rest than I can remember.

And when I fall asleep praying this time, it's mostly the same two words over and over.

Thank you.

Chapter Twenty-Nine

BASH

I'M MORE than relieved when Romilly is finally discharged, nice and safe in my car as I drive her home.

"I could have driven so you could finally get some rest." She glances at me from the passenger seat. Her hands are folded delicately in her lap, and seeing her back in her stunning emerald dress brings back the memory of her on the stretcher.

"No way. Not post-concussion."

"You really should have slept more, or checked into a hotel or something," she says.

I reach across the car and take her hand, winding our fingers together. "But I didn't want to miss out on any time with you."

She laughs. It's her surprised, sweet laugh, the one I can never get enough of. "It sounds funny when you say things like that because we literally see each other all the time. But at the same time, I get it because I feel the same way about you." Romilly says it so matter-of-factly, as if her words don't set my soul on fire. As if every admission from her that she loves me doesn't make me want to write embarrassing poems and do a backflip in public.

Romilly rests most of the drive, and when we get back to Meadow Hills, I park in her driveway. I help her out of the car, placing one hand on her lower back to guide her. It's not that she needs it—she can walk just fine. But I'll find any excuses I can to touch her.

The idea that she's *mine* now feels unfathomable.

"I'm going to take a long nap," she murmurs, glancing up at me through those long lashes.

"But you have a concussion. You're supposed to take short naps, remember?"

She sighs. "That's right."

"I'll call you every thirty minutes or so to make sure you're alright. But mark my words...If I don't hear from you even once, I'm coming right back."

"Fine." She blushes, but smiles.

I kiss her soft mouth and then move to her forehead when it becomes too much. Romilly leans into me, letting me fully envelop her in my arms. It feels so good to hold her like this, but I don't want to keep her from resting, so I let her go and get in the car. I fully intend to let her sleep, but as soon as I start driving, worry creeps through me. I tap her contact photo on the screen in my car.

"Already?" she answers.

"Already."

A laugh. "That's fine. I'm not ready to go to bed yet, anyway. I still need to feed Jasper."

"Good. But even when you are ready, I fully expect you to stay on the line and fall asleep to the sound of my voice."

"Well, that's even better than lullabies. You're spoiling me." Then she gasps like she's distracted by something else. "Guess what?"

"What?"

"I just checked my email and Elena Fererra wants to come interview The Paw Spa next week."

I raise my eyebrows. "You've got this. We're going to knock the socks off her."

I can practically feel her blushing through the phone. "Thank you. And I know you won your fight, but I was hoping you'd at least be there that day."

"Of course. I told you I'll always be here to help you when you need it," I tell her. Though I can't deny, it felt like a giant weight off my shoulders when two sponsors reached out after I won my fight—one energy drink company and an athletic clothing brand. Still, I haven't even started packing my stuff at the lake house to move into my new apartment—which I got approved for, thanks to Mr. and Mrs. Westfall's connection to the landlord.

"Thank you." She yawns. "I can barely keep my eyes open."

I talk to her for a little while longer, muttering stories to her that I make up as I go about dragon slayers and princesses who bake fresh sourdough bread. I make Jasper the main character of one story, and by the time I decide I'm quite proud of where it's going, I realize she's fallen asleep.

When I hang up the phone, I go inside. The lake is visible through the kitchen windows, rippling under the wind like a flag hung full mast. Heading up the stairs, I find Ingrid in her room. She's in the middle of packing her things, and even though we discussed her going back home, the sight of her leaving still causes an ache in my chest.

"I'm, uh, going to miss you, Innie."

She lovingly rolls her eyes over her shoulder at me. "Oh, don't start getting all mushy on me."

"Sorry, you're right. Get on out of here, will you?"

She zips her suitcase and faces me with a grin. "Are you sure you aren't going to starve without me?"

"I make no promises."

She smiles, but it fades away after a moment. "It's going to be odd without you back home. Mum and Dad are going to torment me."

"If they do, come visit me. I'll be in my own place, and you can break all the rules you want in the home of Sebastian Black."

"Oh, please." Ingrid laughs. "As if you won't already be breaking the rules on your own. You should have gotten a two-bedroom so I could stay. Who's going to keep you from smoking while I'm gone?"

I gape at her in mock offense. "I'll have you know I haven't smoked in ages."

"About time." Her eyes turn glossy. "So...I guess this is it, then."

I frown at her. "Stop it. This isn't goodbye. You'll be here soon enough to chase summer, as always."

She hugs me, and I squeeze her back. When her ride arrives, I walk her to the door. "I expect full reports on everything back home. Understand?"

"Yes, sir." She salutes me before shutting herself in the vehicle.

My mother calls me, almost like clockwork, as soon as

I'm inside. I answer the phone. "Don't worry. I just sent Ingrid on her way, and I'll start packing this weekend. You'll have your precious lake house back in no time."

"Sebastian..." Her voice sounds softer than normal.

I frown. "What is it? What's wrong?"

She sighs. "We, um, we watched your fight. I didn't want to, but Ingrid said she'd never come back home if we didn't. And...well, you did really well."

I'm speechless.

Something rustles on the other line. And then my dad speaks next. "I thought so, too, son. Well done."

I clear my throat against the emotion clogging it. "Does this mean...?"

"We're still not happy about you fighting, Sebastian," my mother finishes. "And we still wish you'd come home and finish what we trained you for. But that doesn't mean we're not proud of you."

"Both of us," says Dad.

"Thank you. That means a lot," I say. *More than they realize.* "I love you both."

"We love you, too," says Mum. "We'll see you in June."

When I hang up, it feels much too quiet. I'm still in disbelief that their phone call even happened, but the positive feeling floating through me is proof of it.

They're proud of me.

Thank you, Lord.

When I'm finally done replaying that conversation over and over, I busy myself by looking up the local newspaper, *The Meadow Bee* and anything I can find about Elena Ferrera, which isn't much.

I also try to find out what kind of questions she might

ask so we're prepared. Because most likely, Romilly will be nervous. So if I can, I want to keep things running smoothly. It's almost as if my entire life has prepared me for this moment. All those times I've had to delight buyers at auction houses.

And here I am. Sebastian, the charmer, once again.

Chapter Thirty

ROMILLY

THE FIRST THING I notice about Elena Ferrera is that she means business. I don't know if it's her firm handshake or the way she gazes directly at me through the stylish glasses on her button nose. There's a self-assuredness about her that makes me instinctively stand a little straighter.

"*The Meadow Bee* is so happy to have you. Paige spoke highly of you for our Small Business Spotlight. And she was right. This place is great." She snaps a photo of me standing in the lobby with no warning.

The sharp click of the camera makes me flinch, but I recover quickly. I paste a smile on my face in case she continues taking photos—the smile that's won a dozen pageants and mollified countless customers. "Thank you. I'm honored to partner with you."

She snaps another photo. The flash bounces off the glass counter behind me, leaving me momentarily blinking. "I'm going to photograph the interior if you don't mind, and then I'll let you know when I'm done."

"Of course." I nod and gesture toward the grooming

stations, but she's already moved on, her camera lens trained on the teal-and-pink accent wall. Her efficiency makes me feel slightly breathless, like I need to catch up.

I excuse myself to go find Bash. He's in the back room, already washing a Pug named Winifred. The scent of sweet almond shampoo fills the air, mingling with the tang of wet fur. As soon as I lay eyes on him, some of the nerves leave my body.

As if sensing my gaze, Bash turns, his hands still submerged in the tub. A soapy bubble clings to the end of his nose, and he wipes it off with his forearm. "What is it? What's wrong?"

"Elena is here." I bite my lip, trying to steady my voice. "Could you just...I don't know. Make sure you're on your best behavior?"

He smirks, one dimple appearing in his stubbled cheek. "Where's the fun in that?"

"Bash."

"I'm kidding, pumpkin." His grin widens, but it softens when he sees my expression. "Of course I'll be on my best behavior. I'll charm the pants off her if you'd like."

Jealousy blooms, unbidden and sharp. The thought of Elena swooning over his smirk or his laugh hits me harder than I'd like to admit. "Well, maybe not that far."

"Alright, got it." He winks. "Be charming, but at a level which ensures all pants stay on." He searches my face, probably expecting me to laugh. But he must see how nervous I am because his brows draw together in concern. "Romilly, it will be impossible for her to scrounge up anything bad to say, even if she tries. Trust me. You're not doomed to fail again, I promise."

I roll my eyes but can't stop the smile from spreading. "Thanks. I'm going to see if she's done taking photos."

I speed-walk back to the lobby, where Elena is crouched near the counter, snapping a close-up of my decorative basket of grooming supplies. Her camera clicks rapidly, and her highlighted ponytail sways as she adjusts angles.

She looks up when she hears me approach. "Can you tell me about your color choice for the lobby? Maybe dive into what made you go with teal and pink?"

I chat with her for a while, explaining the inspiration behind the decor—calming tones to make pets feel at ease, paired with cheerful pops of pink to give the space personality. She nods along, her tablet balanced on her knee as she types furiously.

Thankfully, I chose not to schedule many dogs today. Mostly all of them are baths except for later this afternoon, when she'll already be gone. This way, I can spend as much time as possible mitigating any negative impressions of my business she might form.

Elena seems satisfied with my answers, nodding as I speak and typing on her tablet with fingers that fly across the screen. A customer enters the salon, and both of our gazes dart to the door.

Mrs. Long, one of my elderly pet parents, hobbles in. I smile and greet her before turning back to Elena. "I'm going to let my bather know Mrs. Long is here to pick up Winifred."

I head back to the grooming station, where Bash is spritzing pet perfume on the Pug's dry fur.

"Mrs. Long is here," I tell him.

He nods and grabs her leash, securing it to Winifred

with ease and patting her on the head. "Right. Let's get you to your mum."

I follow him to the front of the shop, where the evidence of last night's rain is still visible through the windows. Droplets cling to the leaves of the oak trees lining the street, and the retention pond just outside glistens, brimming from the downpour.

Bash hands Winifred's leash to Mrs. Long. "Here you go, ma'am," he says, and heads to the computer to ring her up.

Elena studies him with open curiosity, her fingers pausing over her tablet before she scribbles something down. "Would you like me to include him in the article?" she asks, looking at me.

"Sure. His name is Sebastian Black and—fun fact—he's also a professional fighter. His fighting name is Bash the Smasher."

Her brows lift in intrigue, and she tucks a highlighted strand of hair behind her ear. "Interesting. I think readers will love that."

After asking Bash a few questions, which he answers smoothly, she sighs in satisfaction. "Perfect. I think I've gotten just about everything I need here."

"Great. I'll walk you out, then. Thanks, Elena."

Mrs. Long is already halfway out the door as we approach. She tries to hold the door for us with wobbling hands, but she loses grasp of Winifred, and the Pug goes running right out the door.

"Winifred!" Mrs. Long cries, reaching out, but it's too late. "Not the water. Not the water. She can't swim!"

The little dog bolts straight for the retention pond.

"No!" I shout, already sprinting after her.

Bash is faster. He darts past me, his long strides eating up the distance. By the time Winifred tumbles into the pond with a splash, Bash is already diving in after her.

The world seems to hold its breath. I watch with my hands clasped tightly over my mouth. Elena's camera clicks relentlessly, but I barely register the sound.

Bash resurfaces with Winifred cradled in one arm, paddling toward the edge with the other. I nearly collapse in relief when he pulls himself out of the water and sets the soggy, but safe, dog onto the grass.

Winifred gives a mighty shake, spraying droplets everywhere, before trotting back to Mrs. Long.

"What just happened?" Elena asks, wide-eyed, her tablet poised mid-air.

I explain quickly, my voice shaky. "Pugs can't swim well. Their flat faces make breathing while swimming nearly impossible. They just—" I stop, swallowing hard. "It's really dangerous for them."

"And your bather-fighter just saved the day?"

I nod. My gaze drifts to Bash, who's wringing water out of his soaked shirt.

Elena grins and resumes typing. "This is going to make a fantastic addition to the article. Do I have your permission to include it?"

"I—of course." My words come out in a stammer, because I'm still having trouble processing what just happened. "That would be fine."

Elena thanks me, packs up her camera, and drives off, leaving me and Bash standing in the damp grass.

Bash trudges the rest of the way over to me, shaking water off him. He looks mildly annoyed, but I'm distracted because of course, *of course* he didn't wear his scrubs today.

He just had to wear a white, long-sleeve shirt and fully immerse himself in a retention pod, only to emerge looking like the BBC version of Mr. Darcy.

"Thank you for saving Winifred," I mutter, still staring at his chest.

He scowls, shaking water off his arms. "Little beast just had to go for the water, didn't it? Does this mean I have to bathe her all over again?"

I can't help it. I laugh.

Mrs. Long approaches us with her dog. "I'm so sorry for the trouble. I don't know what she was thinking."

I take the leash from her. "Don't worry. I'll give her a quick shampoo and dry her off. She'll be back to one-hundred percent in no time."

She places a hand to her chest. "Bless your heart, dear. And you," she says, turning to Bash. "Thank you so much for saving her."

"Of course. It was my pleasure," says Bash. Ever the charming gentleman.

December

Chapter Thirty-One

BASH

IT'S ONLY BEEN a month since Elena's story on Romilly's business. But as soon as the headline, *Fighter Saves Puppy From Drowning,* graced November copies of *The Meadow Bee,* we've both been the talk of the town. I became somewhat of a big deal around Meadow Hills for my heroic act, and then shortly after, even more offers for sponsorship started coming through. My agent sent me a new one practically every day, until I couldn't keep up anymore.

"It's a good thing you saved that dog," said Max. "That's what every business has brought up in conversation with me so far."

Romilly grinned at me. "I promise The Paw Spa will finally sponsor you in addition to your other admirers. After all, it's practically your origin story."

And the best part? She was more than able to afford sponsoring me. Once the article blew up, Agatha practically begged Romilly to take her back. Apparently, some of Agatha's customers in Portland caught wind that they could get their dog bathed by a famous fighter (AKA, me) in Meadow Hills, and they left her for The Paw Spa. And not just the customers, but the groomers, too.

And I can't deny, I'm more than thrilled Romilly hired them all, because now she has so much more time to herself. The woman actually eats now, and it's such a relief.

"Will you please tell me where we're going?" Romilly asks from the passenger seat of my Camaro.

My car is finally back in tip-top shape, which is a massive weight off my shoulders now that it's snowing. I grin past the swarm of nerves in my stomach as I hit the gas on it. "No way."

She crosses her arms. "We're near Orangewood Estates. That's where Addison and Perry live. Are we going to visit them?"

My smile only grows. "Nope."

"Tell me, Bash."

But I don't answer her. Tiny flakes of snow fall from the sky like little cotton puffs, collecting in a line at the edge of my windshield, and falling into piles and little hills along the sidewalks. I pull into the driveway of the two-story colonial we're here to see.

When I get out and come around to open Romilly's door, she frowns at me. My palms are actually sweating in my gloves, but the cold air nips at my nose and turns Romilly's cheeks pink. Her mittened hand feels impossibly small in mine as she lets me help her out. "What on earth are we doing here? I mean, I'm pretty sure this place is vacant."

I thread our gloved hands together, leading her to the door. Swallow. "It is right now. But it won't be for long."

Together, we crunch up the snow-packed path. Our boots leave behind the first footprints this house has seen in months.

"Hang on a minute." Romilly shakes her head, turning to face me. "Are you saying you bought this place? What about your apartment? You just signed a lease."

We stop at the base of the stairs leading to a wraparound porch that circles the blue and white-trimmed exterior. A wooden swing hangs at one end, dusted with snow. I can already imagine Romilly sitting on it with a steaming mug of tea in her hands.

I shrug. "I broke it."

Her mouth falls open. "Wait, you're actually serious? This is your house?" Romilly squeals, clapping her mittens together.

"Our house." My voice shakes on the way out. *Come on, Bash. You got this.* Dropping to one knee, I take both of her hands in mine. "Romilly...I know it hasn't been long, but I love you. I didn't know it was possible, but I love you even more now than I did when I first told you. And I promise to let my love continue to grow for you with every passing day. Will you marry me, live in this house with me, and make me the happiest man in the world? It's even vintage inside, just how you like it. I checked before I bought it."

Romilly covers her mouth with her hand. The glistening on the surface of her eyes makes a knot clog in my own throat.

I reach into my pocket and produce the ring I picked out last week for her. It's shaped like an oval, with clusters of little diamonds surrounding the stone in the center. As soon as I saw it, I knew it belonged with her.

Hold it together, Bash.

She sniffles, wiping her eyes before our gazes reconnect. For a moment, the world around us completely fades.

It's just us.

Me and Romilly.

She takes my face in her hands. "Yes."

Yes.

She said yes.

Taking her mitten off so I can slide the ring onto her finger, I crush her against me, making her laugh. Then I pepper kisses across her hair, her face, and finally, her lips.

"Wait a minute!" She pulls away from me. "I know you're like, a super popular fighter right now, and you have lots of money, but you're still kinda new. Is this house something you'll be able to afford long-term?"

I grin. "So responsible. Don't worry, pumpkin. There are more fights in me where that last one came from."

"Now, that I believe."

We stare at each other for a long moment, both of us grinning. "You're going to be my wife," I say. I still can't believe it. "Officially."

"And you're going to be my husband. Officially."

Kissing her again, I soak it all in—our life right now, and the promise of our future together. It's all too good to be true. I can't help but think back to the person I was before I met Romilly. I was so sure being untethered from anyone else was the best way to go. But loving her has made me feel freer than ever before.

"Wait," she says, pulling away. "What about kids? Do you want them?"

I smile. "Do you?"

"I want to be a foster parent so bad," she says. "But I know not everyone—"

"We're doing it," I tell her. Warmth radiates throughout my body at the idea. "We can start right away if you want to."

Romilly nuzzles her head to my chest, and I breathe in the scent of her skin. "There's no rush. We can take our time. We have the rest of our lives to figure out how we want to live them."

I kiss her again. "As long as I get to live mine with you, I'm going to die happy."

Epilogue

ROMILLY

"I'LL NEVER GET tired of the way your mum cooks," Bash whispers in my ear. "Don't get me wrong, I love the way you cook, too, but there's something about Thanksgiving that makes everything she serves taste unreal."

I giggle. "Trust me. I know what you mean."

We're all standing in a circle next to my parents' dining room table. A table that's currently filled with steaming plates of turkey, stuffing, mashed potatoes, gravy, and the rest of my mother's delicious creations.

My dad says grace with all of us holding hands, and then we find our seats. Bash pulls out the chair next to his for me to take, then helps our four-year-old daughter, Ginger, onto my lap.

"Daddy, I want stuffing," she tells him.

"No fair," he teases. "I want stuffing, too. What are we going to do?"

Ginger gasps. "I don't know."

"Bash, pass *me* the stuffing, first," says Zara from across the table.

"No." He picks up the platter and holds it to his chest. "This is all mine."

My mom laughs. "Honey, I'll whip up all the stuffing you want. Just never stop telling me how much you love it."

"I could never," he says. "In fact, I'm convinced the only person here who likes it more than I do is Ginger." Bash winks at me, and from my lap, Ginger nods eagerly and makes a barking sound like a dog, then licks her lips.

It's her new thing lately—acting like a puppy. Last week, Bash and I let her explore the entirety of The Paw Spa for the first time, so she's been obsessed with acting like a dog, even chasing poor Jasper around until he hisses at her.

Mom laughs. "Well, in that case, pass the platter to my granddaughter this instant."

"Save some for me," says my dad.

Aiden smirks. "Sorry, but if Ginger wants it, you might as well kiss it goodbye."

Even though he's joking, my brother has a point. Ever since Bash and I adopted Ginger through the foster care system, my mom has made it clear she will not be refraining from spoiling her granddaughter any chance she gets. And that was two years ago.

I help Ginger spoon more casserole onto her plate and weave her honey-colored hair into two braids so she doesn't get food on it. I've become a pro at eating from my own plate with her on my lap. Even though Bash constantly offers to take her from me so I can eat in peace, I won't let him. My sweet girl won't be this little much longer, and I already know how much I'll miss having her on my lap once she's too big to be there.

I kiss the top of her head. "Love you."

"Love you, too, Mommy," she says around a mouthful of stuffing. There's gravy dripping down her chin, so I dab it with a napkin. So far, she hasn't stained the cream sweater I just bought her. And I'm glad, because it looks so cute on her, bringing out the golden tones in her pale skin and brown eyes.

When we're all finished with our second and third helpings of Thanksgiving dinner, we gather around my parents' living room to talk about what we're grateful for.

Zara is practically bouncing in her seat on the couch. "Can I go first? I'm grateful to finally be done with college. Now I get to see everyone more."

My mom wraps Zara in a hug. "I'm grateful for that, too, honey. And also for every single one of you sitting here with me today." She tears up a little and wipes her eye, just like she's done every year since I was a kid.

For the first time, I understand why. Just thinking about the past few years I've spent with Bash and Ginger, even for a moment, makes me emotional. It's hard to believe I was so against opening my heart to him when we first met. I would have missed out on so many beautiful memories if I hadn't trusted God to bring us together. And then trusted Him again to help us adopt Ginger and make her our permanent daughter.

We all go around expressing what we're most grateful for this year, and when it's my turn, I say, "I'm grateful that my wonderful husband, Sebastian Black, has become so high-ranking in his promotion that he only has to fight twice a year now. We get to keep more of him this way."

Bash squeezes my hand. His own have become even more calloused over the years, now showing signs of all his training and fighting, along with the labor he's done around my shop, and finally learning to fix cars in his spare time. And somehow, he's only gotten more handsome with time. His occasional stubble has blossomed into a full beard, and in his brown and cream shearling jacket and slacks, it's hard not to stare at him.

"If anyone is wondering what I'm grateful for, it hasn't changed," he says. "I'm thankful for God, for all of you, and for the meal we just ate, which I'll be dreaming about every night until next Thanksgiving."

I roll my eyes, but giggle. Even after all this time, he never stops thinking about food.

When everyone's done, Bash and I leave Ginger with my parents so we can stop by Harvest Valley. Every year, my mother donates a turkey to the soup kitchen, and we eat our own dinner early so there will be time to take the turkey there.

Bash gets in the driver's seat, and I hold the turkey on my lap in the passenger side. The warmth from the glass platter feels good against my tights peeking out from my mustard yellow sweater dress.

My husband sniffs the air. Juicy, seasoned steam is wafting up from the tender bird. "Do you think they'd notice if there was a bite missing?" he asks.

"Just drive, Bash."

He chuckles. "By the way, my parents told me to wish you and Ginger a happy holiday.

A deep sense of longing fills my chest. "I miss them. We really need to go visit soon. Ginger keeps asking about when we're going back to Australia."

"I'm sure they'll love that. But they might try to keep us from leaving, like last time."

"True," I say. "But at least there have been no major fights between you and them lately."

Bash laughs humorlessly. "Well, it's only been a month. Give it a few more days."

Despite his words, I know Bash and his parents are in a much better place than before. Though they still don't approve of him fighting—something they're happy to voice before each of his matches—at least they've stopped bugging him about running the auction houses. That privilege, and burden, now belongs to Ingrid. But, thankfully, she's okay with that.

The turkey is still hot when we arrive.

Bash shuts off the engine, and we both sit in silence for a moment, looking at the dinner line already trailing out of the building.

"It's hard to believe I used to not want to come here," Bash says softly. "There's so much good that happens here. And I feel so close to everyone now, like they're extended family."

I brush back the front pieces of his blond hair. "Yeah, well, sometimes we find family where we least expect it. Like me with you."

He smirks, turning to me. "Oh, come on. You knew you were going to marry me the moment we locked eyes."

"No, I didn't." I shake my head, trying not to smile.

"Yes, you did. I remember. You were practically undressing me with your eyes."

I cover my laugh with my hand. "We're at church, Sebastian."

"Right. Let's hurry up. All this talk about undressing makes me want to take you back home."

I roll my eyes. "You're relentless."

"And you're absolutely gorgeous."

When we both get out of the car, I can't help but admire the way the setting sun is now filtering through the golden leaves of autumn, casting a warm glow over Harvest Valley. Since getting married, we've been here plenty of times together, but now that it's autumn, I'm feeling extra nostalgic.

I gaze at the exact spot he crashed into me, spilling that soup all over me and making me squirm with that attractive voice of his.

I glance to the side to find Bash watching me study the spot, leaning against his car with that familiar, slightly crooked grin. The same one that made my heart skip a beat that first day. The weird part, though, is seeing *him* carry the food now.

"Don't worry, pumpkin." He lifts the pot like a trophy. "I've got a better grip on it than some people I know."

"Very funny. How did you know that's what I was thinking about?"

"Because I know *you*." Bash steps closer, his expression softening. He sets my mom's turkey atop his car's closed trunk so he can wrap his arms around my waist. Kissing the side of my head, he murmurs, "I've learned every beautiful, adorable expression of yours." The sincerity in his voice sends a thrill through me. "Can you believe it's been this long since I spilled soup all over you, and you very politely told me it was no problem?"

I laugh. "That's because I was more worried about how attracted I was to you than the being covered in soup part."

He grins. "I'm just grateful God put us both in this car park together that day so I'd bump into you, because at that time I couldn't imagine ever loving someone the way I love you."

Tears well up in my eyes. "Bash...stop. You're going to make me cry."

He grins. "Why? Because you're stuck with me, wife?"

To shut him up, I grab his face and press my lips against his. It never gets old—feeling his lips and stubble against my own face. Or the way his strong hands turn me to putty with every touch. The way he loves me every day, and makes my heart grow ten sizes whenever he makes Ginger laugh or plays dolls with her.

He pulls away to rub his nose across mine, but it only lasts a second, because I need another kiss, and as usual, he doesn't disappoint me.

To this day, he still never has.

Thank you for reading *The Wrong Kind of Falling!*

If you enjoyed this book, I hope you'll consider writing a small review. Each one, even if it's only one sentence long, helps indie authors like me so much.

Thank you from the bottom of my heart,
Whitney Amazeen

Goodreads

Amazon

Acknowledgments

Writing the acknowledgments page often feels like trying to think of what, or who, I'm grateful for on Thanksgiving.

Is "everyone" an acceptable answer?

I'm thankful to God most of all, and to all the amazing people in my life who endlessly continue to support me and help me.

My husband, Michael. You've never stopped believing in me to this day, and I don't have words for how much that means to me.

My mom. I'll never stop being grateful for you, and you're the greatest blessing in my life.

My kids, Oliver and Phoebe. I love you two so much. Thank you for sharing me with paper, ink, and my imagination every single day.

Cait Elise. You're the best friend a person can have, and my books wouldn't be half what they are if you didn't read them first.

My cousin/bestie Ashley. You always carve time out of your busy schedule for me, and I don't take that lightly. Your voice (on paper or in my ear) always brightens my day.

My cousin/bestie Haley. You're like an injection of energy and confidence, and I want to be like you if I ever grow up.

My family and friends. You all make me so happy. Thank you for everything. Especially Zach for the pep talks and Elijah for the help.

Leni Kauffman. Thank you for reading my mind a second time and using your extraordinary talents to give me such a beautiful cover. I feel unworthy.

Wendy Higgins. Thank you for being such a wonderful, amazing editor and friend. I'm always grateful to know you.

Latisha Sexton. Thank you for letting me pick your brain and handing out the best answers to me every time.

All the groomers and bathers I used to work with, especially Jess, Laycee, Michelle, Savannah, Kayla, Bea, Aline, and Madison. Thank you for teaching me so much and for being such amazing friends.

And you. The person holding this book. You're the whole reason writing is worth it. Thank you for spending your precious time reading my book when there are so many other choices. I know the value of that, and I'm so, so, so thankful. I love you.

Keep in Touch with Whitney Amazeen

Get all my book news, sneak peeks, bonus content, and more exciting stuff by signing up for my newsletter at

WHITNEYAMAZEEN.COM/NEWSLETTER

About the Author

Whitney Amazeen writes cute, cozy love stories with a sprinkle of faith. Her love for books grew into an obsession in third grade and has been going strong ever since. Before pursuing writing, she studied cosmetology, where she used to hide in the laundry room to read and work on stories instead of clients. When she's not writing, Whitney can often be found playing Sims, snuggling with her kids and dogs, and obsessing over Jesus. Whitney is a California native who now lives in Arizona with her family and expansive tea collection.

Please visit WhitneyAmazeen.com and find her on social media @WhitneyAmazeen!

Made in the USA
Columbia, SC
22 September 2025

62323363R00204